I0699626

Copper & Snow

Winter's Verse Part I

Nicole Hayes

Iona Print

Library of Congress Control Number: 2023910121
ISBN (Hardcover Edition) 979-8-9877243-8-5
ISBN (Softcover Edition) 979-8-9877243-9-2
ISBN (Ebook Edition) 979-8-9894105-0-7

Printed in the USA
Iona Print
nicolehayesauthor@gmail.com

WINTER'S VERSE

Copper & Snow

Polar Axis

The Vast Collective Series

To those of us without a sense for appropriate timing.

Contents

Acknowledgments

Batman, once again thank you for humoring my relentless requests for you to read and provide me feedback. This was a special project, and your insights helped make it even more so. I look forward to your response to the conclusion in Polar Axis.

Firefly, this is a special book for you because you asked to read it after it was all done rather than chapters at a time. It kept me motivated to stay the course and finish it with you in mind. Enjoy the fashion show.

Thanks to my awesome editor, Destiny! Without you, this would've taken me much, much longer. I'm so glad you responded to my email that day, and I believe you have a bright future ahead of you.

Thanks to Destiny! Without your editing skills, this book would never have been published.

Rebeca Covers, thank you for all of your excellent illustrations and for bringing my worlds to life in full color.

 ONE

Winter's Mettle

DRIP.
Drip.

Someone really ought to check the pipes in Lexia Tempest's office. How was a girl supposed to take a nap with all this dripping about?

The crop master's daughter withdrew her long legs off her desk and righted her chair out of her dozing position. The stacks of papers waiting for Lexia's gilded seal stood like tall towers, piled hundreds deep, in silent judgment. In fact, during this Founding Season, there wasn't a sound in the entire building aside from…

Drip.

With a sigh, Lexia eyed the culprit. In a room with a dozen copper pipes pumping steam for heat, it should prove difficult to single out the leaky one, but she'd found it yesterday. Upper right corner of the rose-glass room, closest to her desk. A small elbow dripped onto a steam main.

Lexia had just paid for the last copper re-pipe…What? Three months ago?

Well.

Her father had paid for it, and she was sure Gauge Snow had loved that. Although, to be fair, she knew little about the twenty-nine-year-old bachelor since Lexia's father refused to let her set foot in a room with him, let alone reintroduce her to the man. They hadn't seen each other since they were children.

No, instead, Lexia heard all about Snow's arrogance and avarice from her father and Axis. But facing off with this leak in her office, Lexia had a few of her own choice words for the Count of Copper.

Her black leather pants creaked softly as she stood and crossed the room to the exterior wall made of rose-colored glass. Through the fog, Lexia glared at the impractical Cathedral built entirely of the precious metal on a hill in the town's center. Train cars on iron tracks helixed through the humid clouds surrounding the steam empire's most recognizable monument. Once through the Copper Cathedral's security, they'd arrive at the mine depot where their labor made up a third of the planet's occupations. Winter's occupations.

Another third worked the plantations, scattered across the planet, growing food and fibers to supply the world with nourishment and textiles. This was Leon Tempest's domain, and, as his daughter and inheritor, it was Lexia's future.

Factories employed the final third under Axis' father, Valve Flicker. Within the stacks of machinery, laborers took those materials from the plantations and processed them into goods for consumption. All to keep shelter over their heads and food on the table.

Everyone was beholden to the mighty triumvirate: copper, cotton, and construction.

Even Lexia, who worked on her own merit and not her father's reputation. Proof positive seeing as she was the only one in the office today. She glanced at the brass clock on the wall with its fancy scroll. It said one hour until closing. When Lexia blew the air from her cheeks, it fluffed her bangs as she considered how badly she wanted out of this pinstripe corset. But she wore it for a reason.

That reason was six inches taller than Lexia with soft green eyes and short burgundy hair and enough steam coming off his honed body to power all of Winter. Dinner with Axis in an hour. A night with him was the only way to kick off Founding Season with a bang, assuming she could keep his mind off work.

The People's Prince never stopped advocating for laborer's rights, even when facing his father—

No.

Lexia didn't want her thoughts to go there this afternoon. Tonight was about the young couple and not the struggles they'd inherited in their respective industries. With two easy strides, she returned to her desk and retrieved a compact from the top drawer.

Waves of white hair cascaded down Lexia's shoulders. Soft gray eyeshadow emphasized the depth of her black eyes. Was burgundy lipstick the right choice or was it too on the nose? She swept her bangs a little to the side and re-powdered to cover her pale blue freckles, dusted across her temples. Against her white skin, they often drew too much attention. They reminded the public of her mother, and Lexia was her own woman, now twenty-three years old and ready to take on the empire.

Fifty-five minutes left, and she could leave for the most important date of her life. Axis would ask tonight. Lexia was certain. She looked down at her breasts and straightened the blouse beneath her corset to better distract her suitor before spritzing more perfume across her pulse points.

Axis loved the smell of summer rain.

Surely the primping ate up another thirty minutes. Lexia glanced at the clock and frowned. Only one minute had passed.

With a sigh, she poured herself back into her chair and lit her ink pad. The flame ignited, and Lexia took the first page off the pile of work. It was a report of unionizing activity among the orchard employees. One of their lifers, a man named Kol, had provided the findings. The document included a request for more resources. This would prevent an uprising asking for outlandish demands.

Lexia held her hand over the flame and let it kiss the golden gear strapped to her palm. Once hot enough, she sealed the report with her signature and moved onto the next.

Sometimes the only way to move a work day along was to get some actual work done.

The steam whistle sounded the end of the work week, and it wouldn't sound again until after Founding Day. Lexia made it through the last stack of paper and felt better about her time spent. She left her office as tidy as possible, then rushed on her four-inch stiletto thigh-high boots onto the thoroughfare.

There were two major arteries to the city: Tempest Boulevard and Flicker Avenue. Both spread out diagonally from Snow Plaza, forming a triangle in the heart of the city. Most people traveled by streetcar or train. The trains went overhead, roller-coasting on steam-powered tracks. Her family could afford the luxury of personal cars with drivers, but Lexia wanted to take the city's pulse tonight. So she walked through the twilight under lamps fueled by Flicker wicks: a hybrid of Tempest fuses and Flicker engineered filaments.

To Lexia's delight, the Founding Parade had already started down the boulevard. She loved the dancers in their bright costumes, and the bands with their brass instruments and drums. But her least favorite part were the floats.

Each one represented a different stage of Winter's establishment ten years ago now. The first float, which she'd missed, was bright enough to still see on its way. It represented the electromagnetic pulse on a world powered by electronics.

Lexia had gone outside in time to glimpse the worst float, and it made her frown.

A life-sized replica of a younger Gauge Snow warned the planet's congresses of the phenomenon. It was backed by the Copper Cathedral, half-constructed in those earlier times. The replica was just after he'd bought all the copper mines in the Ignis Crater to prepare for what would come next.

His prescience had always bothered Lexia.

The third float represented the fall of civilization as pre-Winter knew it. The old name for the planet was illegal to speak, and Lexia hadn't heard it since she was a girl in braids.

The fourth float boasted another life-size statue of Snow, but this one was made from solid copper. It depicted his rise to reestablish order out of chaos, and he'd gladly donated the copper for it. While fawning at the statue's feet, the young women on the float wore low-cut blouses and bloomers over fishnets.

A chill made Lexia shiver in her ankle-length duster, and she pressed on while trying to enjoy the music on her walk. Further down the cobbled street, she noticed a wall of people blocking the sidewalk. A thrill replaced the chill.

Lexia touched her hand to the steam cannon holstered on her hip beneath the coat as she made her way through the crowd. Some recognized her and lowered their heads in deference, stepping out of the way. This was typical in a throng this size, but she was still polite enough to say, "Excuse me. Pardon me," as she forced her way to the front.

There.

As Lexia had suspected, two men were pressing their backs to one another. Both of them had rapiers! A sword duel was less common these days, and she couldn't wait to see how this one played out. Once they'd reached the ten paces, another man who refereed for them whistled for the duel to start.

The man on the left, with green hair and brown eyes, turned first and brandished his weapon at his opponent.

The second fighter, with blond hair and purple eyes, backflipped away on one hand, dazzling their audience.

Lexia already knew who would win the fight just by their stances, but it was exciting to watch them trade blows. Sparks flew when their swords clashed; the blond man bore down on his opponent with more strength and skill.

The green-haired man, desperate not to lose, reached into his boot and withdrew a dagger. He thrusted it into the blond man's gut.

A dirty move, and the crowd booed. Lexia included.

The blond man with more skill whirled away and swiped the green-haired man's wrist, cutting into the veins. He dropped the cheating dagger with a wounded cry. He couldn't resist the instinct to clutch his injured wrist to his chest, and the blond man sought his opening.

After one deft thrust into the green-haired man's heart, Winter was short another citizen tonight.

Lexia had witnessed a hundred duels in her lifetime. 'Dispute resolutions' were their legal names. It was not only illegal to kill outside of a duel, but pre-meditated, cold-blooded murder would see you cast in copper and hung on the Wall of Pain.

Which just so happened to be the front door to Gauge Snow's Cathedral.

Lexia fought another shiver and moved on through the crowd. She tried her best to ignore the body being lifted by the undertaker. She wasn't cold-hearted; this was simply how things were done on Winter.

Maybe two steps later, Lexia stopped and sighed. Without turning around, she said, "It seems silly for you to hide behind me when I can distinguish your steps in a crowd." When she turned, she wasn't surprised to find her unwanted bodyguard looking disgruntled under the lamplight.

Rhyme never looked happy. His arched brows reminded Lexia of a hawk, and they were furrowed to deepen the frown on his thin lips. His arms were folded across his chest—too broad for her liking. His prosthetic leg with its copper casting and its steam tank jutted out from his hip with entirely too much sass for an employee. Her father's employee.

Rhyme rubbed the stubble on his chin while he contemplated, "What would Dr. Tempest think of you rushing over to witness a duel, endangering yourself?"

Lexia turned around and kept walking, gesturing her nonchalance as she said, "He'd probably thank the bodyguard before you who taught me everything I know in self-defense and dueling etiquette. They were using swords, Rhyme. Not projectiles. I was fine."

As Rhyme followed, his prosthetic made a distinctly empty footstep compared to his boot. He humphed in that gravelly voice of his with his rugged features and his braided hair. He was handsome, but no one could compare to Axis. Not to mention, Rhyme was about ten years older than Lexia, and she never really fancied older men.

Rhyme asked, "Why don't you ever submit your schedule so we can plan your security better?"

Lexia laughed, letting that question answer itself. She didn't have to answer to him, anyway. There was a good chance even her father didn't know about her plans tonight.

Ah.

Lexia couldn't have timed her arrival at the restaurant better herself. She turned to ask Rhyme, "Can you please be discrete tonight? I don't want Axis nervous."

Rhyme looked at the narrow Victorian cottage with its turrets and wrought-iron fencing. It was a secret shared between the couple—a place they liked to go and pretend they were normal without all the glitz and glamor of balls and galas. No pressure. The perfect place for Axis to ask her to—

"I don't think my shoulders can fit through the door, little Heiress." Rhyme smirked.

Lexia rolled her eyes and went inside, ready for the most important engagement of her life.

Axis checked his lapels, sleeves, and waistcoat for the thirtieth time. It was a more respectable use of his nervous energy than allowing his knee to bounce. He was a private man, and public displays of affection were more advertisement about his personal life than he'd liked to air.

However.

When Lexia arrived, her beautiful smile over this crystal dining set would be well worth the anxiety, and there was no better venue than this restaurant to ask for her betrothal. Here, in this quaint setting where they'd had their first date. So, so long ago now. He could almost recall similar nerves then as he sat in the private alcove waiting for her to arrive, she all of sixteen and he only seventeen. They were fortunate their fathers even allowed them to leave their homes at the time, let alone go on a date in a public setting.

How could Axis forget his surprise when she arrived in a dress? His Lexia. In a dress. It had been a magical evening for the two childhood friends to progress into something much more.

Now here they were again. Same restaurant; eight years later. Only this time, Axis knew better than to expect Lexia to arrive in a dress. She wouldn't even attend the Founding balls, where the dress code mandated it.

No, Axis wouldn't dream of asking Lexia to wear one. Not even for their wedding. She'd rant about not being dressed to participate in a duel, should the occasion call for it. The notion was amusing enough to make him smirk into his wine and relax his nerves.

No way.

While Axis waited for Lexia to arrive, he peered at the copper utensils surrounding the crystal plates. Everything else in this restaurant had come from Tempest crop or Flicker manufacturing. But the expensive copperware was an ugly reminder of Axis' day—one he'd hoped to keep from his mind during this special evening. Yet as the parade sounded from outside with its ugly floats on Flicker-engineered rails, Axis had trouble keeping Gauge Snow off his mind.

"We keep losing employees to your mines because your pay and benefits are competitive, which goes against our accord," Axis argued at his father's side.

The older man nodded silently in his approval.

Gauge had steepled his gloved fingers to his lips and smirked behind them. The entire board went silent and awaited his response with bated breath.

Before answering, Gauge removed his rose-tinted spectacles—the copper frames glinted in the whiskey light of his auspicious conservatory. Nothing in the room—not the grand piano, not the scantily dressed servants, nor the table of bespoke stakeholders—could take away from the piercing blue of the Count's eyes. Their striking shade of cobalt emphasized the blue tint of his dark gray complexion.

Everyone in the room went stock still.

Into that silence, Gauge said, "The People's Prince has spoken. I must reduce the pay and benefits offered in my mines should his family's terrible mistreatment of their factories' employees continue without consequence."

What?

What 'mistreatment' was Gauge referring to?

At Axis' frown, the Copper Count continued, "Perhaps you should investigate your own policies and practices—Standardize them, even. Rather than allowing your machine managers to dictate their own, including corrective action and training. With the kind of punishment I hear they dole out over the slightest mistakes, it's a wonder you retain any employees whatsoever."

Axis looked away from Gauge—an arduous task when all the chairs at the table were mounted to face him—and glared at his father.

Valve Flicker did nothing to refute the accusations. Instead, he took his cigar out of his mouth to say, "You'll find the real trouble in the unions which keep forming under Dr. Tempest's diligence."

Deflection.

It was an ugly admission of guilt which Axis abhorred, but, across the table, Dr. Tempest entertained it.

The good doctor said, "Since we've allowed a few crops to unionize, we've received fewer complaints from our more labor-intensive positions. In fact, we've seen an influx of new employees. I could even say a few came from your camp, Master Flicker."

Axis almost shuddered where he sat waiting in the restaurant recalling the use of his father's formal title. They were hand-selected after the previous world had ended: Doctor, Master, and Count. At least Leon held a doctorate in agricultural science in his previous life. But Master and Count?

Axis had rolled his eyes at the arrogance then, and he almost rolled them now. But he caught a glimpse of white from the doorway. It was enough to banish any aggravation from today's leadership meeting. Only two people in all of Winter were born with white hair, and sadly, Lexia had lost her mother two years ago.

As she walked through the door, the smile on her burgundy-painted lips was all that mattered in the world. It lit up the room far better than the wicks in the gas lamps, but Lexia's clothes made Axis think of darker things. How was she even breathing in that corset? And she wore the thigh-high boots he liked to make them nearly the same height.

Stunned.

That's how Axis felt until he shook himself from the trance and minded his manners enough to stand and pull out Lexia's chair. He'd worn a new silk three-piece for her in the color she liked, matching the rich burgundy of her lips and his hair. It could only bring out the soft green of his eyes, and the eye contact between them said that she'd noticed.

They didn't kiss when Lexia arrived at the table, taking her seat and peering up at Axis with the desire to do so in her eyes. But she respected his phobia about public displays of affection, which made him hope all the more that his plans for tonight would surprise her.

It took everything in Axis to brush Lexia's back through the chair, and, when he sat, he could see how the love of his life beamed at him for it.

Yes. Tonight was the night.

They didn't need menus. The wait staff immediately served them their favorite drinks and appetizers, and would return with their entrees soon. In that time, Axis tried his best to work up his nerve, and bless Lexia for breaking the tension.

"I was the only one in the office today. This Founding Season seems to be more anticipated than I can think of any other year."

Axis ate up the small talk as an excuse to slow his pounding heart. He said, "It was in the air at the board meeting. Did your father brief you on it yet?" Some part of him was grateful Dr. Tempest never asked Lexia to attend. She wouldn't stand for Snow's grandiose flexing. But another part of Axis knew how much Lexia wanted her father to respect her enough to let her attend. It was a complex situation, and one which would eventually find resolution.

Lexia beamed as she said, "Not yet. I came straight here to meet you." She didn't have to ask about the surprise Axis had promised. He could see the curiosity naked in her exotic eyes. Despite how much powder she'd applied, she could never fully cover the striking effect of her freckles so near those obsidian irises.

Could they just skip this part and get straight to celebrating their time by sneaking off to his bedroom?

Axis' thoughts must've shown on his face, because Lexia's grin tilted into a sexy, knowing smirk. It was infectious.

This was it.

The timepiece on Axis' wrist was leather and silver, simple and elegant. When he began rolling back his sleeve, he heard Lexia's breath catch in a soft gasp. He said, "Lexi, would you—"

Servers interrupted with the entrees, and Axis hid his exposed arm under the table like a coward. He almost broke out into a sweat. Why was this so hard?

Across from him, Lexia smiled. It wasn't pitying, even though she was fully aware of his command for privacy. It was gorgeous and bright, completely aware of the gesture he'd wanted to make without ruining the surprise.

While Axis tried to recover from an onset of panic, Lexia's boot found his calf and traveled up between his legs. Hers were long enough to span the distance. After Lexia caught his eye and winked, Axis spread his legs further for her.

She was perfection, and he wanted her forever. That's what the exchanging of watches meant. They would share their time belonging to one another, if only Axis could muster up the nerve.

But the entrees came and went.

They'd split dessert with Axis biting his lip because of Lexia's teasing.

It seemed the entire date had passed in the blink of an eye, and now the opportunity to propose publicly had closed. Axis couldn't do it. He'd even unrolled his sleeve and tried his best not to look defeated.

Lexia knew. It was in her eyes, kind as they were. She said, "We'll stick to the rest of the plan for tonight."

Meaning, Lexia would try to ditch her bodyguard who waited outside the restaurant to sneak over to Axis' apartments. She must know that when he'd made those plans, he'd intended for them to be engaged already, but she showed no signs of disappointment. In fact, she seemed eager to get him alone.

That was how Axis liked it, which was also part of his problem.

When he'd asked last year for Dr. Tempest's blessing, Lexia's father had been clear—If Axis couldn't handle a public engagement, then he couldn't handle a public wedding. Or a public lifetime partnership.

One day, Axis would live up to his promise.

Gauge Snow signed an order to increase starting benefits across the board in his copper mines. This ought to amuse Axis Flicker, not that the younger man's father would care. No, the factories would continue to pour dissatisfied laborers into the trains leading to the Ignis Crater, and the Count of Copper was fine with that.

With a sigh, Gauge leaned back in his chair, laced his gloved fingers over his brocade waistcoat, and crossed his polished spats on top of his desk. This Founding Season was more welcome than last year's. So much progress had been made in steam ingenuity, mostly thanks to Dr. Tempest's contributions. Meanwhile, as the man in charge of progress, Valve Flicker proved more nauseating by the minute. Quotas weren't being met, and Gauge tired of the Factory Master deflecting concern onto crops. It was a maneuver, a pawn offered on the chessboard, but for watching the vein pop in Axis' forehead, it was losing its entertainment value.

Not to mention, it was a waste of the twenty-nine-year-old Gauge's precious fucking time to deal with middle-aged stalwarts.

There were ceremonies to prepare and balls to arrange. Every wedding required Gauge's officiation, but it served more as a way of keeping track of post-Founding lineage. Not every genetic pairing was optimal, and he oversaw the matches to guarantee the survival of the best traits. Though it wasn't as if anyone knew that. They all assumed it was his right as the man who'd led them to their salvation.

Winter's children were so easily manipulated.

Tired from four days of insomnia, Gauge sat up straight and swiped his gloved hands down his face. He was getting old if less than a week without rest was wearing him down this badly. Or perhaps it was a byproduct of too much work. It kept coming and hadn't looked likely to slow down over the course of the ten years since the electromagnetic pulse had rendered electronics useless. What a glorious age of steam and copper it had heralded, and oh, so many secrets.

Gauge got up from his desk, left his conservatory for the library, and climbed up the rosewood spiral stairs. At the top, he went to the southwest corner and moved a set of false books aside. He reached behind them to dial his combination into the lock. When the tumblers released the mechanism, he pushed the wall of books inward. Steam hissed as the hydraulics allowed him into the vault.

The darkness inside smelled of leather and blackmail. Gauge inhaled it as he turned up the lights. Their rose glass fixtures illuminated the columbarium of extortion in soft pink hues. Every cremation slot held a wealth of persuasion, but none so valuable as the two in the center, aptly labeled Tempest and Flicker. Each of their columns were twenty slots tall and three slots wide.

Ignoring the good doctor's dossier, Gauge went to the Flickers' files, hoping for some inspiration to motivate the Factory Master into doing his job. Gauge's spies kept comfortable supplying this treasure trove, living handsomely above the table of obligatory labor. While he studied the material on Valve, Gauge helped himself to a drink, sat in one of the tufted chairs, and frowned at the reports until his vision blurred.

It surprised Gauge to find nothing on Axis. The People's Prince didn't liaison with his employees, nor did he abuse his position of power. He didn't even embezzle from the company pot. The only news in his file pertained to his relationship with Lexia Tempest, and that included a forthright request from her father for Axis to marry Leon's daughter.

So wholesome.

So boring.

But the mention of Lexia made Gauge glance at the Tempests' slots. She was old enough to marry now, and he realized she must be about twenty-three. Not that he would know this information offhand. Gauge hadn't seen her since they were children. He set his drink aside, left his chair, and crossed the vault to the Tempest collection. He opened the slot and rifled through the papers until he found a signed trade agreement with Lexia's seal.

A gilded butterfly.

"Butterflies are so pretty. They're my favorite. What do you like, Gauge?"

Gauge, nine at the time, wanted to make friends with Lexia and Axis, and he knew the perfect gift to give her for an upcoming birthday. Sickly as he was, Gauge went outside every day for a month and collected twenty-five butterflies. Excited, he prepared his present for Lexia, hoping that by winning her approval, Axis would teach him to climb trees. Yes, they were younger than him—four and five respectively—but Gauge was small for his age. 'Little Bones' his father would call him.

After a bad bout of his illness, Gauge was too weak to attend Lexia's birthday, so he made sure to rest and take his medicine. In a week's time, he was allowed to visit Dr. Tempest's home again. There, he gave Lexia her birthday present.

Twenty-five butterflies pinned and labeled.

But the surprise went all wrong.

Lexia saw the dead butterflies and began to cry.

"Please, Lexia, I'm sorry. I didn't mean to make you sad—"

"Get away from her, Gauge." Axis pulled Lexia's face, yellow with tears, into his chest and held her. "Don't come near us again."

Gauge blinked and found himself aware of his vault once more. He refocused on the present issue.

It was a known fact that Axis didn't like public engagements. He abstained from the Founding events and only attended factory functions under threat of being disowned. Gauge wondered how the young man would fair in such an ambitious relationship. Every single detail of their marriage would fall under public scrutiny, including the engagement and wedding. And what sort of match would the two make?

Lexia was a genetic marvel, so similar to her mother. If it were up to Gauge, he would clone the girl to keep her genes pure, but Axis wasn't an unworthy match. His intellect and coloring would make for a positive contribution to Winter's pool.

However, it was in Gauge's best interest for the two to separate immediately. Tempest and Flicker together, uniting their families and their industries.

Against Gauge.

No. He needed some dirt on the squeaky clean Prince as soon as possible, preferably before his father's death and Axis' subsequent inheritance over Flicker Industries.

And as for Lexia, Dr. Tempest kept her like a princess locked in a tower. She attended nothing. Ever. The last time Gauge had glimpsed her white hair and black eyes was the first Founding Day when she'd been thirteen and the world went by another name.

A lesser name.

Winter suited the planet better amid an ice age. Only steam-engineered glass domes kept the cities safe, and they were connected by steam-powered underground tracks. All of which were supplied by Gauge's imagination. Without him, there would be no cities on Winter. Without him, there would be no people at all.

The Founding Parade sounded outside, and Gauge cursed. He swept on his coat, grabbed a top hat, and his cane—

With a quick about-face, he went to his desk to reclaim his glasses. He couldn't go outside without them. The copper along the side of the lenses blocked his peripheral vision, but also kept out the light from the sun, which was almost prismatic through the glass domes. It blinded his weak corneas.

It was one reason Gauge had removed himself from the gene pool, but that was more negativity than he cared to entertain during the first day of his favorite season. The season all about Gauge and how he saved Winter.

The second he left his library, half-dressed servants descended upon him.

"Count Snow, we have prepared your speech for today."

"Don't forget your cane, sir."

"Will you require refreshments once you commence the Season's festivities?"

To labor in the Copper Cathedral was an honor. Gauge was not a demanding master, and his people luxuriated in the finest of everything not only for *their* lifetimes, but for the lifetimes of their children and so on. However, their loyalty came with a price. Wrong him—betray him—and Gauge would cast their entire family in the Wall of Pain. The doors to the Copper Cathedral were a permanent reminder of his expectations and the punishment for failing them.

The copper entry opened now, revealing a gathered crowd in Snow Plaza. Gauge set his top hat on his midnight black braids and leaned a little more heavily on his jeweled cane as he stepped outside. The parade and those who followed it into the Plaza cheered at his appearance. He stepped out onto the veranda, standing half a story above the cobbles, and waved.

From the apex of Tempest Boulevard, the good doctor, Leon, fired a flare, and blue streaked the sky. From the left, where Flicker Avenue intersected with the plaza, Valve shot a red flare. Gauge fired the copper-colored flare into the night. When the three lights joined in the sky at a triangle, the music started up again, and their people danced in the streets. The half-naked men and women on the floats joined the dancers with the band, and merriment ensued.

While Axis avoided public events, Gauge relished them. He loved the colors and sounds—the smells of delicious treats from concessions. The glitter and glitz dazzled him and filled his heart with pride.

He did this.

Gauge's hard preparation had earned him this reward, and it never got old.

{AN HOUR LATER}

Lexia trailed a circle on Axis' bare chest. His topaz skin contrasted starkly against her pale hand. She loved the marriage of the colors and often imagined a child with such a complexion. They laid together, satisfied for now, and discussed their futures. Mostly work. Meanwhile, she drew a map of their lives across his abdomen, careful to avoid the ugly round scars. The coin-sized imperfections constellated his entire body in small circular reminders of pain, and Lexia hated them.

It's why she never asked Axis to be rough with her, even though she craved the knife's edge between pain and pleasure, control and choice. Lexia loved him too much, knowing Axis could never hurt her after the abuse he'd endured all his life. She was happy with how he liked things, gentle and drawn out to prolong the climax.

It had taken Lexia the better part of an hour to stealth out from the cover of Rhyme's watchful eyes, yet still, it shouldn't be too hard to find her. Lexia and Axis' relationship was growing more and more public with every stride her lover took to propose. The newspapers reported every picnic in the park or lazy stroll. A local writer created a play after catching the couple making eye contact across the street once. When they first held hands in public, someone changed Winter's anthem to include lyrics about their perfect match.

Axis hated it, but Lexia didn't mind. Their eventual union would dominate gossip about children and inheritance, all things expected when born into the most prominent families on the planet.

"Come back to me, Lexia." Axis kissed the top of her hair and took her tracing hand in his, kissing it next. "Am I boring you with my recap of the meeting?"

She wanted to laugh about his choice of pillow talk, but it had always been this way. Gauge Snow was never far from Axis' mind. Lexia said, "I think the unions are a sign of growth, and, although it often comes with a little pain, this change will ultimately result in a stronger force."

"Much stronger than our factories, apparently. I can't believe father is letting the machine managers abuse laborers, and I'm especially aggrieved to learn this from Snow of all people."

Yes, Lexia supposed it was quite embarrassing. She wasn't sure why, but she always imagined the Count of Copper with a smug smile on his face. At least that's how Axis painted him. In her lover's defense, she said, "I wished I could've been there."

Axis barked out a laugh. "You would eat him alive." Still holding onto her hand, he turned it over and peered at the timepiece on her wrist.

The metal twisting around it to form Lexia's seal was gold, and the harness was a soft black leather. It fastened the small clock to the pulse point on her wrist.

Axis' voice was soft as he peered at it, saying, "I wish I were a braver man for you."

Lexia shook her head. "Don't say that. My father's expectations are unfair—"

"No, Dr. Tempest is right. If I'm to marry you, I need to get over my issue with privacy." Before Lexia could argue, Axis sat up and stared down at her in his arms to say, "And I will. I vow to you, Lexia. We'll be together."

Lexia pressed her hand to his jaw. "We are together right now. Just give me your timepiece, and I'll give you mine. We'll tell father you proposed at the restaurant."

But Axis was already shaking his head. "I respect your father too much to lie to him. He protected me as much as he could. If I'm to be a man fit to marry his daughter, I only have to overcome this one thing. This Founding Season, I know I will."

There was nothing else for it. Lexia beamed at Axis and brought him down to kiss her. Until they made it official, sneaking out and spending their nights together would have to do.

For now.

Lexia walked home, sore and sated. About two blocks ago, Rhyme had picked up in step behind her, and she didn't have the energy to tell him off. Plus, she wasn't stupid. Some protection for the Tempest Heiress made sense, but crime wasn't necessarily the problem here.

People wanted for nothing. By participating in any of the available labors within Winter's city domes, they'd earned their shelter and food. However, the closer to working for one of the three prominent families, the better they lived. Which meant Lexia was often accosted for work in the manor or in the offices. Sometimes it formed a crowd, and sometimes the crowds might become unfriendly.

So Lexia tolerated her large, muscular shadow for the walk home, especially with all the activity in the streets.

From behind, Rhyme called, "This is why I don't give you a centimeter, Heiress. You took a kilometer by disappearing and leaving me with a story to tell your father."

"Perhaps we ought to keep it between us," Lexia offered without turning around or pausing in her stride.

Rhyme asked, "Now why would I do that?"

She said, "Because if you don't, he'll know you lost me and failed in your duties."

Rhyme was quiet for the rest of the walk through the streets of dancing and singing people. Someone took her hand and twirled her around. She held up her hand to stop Rhyme from interfering and curtsied away from the drunken dancer. Maybe tomorrow he would wake up and realize what he'd done, but Lexia hoped not. Founding Season was the perfect excuse for a good time, and she welcomed it.

Wrought-iron fencing between stacked rock columns announced their arrival home. The gate was closed to the street, and the Victorian manor was set back a hundred meters from the public eye. Rhyme went ahead of her to tell the guard to open up, and she sauntered in with a wink for her bodyguard.

Lexia wouldn't tell if he wouldn't.

Before she entered the property, Lexia glanced over at Snow Plaza on the hilltop. There, the parade had exploded into the grandest party she could ever remember seeing. Beyond the ruckus and the floats, the Copper Cathedral shimmered in the lamplight, its doors an ugly reminder of the kind of man who lived inside.

Well, the kind of man Axis and Lexia's father had described, anyway.

Lexia gathered her coat around her, but it wouldn't fight off the chill. Rhyme followed her inside and down the long paver walkway to the beautiful house she called home. Would Lexia miss the pastel blue siding and soft gray shingles with its wraparound porch when she married Axis? Would she move into the Flickers' ugly brick mansion, or could she talk her future husband into a compromise of their own home together?

These thoughts concerned Lexia as she stepped inside the warm sentinel of her childhood.

Rosewood stairs wrapped around the walls up to the fifth floor, comprising the grand foyer. Her father stood on the second floor landing with a warm smile.

Dr. Tempest's voice held a wealth of affection for his headstrong child as he asked, "Should I ever expect you to arrive on time?"

Lexia beamed up at him. "Only for work, father."

"That's my daughter. Punctual only when it matters." Leon's watchful gray eyes fell on the timepiece on her wrist, and his face softened. "How is Axis?"

Lexia wanted to cry. Perhaps, she'd hinged too much on this date—too much on Axis. She reinforced the smile on her face. "Lovely as always, father." For good measure, she said, "Rhyme was diligent, as only a professional of his caliber could be." She turned and extended the smile to her bodyguard.

Rhyme's eyes widened a touch.

Leon asked, "Did you keep her out of trouble?"

Rhyme glanced at Lexia before answering, "Yes, sir. There was nothing out of the usual."

Lexia relaxed a bit and made a note to send Rhyme a thank you gift. She turned back to the stairs and took them two at a time, with a pause on the landing to hug her father. "I'm tired from working—*alone*—all day. Good night."

"Good night, love."

Lexia's room was the only room on the fifth floor, where her father insisted on keeping her private apartments. It was covered in sketches of Axis and butterflies which no one was allowed to disturb. A desk, a bed, a vanity, and a wardrobe consumed the bedroom in soft white. More white furniture made up the sitting room. The parquet floors were painted black—much to her father's dismay and much to Lexia's delight. And a bathroom accounted for the rest of the upstairs.

After a hot soak and writing a letter to Axis, Lexia went to bed with entirely too much on her mind. Dreams of copper and snow haunted her.

She awoke the next morning to find a stack of missives in the sitting room. The only one she cared about was the one in the burgundy envelope. It boasted Axis' flame seal.

My dearest Lexia,
I will keep my vow.

Lexia's heart soared, and she almost missed the shiny envelope at the bottom of the stack.

Copper leaf.

A surge of adrenaline sent Lexia's pulse pounding. She opened the envelope to find a slip of black paper with a signet in the shape of a shooting star, and only two words were written on the invitation.

Founding Ball.

Lexia would need to find a dress.

After spending last night with Lexia in his arms, Axis felt revived and ready to conquer the empire. Which meant dressing down to blend in at the train depots. The spiraling tracks twirled around buildings only ten years in their infancy, but designed to look two hundred years old with turrets, parapets, and verandas. It was a stark contrast compared to the pristine, brick offices at Flicker's Factories.

Here, at the train stations, people filed in and out, all in higher spirits thanks to the Founding Season. Mandatory vacation sent shoppers on their way to stimulate the economy throughout Winter's capital city. With gifts to share and balls to attend, there was no shortage of intellectual property to barter and exchange.

In his hand-woven sweater and tailored slacks, Axis still stood out. He was already taller than most of the citizens at six feet, four inches, but there was little he could do to change his skin and eye color—a trademark of his family's genes. Most people politely ignored him, but some stared and whispered.

Axis smiled for everyone, searching the crowd for a familiar face—There.

Mrs. Tenz stepped off the train and noticed Axis immediately. He was sad to see her smile lessen as he approached. He hoped it had more to do with her leaving the factory after six years rather than something to do with him personally.

"Good morning, Mrs. Tenz."

She blushed a little as she took the hand Axis offered. "Good morning, Master Flicker."

He almost gagged before saying, "Just 'Axis' will do." He hated being associated with his father. "Do you mind if I ask you some questions about why you left the factory for mining in the crater?"

Mrs. Tenz's resolve hardened in her brown eyes, and she led Axis to a bench, saying, "I think you should take a seat." He did, and she sat beside him. "You're a hero to us, Axis. The way you fought for our benefits increases last term gave me the means to send my son to Dr.

Tempest's university for medicine. I bartered an entire year of leave for that privilege, but I only had it because of you."

In such a public setting, Axis swallowed and tried to maintain eye contact despite the emotion coming from the older woman.

"But the machine managers and shift enforcers are…handsy."

Axis' brows shot up as Mrs. Tenz continued, "I've been working the looms for six years now. I don't need a lineman showing me how to do it, especially not by pressing the length of his body against me."

This was an outrage. Axis' skin felt hot as he said, "I'll challenge him to a duel today. Which one was it?"

Mrs. Tenz shook her head. "No, young man. The People's Prince. I won't have you dying for my honor. I left, and that was enough."

Axis frowned and ran a hand through his hair with a sigh. "Would you at least tell me who it was so I can begin the removal process?"

"Your father knows. I filed a complaint with him."

Axis didn't bother hiding his wince. His father knew. Of course the tyrant knew. He said, "I appreciate your honesty, Mrs. Tenz. Now can you please tell me what else my father knows that I don't?"

Axis spoke to three other former employees to complete the full picture. Trusted and long-term professionals complained of sexual harassment, verbal abuse, and even beatings on more than one occasion. It was enough to turn his stomach, especially since every one of them had filed a complaint with the Factory Master's office.

How did this fall off of Axis' radar? And why in Winter would these people, with such esteemed positions, start behaving this way after a decade of compliance?

Something smelled foul.

Axis was too conspicuous to investigate on the factory floors where the managers would spy and report back to Valve. He'd need to hire a few spies of his own to gather concrete evidence before taking this to his father. It plagued his thoughts the entire car ride home. Only after he arrived at the brick mansion and received a butterfly-gilded letter did his mind stray to Lexia.

She was Axis' angel, his guiding light. Lexia was all that was right in the world. If she wanted to live in her father's manor after the two wed, he would gladly do so. If only he could bear Dr. Tempest's sole condition to asking her.

Wait.

The letter.

My loving Axis,

I know this is sudden, but would you escort me to the Founding Ball? Gauge Snow invited me, and I would love to dance the night away with you. In a dress. I'll consider it practice for our someday wedding.

Sincerely yours,

Lexia

Axis' chest felt tight, and he clutched the collar of his sweater. By planting both hands on his desk and drawing slow deep breaths, he managed to beat back the worst of the panic.

There was no place more public than the Founding Ball, and Axis' brain just tried to short circuit because he knew.

This was it.

This was the best opportunity to ask Lexia in front of hundreds, in front of their friends and families. In front of the officiator, Snow, himself. This was it.

Axis breathed deep until he fell calm and imagined the gorgeous smile on Lexia's face after he'd given her his timepiece for all of Winter and her father to see. And Dr. Tempest's pride in Axis, after all these years of tending his injuries, would only elevate the moment to the most unforgettable engagement in Winter's history.

The hard brown glass of Mrs. Tenz's eyes flashed in Axis' mind. It wasn't really the appropriate time to imagine his betrothal with the factories losing good laborers and Snow benefiting from the misfortune. But before Axis could confront his father, he'd need evidence. So Axis picked up the phone and called in a few favors.

First, settle this business on the factory floors.

Then, ask Lexia for her hand in marriage.

Given enough determination, nothing was insurmountable.

Two

Silk Bindings

IN THE LATE MORNING, GAUGE AWOKE IN HIS BED FILLED WITH STRANGERS. He only knew they'd been brightly dressed the night before and proved extremely flexible. The lovely dancer was treating Gauge to some morning delight, waking him with her mouth hard at work. It left her ass free for the burly drummer to practice some rhythmic work before Gauge sent the pair on their way. He groaned, gripped her hair with his gloved hands, and arched his back as the female's draws quickened in time to her other lover's furious beat.

It was a glorious way to start the day—Hell, to start the Founding Season. Now the pair would have an unforgettable story to tell, seeing to Gauge's needs. Jan, the Cathedral's butler, showed Gauge's bed fellows out while the Count showered alone. As he washed through his braids, he glimpsed his hands. They were paler than the rest of him from lack of exposure, but it was a necessary precaution.

Gauge gloved his fingers before allowing the servants to dress him for the day. A high collar and hand-sewn slacks might seem overdressed and impractical for the work ahead of him, but there really was no remedy for good taste.

When breakfast came, Gauge took out a vial from his kit and dusted its contents across the eggs and bread.

No reaction.

Then for the juice, he took out a dropper and tested it.

Nothing.

Yes, doing so altered the experience, but Gauge had long become accustomed to the tangy aftertaste coating every meal and every drink save for his private bar in the vault.

Afterward, Gauge slipped into another three-piece suit and sorted through his mail. He took the guest list and seating arrangements seriously. RSVPs were a necessary chore for the Founding Season events, including the ball and opera. One RSVP in particular caught his interest.

It was a white lace envelope with a black card inside. There was no message on it save for Lexia's gilded seal.

Style.

So few people had it on Winter, and her response left Gauge intrigued as to the sort of woman she'd become. Which brought him to the question—Where would he sit Lexia for the dinner? This late in the preparations there was only one table with an open seat, and he couldn't wait to see Axis' reaction.

It was enough to keep Gauge smirking on his way to the Cathedral's back entrance. There, a team of essential workers joined him on their time off to inspect the conditions in the mines. Each held a clipboard and wore the appropriate safety gear, while Gauge tipped his top hat to them on his way through the black iron door. His shiny spats glinted in what sunlight streaked through the domes, threatening his eyes but for their copper and glass shields. Everything appeared to him through a purple lens.

The copper mines comprised Gauge's backyard. He wasn't subtle about his ownership over them. Well, he wasn't subtle about anything. Steam lamps featuring Flicker wicks illuminated the cavernous pit perfectly, and, since Dr. Tempest fitted them with a slow-burning fiber, they never seemed to dim. They were the first tick in the box on his team's checklist. The next were the walkways and railings.

Gauge said, "Test these," and then he tried to wiggle a rail, much to his team's horror.

"Sir!"

"Careful!"

He didn't resist grinning at them as he repeated, "I want to know if any of these have lost their integrity. Check for signs of rust and warping."

They spread out like insects scouring every inch of the crater while Gauge amused himself by recalling his father's lessons.

"The Ignis Meteor site was a gift, holding enough copper to finance the future."

The old man was right, but he hadn't lived to see how much so.

Gauge strolled down the gangway, touching his gloved fingers along a vein of shiny ore. Fixed beside it were the pickaxe schedules with this spot high on the priority list. It bore Mrs. Tenz signature. Gauge recalled Axis' outrage from the day before, and it struck Gauge as sentimental. Perhaps, there was cause to check on the woman's progress, to see how she was settling into her new role as forewoman. Surely it was an improvement over having some lineman sweat all over her day in and day out.

And what about Valve? Why was he allowing such discontent in his factories?

Why, it was almost as if he was intentionally spoiling his son's inheritance, here on the brink. And as much as Gauge truly enjoyed the young man's discomfort, it wouldn't do to see their balance disturbed in any lasting way.

"Sir?"

The team leader joined Gauge on the top floor. "Yes?"

This annual inspection hinged on him employing the best, which was evident by the man's list of concerns as he said, "There's some rust and calcium buildup on the bolts on thirty-second sub level at the second intersection…" He carried on for quite some time.

Long enough to see Gauge lean on his cane after standing in one place for so long. When the team leader finished, he said, "Excellent work. You'll see additional time off in your benefits if you can oversee the improvements before this Founding Season ends and the other employees return."

"It will be done, sir."

Gauge nodded. "Dismissed."

Once the team leader set off to delegate his tasks, Gauge went to turn and nearly winced for the creak of his bones, and he was slow to exit the mine. Curse the malady. But the stiffness was his own fault. He'd fallen behind on his physical therapy again, and this was his price to pay.

Gauge refused to let it sour his mood as he submitted the new seating arrangements to his butler. It was well worth Jan's eyes doubling in size. He even did a double-take as if to check and make sure Gauge wasn't joking with him.

The Count of Copper asked, "Is there a problem, Jan?"

The butler blinked his eyes back to their normal size and shook himself out of the shock. "No, sir. I will see to it."

"Good. Oh, and invite Mrs. Tenz to dinner tonight. I have some business with our new forewoman."

Jan went off in search of the crew manning the upcoming Founding Ball, while Gauge returned to his conservatory. He looked forward to investigating this business with Flicker's Factories. Perhaps, he'd even solve it right under Axis' nose.

Now there was a notion to bring a smile to Gauge's face.

———————————————

"And Snow will protect Winter. May it never thaw."

Lexia's students finished the last line of Winter's anthem, which always left her a little melancholy. Why wouldn't they want it to thaw? Perhaps, the Copper Count wasn't the best protector for Winter's people?

A tiny throat cleared, bringing Lexia out of her thoughts. She'd been staring down at her hands on the piano while the children of Tempest Manor waited expectantly for their next lesson. Five in the front, the tenors and altos, and four in the back, the sopranos. They varied in age and maturity, but all of them had been born under Dr. Tempest's care.

A little girl in the front asked, "Ms. Tempest, can we play our instruments now?" She swiped a hand under her nose and gave a sniff.

Lexia smiled. Kids. She said, "Of course."

Each of them left their places on the stands to break out woodwinds, violins, and brass. The music room doubled as the ballroom, so the draperies softened the acoustics and made for a perfect room to give lessons.

This time, when Lexia played accompaniment to the anthem, her students played along. Despite a few off-tempo moments or the occasional mistake, they finished their practice without a hitch.

"Excellent. Well done!"

The children beamed at Lexia while they all clapped. She stood from the piano and gave a deep theater bow. The kids clasped their hands together and did the same.

The head chef entered the room, calling, "Marey!"

The little girl with the sniffles stood and said, "Coming," before running into her mother's arms.

"Thank you, again, Ms. Tempest for the instruction." The chef half-curtsied with her daughter in hand. "Say thank you, Marey."

Marey swiped her nose on her mother's arm before saying, "Thank you, miss."

Lexia beamed and closed the lid over the piano keys to hide the extra shine in her eyes. "You were a treasure as always."

More parents filtered into the room to collect their children—the drivers, cobblers, and the seamstresses. The last of which Lexia asked a favor.

They both gaped at her before breaking out into full grins. "We would love to design a gown for you. Although it's last minute, I think I have the perfect fabric in mind."

"And the accessories—We can compile it all out of materials we have here. You'll steal the floor, even from Count Snow."

Well, wasn't that a bonus?

They took her measurements there on the spot and fussed over her height, while Lexia gave her input here and there. They didn't agree on every choice, but on one, she refused to back down.

"Lexia?"

She looked up to see her father walk into the room with a curious and slightly bemused expression on his gentle features.

Oh, right.

Lexia said, "I'd planned to tell you while we inspected the combines, but this afternoon got away from me. Gauge Snow has extended an invitation for my presence at the Foundation Ball, and I accepted."

Leon went still, blinking at his daughter.

The tension mounting in the room brought the seamstresses to excuse themselves, and Lexia frowned as she thanked them for their time. When they were alone, she tried to cut the tension with some news. "The Eastern orchards are asking for a union. I gave our task manager permission to meet their current demands before they escalate out of control—Father, did I do something wrong?" Her voice shook a little. She hadn't seen her father this way since her mother died.

With a shake of his head, Leon transformed back into the familiar figure of her childhood, saying, "No. Of course not. Did you say he sent you a personal invitation?"

They were back on the subject of Snow. Lexia went to his side and took the arm offered, saying, "Yes. On his signature stationery, or I suppose it must've been given it was made entirely out of copper. I returned the favor as is polite, of course. If that's what you're worried about." She couldn't shake the feeling that something was wrong.

Leon ran a hand through his sandy brown, chin-length hair while blowing the air from his cheeks. "It's not the stationery or even the manners that have me concerned, sweetheart." He led her outside into the acre of gardens off the ballroom's veranda, collecting his thoughts and considering his words.

It made Lexia more nervous, but she tried to put on a smile for him.

Twinkling lights in the birches and along the hedges illuminated Leon's weariness as he said, "We have an accord with Count Snow's mines and the Flicker Factory Masters. It's a delicate power structure, but it ensures the happiness of everyone who works under us, including you and I."

"Yes. I've read the treatise." More like memorized it.

Leon peered down at her, almost the same height but with worlds more experience lining his kind gray eyes. He said, "What isn't written there are the politics at play. One cannot simply trade silk to the loom weavers without it coming under scrutiny of each party at play. There are bids to make and egos to stroke. None of them quite so mercurial as Gauge Snow."

Oh.

Lexia bit her lip, as her father continued to make his point. "Until this moment, Gauge has ignored your piece on the board, the queen protected by the rest of us pawns. Together, Axis and I kept his attention from you, hoping it would last until you took my seat at our offices on the Boulevard, but it seems we have failed."

Leon turned and faced his daughter, taking her hands in his. He wouldn't meet her eyes, and it bothered Lexia. She said, "Father, you're forgetting that the queen is the most formidable piece on the board. She protects the king and the kingdom."

That got a smile out of Leon, bitter as it was. "That's what concerns me." He lifted his eyes to meet hers, no longer filled with concern. There was irony there, instead. "You are formidable, my child, and there's no way of knowing how Gauge will respond to you. He could banish you to one of the other cities, or force you to work in the mines. Or, heaven forbid, he might propose to you on the spot."

Lexia couldn't contain her laughter, but the slight tightness around her father's eyes sobered her quickly. She hugged him, saying, "I understand, and I promise to do my best not to shame you or find myself betrothed to the most loathsome man in all of Winter."

Leon shook his head on top of Lexia's hair. "That's the kind of talk that worries me."

———————————————

Axis despised dining with his father, but on condition of remaining the Flicker heir, he was required to eat with the monster at least once per week. Fortunately, a long dining table of iron-wrapped wood separated them in the formal space. The servants had parted the red velvet drapes to reveal the city's seasonal light displays. It was a cheery backdrop to a drab evening.

One day, Lexia's kind eyes and radiant skin would lift this house into a home.

One day.

Until then, Axis tolerated his father's chronic chest congestion, reverberating off the walls and putting Axis off his meal.

Valve coughed into his Tempest linen napkin, but managed to suck in enough air to say, "I understand Snow has invited our darling Lexia to the Founding Ball this year. It makes one nervous, does it not?" He quirked a heavy burgundy brow on his thick face.

Axis hated to admit it, but Gauge's interest in Lexia had been on Axis' mind. He said, "It only makes sense. She *is* the crop heiress." And that's all the stakes Axis hoped Gauge had invested in her.

Valve gulped for air, and somehow smirked while doing it. A knowing, rotten expression. "Let's hope he behaves himself. You know how laser-focused he can get. Do you have any diversions planned to spare the poor girl from his attentions?" Where Axis' green eyes were soft, Valve's were hard as stained glass, and they shone with malice.

Axis had one diversion in mind, but he wasn't about to share it with his father. Instead of answering, he tapped his napkin to his mouth and pushed his untouched plate away. "It's been miserable, as usual, father, but I must see to some business—"

"Light my cigar first before you go."

Bastard.

All the muscles in Axis' body seized, and he clenched his jaw to keep from shouting. "No."

Valve chuckled as he lit the Snow exclusive himself. The round cherry glowed when he took a drag, and Axis shuddered. His father ignored him, saying, "The doctors tell me my one vice will eventually be the death of me."

It certainly seemed so as a coughing fit seized the heavy man. He gasped for air like this breath would be his last. One could only hope.

Seeing the weakness in Valve returned Axis' strength, and he stood, gliding to his father's end of the table. He glared at the coughing tyrant. "Whatever you're scheming, leave Lexia out of it."

Valve's fit eased, and he wasted the air in his lungs to say, "Be sure to tell Snow the same."

Before Axis left the dining room, he turned back to see Valve staring at his napkin.

It was coated in blood.

Axis couldn't wait for his father to die, and it looked like he wouldn't have to wait much longer.

The factories on Flicker Avenue were quieter than usual with most of the staff off for the Founding Season. Axis met the inspection teams at the site in the Factory Master's offices, spanning the entire top floor of the textile mill. It was the closest to the Avenue with the paper mills being the farthest to keep the smell from permeating the more populated areas under the dome. Acres and acres of factories stretched out to touch the horizon and then some.

It wasn't a small dominion to inherit, and Axis took his role seriously. To the inspection teams, he said, "Check every safety precaution, including pinch points. Update the documentation to reflect any hazards, and I expect recommendations on how to prevent them. We went an entire year—" An entire year since the last Founding Season when Axis took over, "—Without a single injury. I plan to keep the streak going."

"Yes, sir!"

Axis beamed at them, saying, "See to it."

All but one took off to their respective tasks. A petite woman with long black hair and big blue eyes lingered.

Axis hated to ask this of anyone, but… "Do you understand your role, Ms. Cloud?"

Tija Cloud lifted a compact and applied some bright red lipstick in the mirror. She said, "It will be done, sir, and don't worry. I'll enjoy this." She gave him a wink.

It actually made Axis laugh. "All right. If you run into trouble, come find me."

The young woman smiled and headed out. She stopped in the doorway to say over her shoulder, "Ms. Tempest is a lucky girl, sir."

"You're dismissed, Ms. Cloud."

The salute she gave as she went about her business left Axis incredulous. He chuckled into the files on his desk. There was no shortage of young women and men with compliments for Axis, but he found only one person desirable. He knew the same was true for Lexia. They were made for each other.

Tija was a friend, but… Well, there were more reasons than her looks for why he'd selected her for the task. Hopefully, this would reveal the truth.

After some time at work, Axis pulled up his sleeve to check his timepiece. An hour had passed. How long should he give Tija to work? He considered the glossy red of her full lips and decided she'd had enough time to draw some attention.

Axis left the office and tried to tread lightly as he strolled from dyes to the looms and deeper into the textile plant. He kept his hands in his pockets, trying to appear casual as he encountered a few of his inspectors. It was a required chore of the foremen, but Axis was searching for one in particular.

Mrs. Tenz had complained about a lineman on the looms, and the foreman in charge was equally aggressive when she filed her formal complaint. Walker was his name, and Axis sought him for answers—

A crash sounded from above in the crow's nest, and a woman's scream resounded.

Axis bounded up the stairs into the foreman's office and…

Lost his damned mind.

Walker had wrenched Tija's wrists behind her back and bent her over his desk. Axis arrived just in time to stop the bastard from hurting her. He gripped the broader man by the shoulders and threw him across the room.

"Tija, are you all right?"

She cried, "Look out!"

Axis stepped aside before the Foreman could drop a terracotta pot on Axis' head. Was this fool trying to kill the heir to one-third of the occupations on Winter?!

Axis punched the man in the throat and kneed him in the crotch.

Walker fell to his knees, clutching his sensitive areas as all the air whooshed out of him. He turned red in the face and spittle gathered on his lip like he was about to vomit.

Axis growled, "Stay down." He turned to the woman. "Tija?"

One of her eyes was wincing closed with purple swelling at the site. "I'm fine," she lied while blood dripped onto her lashes.

Axis grabbed her by the biceps and looked her over. "It's bad. I think you may need surgery on the bone." Hot rage boiled in his veins. "I'll kill him."

"No, no, Prince. You got what you needed to bar him from any employment. It's better than he deserves, but you've done enough. Thank you."

No matter how Tija put it, guilt and shame suffused Axis and dampened his anger. He'd put her in this position, exploitation and all.

Under Winter's watchful dome, was Axis any better than Gauge?

The crater's inspection went smoothly, not that Gauge had expected it to go any other way. The mines were in tiptop shape, ensuring the safety of workers and his peace of mind. No complaints meant no protests which could risk becoming riots. And Gauge couldn't have discontent on his planet, now could he?

Which was why he'd invited Mrs. Tenz to dinner.

Gauge was in the conservatory when Jan let her in. Gauge stood and extended his gloved hand, which she took with a pink flush to her cheeks. This amused Gauge, and he brought her knuckles a breath away from his lips.

Mrs. Tenz looked away, more flustered than enticed.

Gauge let her go, not willing to risk making her uncomfortable. "Thank you for joining me, tonight. I hope Mr. Tenz doesn't mind." He gestured at the seat across from the bistro set.

She sat down, saying, "I was widowed during a duel after the fifth Founding Day. I have seen little point in remarrying."

"My condolences." Gauge waited until she was settled to take his seat and gestured for Jan to begin the dinner service.

Mrs. Tenz smiled kindly as she said, "It's not for you to worry about, dear Count. You're busy overseeing the mines. They were much cleaner than I imagined."

Gauge found her smile infectious and returned in kind. "You know? You're not the first person to say that, but I take the health and safety of every one of my employees seriously. There's no miner's lung in my crater. How were the conditions at the factory for you?" He eased into the point.

Jan served the soup course, and Gauge ignored it. No vials and droppers in the presence of company.

Mrs. Tenz took to it gently, trying to imitate an etiquette she'd never had the privilege to actually witness. It wasn't a poor imitation. She just forgot to slip her napkin into her lap, but she did sip from the side of her spoon. After dabbing her lips, she said, "It's delicious."

Ever the gracious host, Gauge bowed his head, but spurred, "I assume the loom weaving in the factory was quite sterile."

"Are you and Axis working together on this investigation?" Mrs. Tenz surprised him with her question.

So Axis *was* oblivious to his father's mismanagement. The poor genuine fool. Gauge nodded. "Yes. We're interested in how Master Flicker mishandled the situation. Only I believe I'm a few steps ahead of the young Prince. He's still misinformed, while I'm aware of how your Factory Master ignored your complaints. I'm only interested in why, and I was hoping you might know."

Sure. One might assume a woman working on the factory floor wouldn't know a damned thing about the happenings within the top tier of the hierarchy, but being small meant being invisible. Being invisible meant hearing and seeing things others might otherwise keep secret. Gauge would know. He'd been small most of his life.

Mrs. Tenz finished her soup in silence, while emotions warred within her eyes. Loyalty. Safety, even. She had to look after herself and her son. If she was privy to behind-the-scenes knowledge, it might endanger her.

Gauge said, "I understand you traded a year of your time off benefits for a year of enrollment into Dr. Tempest's university for your son. I could guarantee the young man's continued enrollment with no need for you to barter anything at all."

The woman dropped her salad fork and gaped openly at Gauge. The shock conveyed even as Jan took her plate and exchanged it for their roasted entrée. Eventually, she blinked down at her plate as if she'd only just realized the change. With her eyes averted, Mrs. Tenz said, "Sir, I don't think I could accept such a generous offer."

"It's not charity, my good woman. You have information I want, and I'm willing to support your son's education for it."

That got Mrs. Tenz thinking. There was so much intelligence behind the cognac glass of her eyes. She could be shrewd; Gauge saw it in the clench of her jaw as she considered. She said, "I want protection."

Again, he bowed with his head. "Consider it granted. From hereon, you will have a shadow that will prevent any harm coming to your person—" He held up his hands to stave her and continued, "And your son's."

A tension left Mrs. Tenz body in a physical sigh of relief. "Thank you. The foremen talk, and sometimes the Factory Master would join them. Most of it was typical barbarism: sex, gambling—any vice, you can name it. But sometimes it bordered on…"

"Yes, Mrs. Tenz?" Gauge kept his voice neutral when he really wanted to accelerate the conversation.

She closed her eyes before saying a word that made her shudder. "Hedonism."

The conversation had taken an unexpected turn. "How so?"

With her eyes still closed, the woman paled until she turned green. A tear forced its way from her lashes and streaked down her cheek.

Gauge steepled his gloved fingers to his lips and waited. Pushing her now might break her.

"Child abuse." Mrs. Tenz's voice broke on a half-sob. Then the floodgates opened, and she let everything out on a rush as if purging herself of a toxin. "Violence. Perversion. They boasted of the terrible things they subjected onto their own children, too, and it seemed boundless in its sin. Master Flicker wasn't above it, and now I know things about our Prince that I wished I didn't see whenever I look at him."

Gauge stilled. Everything in him went quiet, except for a ringing in his ears.

Valve had abused Axis?

Mrs. Tenz wasn't finished. "And then I heard him say, 'The factories will go to the people before I ever let my parasite of a son have it.' Can you believe it?"

Yes.

Gauge could.

He personally saw Mrs. Tenz out after he insisted she enjoy the rest of her dinner. She was kind enough to ask Jan for the recipes, and Gauge made a note to invite more of his employees over for intimate dinners.

"Sir, the ballroom is prepared for tomorrow afternoon's events. Would you like to inspect it before you turn in for the night?"

Gauge went through the motions of approving the table settings and the decor. "Everything is perfect," he said, but his mind was elsewhere.

It wasn't until he was alone in his room that he replayed the conversation with Mrs. Tenz. Gauge left his spectacles on his dresser and his gloves on his desk. The massive bed with its Flicker silk sheets welcomed Gauge and his melancholy for a long sleepless night.

Valve.

Abused.

Axis.

This was new information. Now only one question remained.

What was Gauge prepared to do with it?

THREE

Black Chrysalis

LEXIA WOKE THE NEXT MORNING, SQUEEZING HER PILLOW. She couldn't wait to sleep an entire night in Axis' bed. Truth be told, it was the primary reason she wanted to marry him. To sleep in his arms and feel his even breathing through his broad chest. She hated the laws preventing them from doing so before marriage, including the ones about children. As in, it wasn't permitted without Snow's officiation. But enough with the negative thoughts.

It was the big day, and Lexia found herself looking forward to the ball. Yes, some part of her hoped Axis would propose, but less so than their last date night. It was an extremely crowded venue, and therefore less likely to be the place.

But a girl could dream.

Especially as Lexia snuggled into a sweater she'd stolen from Axis. The sophisticated woodsy scent of him lingered in the cotton, and she cherished it.

A knock sounded from beyond her sitting room, interrupting the cozy moment. The seamstress' voice carried through the oak door. "Miss? It's time."

Lexia blew the air from her cheeks, fluffing her bangs. Would it seriously take all day to fit her into the dress? She said, "I'll be right there." It surprised her to find a handful of servants waiting outside her door, arms full of supplies, and two of them had thought to bring Lexia's breakfast. "I take it we'll be at this a while?"

Three set her down at her vanity and attacked her hair immediately. Two set down kits and went about her makeup. And the others laid out fabric in striking colors and luxurious materials, prepared for phase II. Lexia had never felt so fussed over.

But four hours later, as the entire picture was coming together, Lexia was near tears. She said, "Thank you for all the thought you've put into this."

"Don't ruin your makeup, miss," one tutted at her.

Lexia peered over at the sweater laid out on her made bed and imagined Axis' reaction to her appearance tonight. Perhaps today *was* finally the day. It certainly wouldn't be a waste of all this hard work.

"Lexia?" Her father was at the door.

Lexia said, "Don't come in! You'll spoil the reveal."

She could hear his chuckle on the other side. "Very well, dear. I suppose you won't join me for the drive over?"

"Go ahead, father. I want to make my own entrance."

"To Axis' delight I'm sure. Rhyme will be waiting for you."

When Lexia stuck her tongue out at the mention of her bodyguard, the ladies and gentlemen in the room fussing over her broke into giggles and chuckles. She said, "Sorry. I know that's not very mature of me."

"It's why we love you, dear."

Lexia beamed for a moment before a thought made her frown. Tonight, she would meet Gauge Snow for the first time since they were children. The thought made her glance at her desk drawer, where memories waited inside. The Count of Copper.

This would make for one hell of a first impression.

Axis had been fourteen when the world by its original name ended. He remembered it better than Lexia, being a year older than her, but he couldn't recall much about the apocalyptic event itself. He only knew that every year he had to hear about how it was saved and made into Winter.

The Founding Season.

Thousands celebrated on the streets and hundreds celebrated at the Copper Cathedral, but only dozens were invited into its interior for the ball. The spacious room was immaculate in its decor and arrangement with every diner dressed in their best fashion for the year.

Axis among them, especially since Lexia would attend this year. With her eyes in mind, he'd dressed in a black double-breasted tuxedo with a butterfly pinned to his breast pocket. He ensured the sleeves of his button down and jacket combined were loose enough to slide over his timepiece when the time came. He could only imagine the look on her face when he finally asked her in front of all these people.

Unfortunately, it was a rather packed room.

Gauge had sat Axis with his father and the other higher ups among Flicker's Factories. He'd rather be seated with Dr. Tempest across the way. The kind man toasted his champagne at Axis, and he returned the gesture.

Where was Lexia?

As far as Axis could tell, there were no other seats available at Leon's table—

The entire room stood, and Axis joined them with a roll of his eyes.

Their host and Winter's Founder strode into the ballroom. His tux and tails were black with copper piping sewn throughout to emphasize his long legs and the breadth of his shoulders. Neither of which were as impressive as Axis's features, but the boxer's build suited the Count at six foot, two inches. However, Axis noted, the older bachelor wore his signature gloves and spectacles per usual.

"Welcome. Welcome, friends, to another Founding Season."

People cheered. Axis faked his clapping. Where was Lexia?

Gauge continued with his speech. "This year marks our decennial anniversary into our quaint way of life, uncomplicated by our dependency on electronics. While, yes, Winter still endures an ice age, it no longer keeps us prisoner."

Sometimes Axis wondered how Gauge, a budding scientist all of nineteen years old, had predicted the electromagnetic pulse from their star to begin with. Axis had asked once as a teenager and suffered greatly for the inquiry. He'd never asked again.

Gauge twirled his jewel-topped cane, implying excitement, with a hint of mischief in his smile. "And this is no ordinary Founding Season. I'm proud to announce, thanks to the talent and dedication of our engineering team, we are opening our fourth city in sector twelve!"

Axis blinked. Sector twelve was a tundra...

"Through the power of steam, we shielded the site and thawed the ice until it became habitable once again. As we grow our communities, it is essential we make room for all this progress. It couldn't be done without each of you. Give yourselves a round of applause."

Thunder erupted from outside the Cathedral as people in the streets burst into applause.

Even Axis clapped sincerely this time. Gauge always planned for the future, but to Axis, it was almost like the man was running from the past.

Gauge waited for his audience to quiet down before saying, "We break ground once the Season is over. Until then, enjoy yourselves. We have much to celebrate."

Guests took their seats, and musicians played their instruments in a soft ambiance to the dinner.

Before Valve took his seat beside Axis, he muttered with a half-cough, "Let's get to him before Leon does."

Axis was busy looking at the doors. He said, "You go. I intend to enjoy my time off."

"Oh, like you enjoyed breaking Walker's jaw yesterday afternoon?"

That brought Axis back around and glaring at his father. "He deserved worse." There was an implied, "So do you."

Valve humphed and went to intercept Gauge, already swarming with guests. The second the old man stepped into Gauge's line of sight, the Count handed him a fresh box of cigars, saying, "You'll need these for all of our planning meetings."

Axis shook his head. It was enough to make him nauseous—

A hush fell over the crowd again, but this quiet was more natural, less forced. All the guests stared at the door, including Gauge, who lowered his glasses to peer over the lenses without their filter. When Axis turned and saw why, his heart jumped in his throat, forcing him to swallow it back down with an audible gulp.

Lexia.

Her gown was black matte velvet with accents of glittering gold interlaced throughout her skirts, bustle, and bodice. Gold lace stretched across her sweetheart neckline to wrap around her biceps delicately. Her signature timepiece stood out on her wrist and black gloves covered her skin to the off-the-shoulder sleeves. What made her stand out even more amongst the ladies in the room was that the front of her skirt only consisted of a tufted apron, revealing her long legs wrapped in thick black tights. Her stiletto-heeled boots went over her knees with gold strands lacing up the length of them.

As if nervous from the sudden silence, Lexia brushed aside some of the loose strands of her white wavy hair. The rest was braided back and knotted from her face, interlaced with strands of gold. She wore a strip of gold around her neck and that was all, letting the dress decorate her enough for the entrance.

When Lexia met Axis' eyes across the ballroom, hers lit up with a smile far more beautiful than any gown.

"What happens behind closed doors, stays behind closed doors, Axis."

The memory of Valve's breath, hot on Axis' neck, never faded, and he was shamed into looking away from the love of his life. Yes, everyone in the room knew they were in a relationship together. No, Axis couldn't handle all of their eyes on the couple.

Even though this was the perfect public venue and Lexia had never looked more beautiful outside of his bedroom, Axis couldn't do it.

He just couldn't…

Lexia Tempest was the most beautiful person Gauge had ever laid eyes on, and he couldn't fathom why Axis would look away from her—*How* Axis could look away from her. No one else in the room seemed able. Her response to Axis' downcast eyes was even more astounding. Her radiant smile transformed into one of sweetness and elegance. She tipped her chin politely at her suitor before joining her father at his table in a graceful glide across the room.

Soft tendrils of her white hair kissed Lexia's pale shoulders and brushed the golden laced back of her bodice as she made her way across the room. Only then did Gauge realize he was looking over the brim of his glasses. The light from the gas lamps lanced into his corneas, and the pain was enough to break Lexia's spell over Gauge just in time for her to notice there was no table setting for her. Even perplexed, she looked magnificent.

It was about the same time Gauge noticed Leon staring at him from across the room. There was icy terror in Dr. Tempest's gray eyes, and only now would Gauge think her father had cause for concern. Lexia was an eligible heiress of marrying age, and Winter's best kept secret from Gauge.

She peered around and waved down Jan with another sweet smile. Lexia's voice was warm and a little husky as she said, "Excuse me. Where am I seated?" She spared Axis a hopeful glance.

He finally managed to meet her eyes again across the room.

Gauge was invested in the interaction, and so was everyone else. He signaled for the musicians to continue playing, and they startled from the scene unfolding before them as if they'd only remembered why they were at the ball to begin with. At least it was amusing.

Jan said, "Come with me, Ms. Tempest," and Gauge almost laughed at himself for how perfectly this was working out. Axis and Leon both watched closely as the fair maiden followed the butler across the room to the only table with an empty seat.

Valve leaned in to murmur, "Excuse me, Count, but I believe a deserving important guest has usurped my position here. Enjoy your evening. I plan to immensely." Old man Flicker coughed into his handkerchief as he went back to his table leaving Gauge alone with Lexia.

She looked surprised, and he couldn't help but notice how it affected her with the neckline of her bodice being so low. Every shallow breath she took was tantalizing.

Gauge felt the men of Lexia's life boring holes into the back of his head, but this was the Founding Season. The festival of Gauge's accomplishments. Not a damned thing would deter him from enjoying himself.

When he took a step toward Lexia, she stiffened, a response Gauge ignored to pull her chair back for her. He said, "Ms. Tempest, I'm afraid your invitation and RSVP came too late to squeeze you into another table arrangement. But perhaps you won't mind joining me for dinner."

Lexia glanced over Gauge's shoulder toward her father before saying, "You honor me, Count Snow. Of course I will join you." She sat down, accepting the scenario with class and grace.

Gauge tried to resist getting close to her ear as he leaned down to scoot her forward and said, "Splendid. I hope you find the meal to your liking," before taking his seat across the table. "Would you care for some wine? Or champagne? There's much to celebrate."

Lexia bit her lip.

While Gauge understood she was considering her words, the gesture drew attention to the deep burgundy of her supple mouth. The deep red was the same shade as Axis' hair.

As Axis glared at them from across the tables, Gauge sympathized with the younger man. Lexia was easily the most beautiful person in the room, certainly the most exotic in all of Winter, and losing her to Axis' phobia of public engagements would be a hard loss from which to recover. But that didn't mean Gauge wasn't entertained with the daggers shooting his way.

Lexia said, "I heard your announcement about the new city. You must be very proud of your engineers who worked so hard to expand your dominion."

Interesting.

Gauge resented the purple filter of his spectacles because he'd give anything to see how her coloring changed with the last word of her remark. "Your choice of words intrigues me, Ms. Tempest. Would you care to elaborate on why you consider this 'my dominion' rather than an advancement for all of Winter?"

When she bit her lip this time, Gauge wanted to lean across the table, thoroughly curious as to her next statement. She was clearly putting forth a great deal of effort to weigh her words carefully.

"All of Winter is yours, Count. Every advancement is made under your watchful eye, and there won't be a soul in this new city who isn't indebted to your genius. As are we all."

Was Gauge detecting disdain from the young woman? He laced his gloved hands against his mouth and stared at Lexia.

Despite the weight of his gaze, the brave and eloquent young woman didn't squirm under his scrutiny. Lexia only stared at him with her black eyes open and full of honesty. Her opinion of him was low, and this stimulated Gauge. So few people were ever honest with him, Axis being the rare exception. But Gauge imagined if the younger man were seated at this table right now, even his jaw would've dropped onto his plate.

Lexia was rare, indeed.

Lexia's heart pounded as she assessed Gauge's reaction to her dangerous words. She could practically feel the panic coming from her father and Axis across the grand ballroom. But Gauge's reactions challenged her diplomacy.

"Do you consider yourself 'indebted to my genius,' Ms. Tempest?"

She almost closed her eyes to hide from the scrutiny of his gaze. Gauge stared hard at her from behind his violet lenses, assessing her every response. Lexia was endangering the accord, but she wouldn't compromise her integrity. She said, "I suppose if there were any man to whom I was indebted, it would only be my father for the privilege of being his daughter."

While Gauge's gloved hands remained laced at his chin, he quirked a brow. "Then what do *you* owe me?"

Lexia treaded less carefully. "According to all of Winter, I owe you whatever you can imagine."

Gauge's eyes flared a little wider behind his glasses before he asked, "And according to you?"

"Nothing."

His laughter was incredulous and amused. Lexia was reluctant to admit it was a pleasant sound, rich in its warmth, and she guessed it wasn't a sound often heard. At least, the people flinching around the room let her assume as much.

Gauge hadn't touched his food, but neither had Lexia. Their conversation had proved too engaging. He said, "Well, you may not owe me anything, but *I* would be honored if you promised me your first dance of the evening."

It wasn't a question.

Lexia took a deep breath, straining against the corset of her bodice to take in enough air to think. These things were ridiculous—

Gauge cleared his throat and shifted in his seat. Lexia wondered if he was getting impatient for her response. Should she dare hazard a glance at her father or, worse, Axis? She wasn't a damsel in need of rescuing, but Leon's words yesterday about the delicate balance made it less easy to speak without heavy consideration.

"You flatter me, Count Snow. What have I done to deserve such a distinction?"

This time, Gauge's chuckle was more familiar, reminding her of their distant childhood. He said, "You upstaged me at my own ball and spoke your mind in my presence. Both are uncommon and, in your case, welcome. Feel free to tell me what you think of me anytime, Ms. Tempest."

Lexia hid her surprise. Every word rang as sincere. The rumble of her stomach reminded Lexia she hadn't eaten since breakfast.

As if Gauge heard it, too, he said, "The soup is delicious."

Hungry and unwilling to be completely impolite to her host, Lexia took a sip and instantly fought not to moan. She waved Jan over while Gauge scrutinized her every move.

The butler arrived. "Yes, Ms. Tempest?"

Lexia smiled at the older man with chocolate brown eyes. "Can you please extend my compliments to your chefs? And to whomever decorated. It's all divine."

Jan bowed deeply. "I certainly will, miss." He half bowed to Gauge before leaving. "Sir."

Curse his glasses. Lexia couldn't read a thing on his face at times. Like right now, he was staring at her, unreadable in every way. It bothered her enough to say, "Count Snow, a lady might think she had soup on her face."

The man smiled. He didn't smirk smugly or grin evilly. It was a beautiful spread of his full lips, one she imagined reached his eyes if she could see them. Gauge said, "You possess no such flaws, nor any at all that I can see."

Lexia's cheeks warmed, and she looked away from his radiant expression. Before she could stop herself, she said, "I suppose you've told many a woman she was flawless."

Something about Gauge's expression darkened. "No, Ms. Tempest. As you've already said, all the women of Winter are indebted to me. I have no need to pay compliments in exchange for my heart's desires."

Lexia almost winced. She'd offended him. Well, of course she had.

A servant came to clear the plates, after which Gauge asked, "What else would you like to speak openly about? I know there's more, and you'll never have a better chance."

A bitterness sharpened the edge of his words. Had Lexia done worse than offend Gauge? Had she truly wounded him? But when she met his eyes through the purple lenses, she wanted to oblige him.

Lexia let the words spill from her without filter. "I think it's despicable of you to dedicate an entire season to yourself every year under the disguised virtue of mandatory paid time off."

Gauge didn't seem surprised by this approximation, but he'd remained silent for so long, Lexia wanted to squirm. Her bodice was too tight, and it threatened to steal her breath away—

For one second…

No, surely Lexia had imagined it.

Did Gauge's eyes flick briefly to her breasts? After she'd insulted him?

He broke through her thoughts by asking, "How is it any different to the plays about you and Axis? The songs…?"

Lexia said, "Those are built on love."

"So is the Founding Season."

"It's built on fear."

Gauge looked away finally and signaled for his staff to bring dessert. Without meeting Lexia's eyes again, he said, "You're under no obligation to dance with someone you find so despicable. I'd said I welcome your honesty, and I meant it. However, I find your observations lacking perspective, and you seem like an otherwise insightful woman. A strong willed one at that. It makes me want to challenge your notions and encourage you to tolerate my presence enough to broaden your predetermined inclinations. So what say you?"

Lexia blinked at Gauge. He still wanted to dance after everything she'd just said? To 'broaden her predetermined inclinations…'

"I didn't mean to upset her. I only wanted to give her this present for her birthday. Lexia, I'm sorry. Axis, please don't make me go home yet."

Lexia remembered little of her time with Gauge as a playmate. She'd been so young, and he was around so sporadically because of his illness. But there was one thing she couldn't forget. Gauge never wanted to go home.

"I'll dance with you, Count Snow."

If only for the sad little boy Lexia once knew Gauge to be.

Axis couldn't wait for the dinner portion of tonight's events to end, so he could steal Lexia away from Gauge's rakish gaze. Even with the glasses, Axis had seen the man's eyes lower to the elegant neckline of her bodice more than once. Why wasn't anyone doing anything?

Across the room, Dr. Tempest stared as if petrified—a frozen witness to the unfolding events. And Rhyme? Lexia's bodyguard stood behind Leon, watching her eat with their rogue of a host. He glanced Axis' way and gave an unhelpful shake of his head.

"She's breathtaking, isn't she, son?"

The last thing Axis needed right now was his father investing any attention to Lexia. He touched his timepiece beneath his sleeve, refusing to respond to Valve's barbs.

But the sickly man persisted after another round of coughing. "Lexia has grown into a fine young woman, and Gauge is a man of influence. Perhaps you were but a rung in the ladder on her way up to the top. I tried to warn you—"

"Father, I've learned quite a wealth of information from foreman Walker about your part in the recent dissension in our factories. I'd say it's enough evidence to sway the other Founding Families into legitimizing my challenging you to a public duel." Axis turned and faced Valve across the table, let him see the resolve in his son's eyes. "It would be the first permitted patricide in our brief history, but don't underestimate Dr. Tempest's and Count Snow's disdain for you."

Valve wheezed into his napkin, staring over it at Axis. He said, "Snow would never allow it."

Axis smiled, and he knew it was cruel. "Snow would allow anything if it provided him with enough entertainment. He could make a spectacle of it and demand the presence of every citizen in Winter. Why, I'm already certain that's how I'll pitch it to him. Threaten my inheritance again, and I will see it done."

There was a slinky shift to Valve's eyes, and Axis approximated he was already scheming other avenues to spoiling the factories out from under his son. But Axis couldn't care less so long as the man did it in silence.

Laughter burst from the front of the room, and Axis turned to see Gauge smiling at Lexia. It had startled many others who flinched at the unfamiliar sound. Dr. Tempest had closed his eyes like he was praying. Axis was relieved to see Rhyme re-sheathe some kind of weapon. At least they were all treating this with the gravity it deserved.

Reassurance.

That's what Axis needed, and he sought it in the same place he'd done his entire childhood. He didn't bother excusing himself from the Flicker's table as he made his way over to Dr. Tempest. The man's sandy brown hair boasted gray at the temples, but he still looked as kindly as always. He whispered to the associate beside him, who abandoned their seat for Axis.

Lexia's father tried to keep the conversation professional. "I heard you had some trouble in the looms yesterday."

"An opportunity presented itself which took a moment of physical exertion to seize."

It warmed Axis to see the older smile fondly at his choice of words. Dr. Tempest said, "Admirable. Let me know if I can help in any way." He kept his eyes on Gauge's table all the while.

Axis loosened his tie a bit to say, "Well, you could help with the situation at hand."

That tore Leon's eyes away from Lexia. He fell still, blinking at Axis.

Perhaps, he'd been too subtle, but the slight tick of the vein at Leon's temples said otherwise. Axis said, "Dr. Tempest, spare Lexia and insist she spends the rest of the night under your escort. When she accepted the invitation, I doubt she expected to be Snow's amusement for the night."

Behind Leon, Rhyme disguised a bark of laughter into his fist like a cough.

Lexia's father swallowed hard. "I'm afraid I can't do that, son."

Son.

From Valve, the word coated the back of Axis' tongue like a toxin, but from Leon it swelled Axis' chest with pride. Every time. So it twinged a bit in this context. "Why not?"

"Gauge Snow is the Founder of our way of life, including Lexia's. If I interfere, I risk breaking the accord, and I risk her in ways you cannot imagine. The man is civilized, and so far, has only treated her to his company over dinner. The only man who can escort Lexia from such a simple engagement—the only man with any right to do so—would be her betrothed."

Leon gave Axis a pointed look which burned through his eyes and into his soul.

What must Lexia look like to a man such as Snow? Gorgeous and sweet but also honest in her eloquence. She was a fair arbiter at work and destined for greatness, surpassing even her father in ensuring the happiness of her employees. With a smile to light up even the darkest corner of a man's soul.

The anxiety in Axis' chest loosened its grip. Lexia was worth conquering his fears.

FOUR

Conquered Resistance

D ESPICABLE.

Built on fear.

In his twenty-nine years, Gauge had heard it all before, but only in reports from his spies. No one had dared say it to his face. Perhaps if it'd come from Axis, Gauge would've simply laughed into the younger man's chiseled face. Or if he'd heard such talk from Valve, it would make Gauge roll his eyes.

But hearing it from Lexia stung the little boy in him, always vying for her approval. Gauge had thought, as Leon Tempest's daughter, she would see the merit in the Founding Season—in Gauge. He'd saved Winter. He'd saved her...

The music picked up tempo. It was the assigned cue for the dancing to start. As host, Gauge had to swallow his momentary disappointment and stand to address his guests. There was no need to clink his glass with a copper utensil, because everyone looked up when he stood. "Distinguished ladies and gentlemen, please enjoy the atmosphere. Tonight, we dance under starlight."

The heavy lamps dimmed as a new chandelier was lowered over the dance floor. Hundreds of teeny flames twinkled against the crystal and antiqued mirror surfaces, submerging the dancers in a night sky they'd not seen in ten years.

Gauge clapped with the guests, but his eyes were on Lexia and her reaction. Her eyes were so black the chandelier reflected off of them like a mirror, and she smiled despite herself.

Now.

Gauge reached out his hand to her, and after a slight hesitation, Lexia took it. They made quite the pair as he led her to the center of the dance floor, with the polished marble reflecting the chandelier above. Years of balls, galas, and parties had made Gauge into a confident dancer, but he wondered how well Lexia would fare given her sparse history of social affairs.

She surprised him by letting him lead. He took her hand in one and wrapped the other around her waist. This close, he could see the blue freckles at her temples hidden beneath pale powder. Even in those heels, he could see she was tall for a woman on Winter, and the boots brought her up to nearly eye level with him. It was more intimate.

It proved difficult not to flex when Lexia's free hand rested on his bicep, but Gauge contained himself. Not his smile though.

She peered at him curiously, and he responded by pulling her into the first of many turns around the dance floor. More guests joined them as the music carried on, but here in each other's arms was plenty of privacy to get to know one another.

"I understand you're quite the protégé." Gauge spent every night before an event brushing up on the ins and outs of his guests. Even though last night he was particularly focused on Valve and Axis, he'd found time to learn the business side of Lexia Tempest's mind. It had impressed him in a clinical sense—a professional one—but since seeing her tonight, it moved him on a more personal level.

With her reflective eyes on Gauge, Lexia said, "My father wanted to entrust our employees and produce to a well-educated and capable inheritor. Once he retires, I intend to not only honor the family name, but to elevate it."

Confidence looked good on the crop heiress, whose bodice was driving Gauge insane at this level. It was hard not to notice the graceful glide of her long legs as they danced. He wondered what it would feel like to have them wrapped around him—

"How do you intend to 'elevate' such an already prestigious name as 'Tempest?'" Gauge asked to stem the direction of his thoughts. He wasn't a teenager. He could control himself.

Lexia tossed her hair a bit, moving her bangs out of her eyes in a cute habitual gesture before saying, "Unions."

Gauge quirked a brow. "Unions?"

They made another turn around the dance floor, the other dancers swirling into oblivion, leaving them the only two on the marble sea of stars.

Lexia said, "Yes. Our fields and plantations are enormous, expanding even more now with your new city. The people need fair representation, and they aren't receiving it while scattered as individuals across a densely populated farm in separated cities. So I'm encouraging them to organize and make reasonable demands regarding their benefits and how those benefits stand up to the cost of living on Winter." She'd gotten so passionate about her little speech that she'd miss the song ending and the next one beginning.

Gauge wasn't about to tell her she'd technically honored her vow for one dance. Instead, he pulled Lexia closer by the small of her back and twirled them further around the room. He wanted to see the look on Axis' face, but he knew breaking eye contact with the intelligent young woman in his arms would ruin the moment. So instead, Gauge said, "I'm experiencing the same lack of representation in my mines. Gold, iron—the lot of them. I suppose unions are the reasonable and inevitable solution."

Lexia looked taken aback. "You agree with me?"

"Yes, but I wonder if we could standardize the expectations a little. To keep things fair across the board. One would hate to see cotton treated with higher regard than corn. Would you be interested in brainstorming some models with me sometime?"

The heiress did not blush like other people on Winter. Her cheeks warmed to a soft yellow in the starlit room. The beautiful young woman broke into a smile, and Lexia's scent beckoned the edge of Gauge's memory—rain on a hot summer's day. Fresh and full of life, she emanated the same warmth from her expression.

Lexia said, "I would like that very much, Count Snow."

"May I cut in?"

The dancing couple stopped twirling and peered up at the only man in the room taller than Gauge.

Axis would be so much fun to play poker with because the boy couldn't hide a thing on his face. His soft green eyes had hardened into stained glass as he seethed at Gauge. The censure immediately melted as he looked down at Lexia. They shared a smile so bright it dazzled the room, and Gauge now understood the epic tales of their romance.

Truth be told, Gauge couldn't afford a duel with Axis. He was too weak and would die pitifully quick. And although he'd loved his time with Lexia in his arms, he had to admit that his bones ached. It was the perfect excuse to sit down and rest.

But...

Gauge lifted Lexia's knuckles to his lips, and when she didn't slip her hand out of his gloved one, he took it as permission to kiss them. He put a lot more promise than necessary into his next words. "I'll call on you tomorrow, Ms. Tempest." He gave a cheeky nod to Axis, saying, "Master Flicker," before leaving the couple to their dance.

Cane.

Gauge needed his cane and possibly some adrenaline because he'd nearly let Lexia dance him to death.

———————————————

Lexia loved dancing under the artificial stars with Axis. She'd hardly noticed the striking reflections of the twinkling lights while she'd danced with Gauge and blamed her engrossment on the topic so near to her ambitions for Tempest crops. It had nothing at all to do with the intriguing and mysterious man who she'd been dancing with. Whose cedar scent still lingered on her.

Stupid purple glasses.

"Lexia."

She beamed up at Axis, floating with him on this nebulous cloud. She was so proud of him for overcoming his public phobia and asking her to dance. "Yes?" Lexia glanced down at the butterfly pinned to his tuxedo and smiled even more. He was so thoughtful.

Axis pulled her closer until he could lean down and whisper in her ear, "You look gorgeous tonight, but I can't help but wonder what you've saved for me under this dress."

Lexia flushed, and she felt a tingle down to her toes. She couldn't wait to show him how it all came apart in a slow reveal of lingerie for him, not that the seamstresses had intended it so. It was all a rather pleasant coincidence, but as a fine tremor came over Axis, Lexia knew not to push his fears. Instead of teasing him about it, she said, "I left the front open in case someone challenged me to a duel, and my steam cannon is stored in a well-hidden pocket."

There was the rich laughter Lexia loved. No one laughed like Axis, and her heart swelled knowing she was responsible for the cherished sound.

Axis changed the subject to work, per usual, but at least they were dancing for it. He said, "You may hear some rumors about yesterday and a factory foreman. Try not to think the worst of me."

Lexia blinked and shook her head. "I could never think ill of you, Axis, but I would rather hear the news from you. What happened?"

They spent another song with him telling her the story, even the parts which shamed him. Lexia said, "You have nothing to feel ashamed about. I would've cast the man in copper."

Axis looked like he wanted to kiss her. "You could never do something so cruel."

For attempting to rape one of her employees? Lexia just might, but Axis thought so highly of her, she didn't want to disappoint him by repeating her sentiment. Instead, she said, "I insulted our host to his face. A few times."

Again, Axis laughed. His eyes twinkled with mirth. "I'll bet you did. I was impressed you could stand to dance with the tyrant for three songs."

Three songs.

Lexia had found herself so captivated by the topic that she'd danced with him longer than she'd intended. What did that say about Gauge? She shook herself and returned to the conversation. "What will you do about your suspicions? You can't challenge your father to a duel for sabotaging the factories. Can you?"

Axis frowned with a faraway look in his eyes as if he were imagining something awful. He said, "It's not like I haven't thought of it a million times before. Only now, I'm big enough to actually win, and I'm right. Snow would indulge it if not for the unprecedented spectacle."

After spending even a short time with their host, Lexia could agree.

With a gentle pull, Axis separated them enough so he could meet her eyes again. He said, "I was worried about Snow taking an interest in you."

Lexia glanced over at her father, who also looked visibly more relaxed at his table. Rhyme gave her a nod as she twirled by. She looked back at Axis. "I was surprised to learn Count Snow had manners. By the way you speak of him, I thought he would sprout horns from his head while we danced."

The chuckle from Axis rumbled deep in his chest against Lexia. Still…

She asked, "Do you remember what he was like when we were children? I never would've thought he'd grow to be so tall." Or that he'd have such an infectious smile…

Axis said, "I remember he was sick, and that he never—"

"—Wanted to go home," Lexia finished.

In a quieter voice, Axis said, "I wonder why." Perhaps he could sympathize.

"All I know is, if Snow had pulled you any closer, I might've challenged him to a duel."

Or maybe not so much on the friendship thing.

Axis smirked and shook his head in disbelief. "But, and I can't believe I'm saying this, Snow *did* help me with one thing." He stopped dead in the center of the dance floor and reached for his timepiece. "Lexia Tempest, will you spend the rest of your time on this planet with me?"

Lexia didn't hesitate to take off her timepiece and hand it to Axis. "My time belongs to us."

Nothing was closer to the truth.

Axis felt every eye in the room burning his skin, adding to his collection of scars. He embraced Lexia, if only to bury his face in her hair, breathe deep of her fresh scent, and hide from Winter's scrutiny. More than anything, he wanted to kiss her and celebrate their engagement. But first… People…

Someone clapped, and Axis peered over to see it was Dr. Tempest. Others joined until it formed a chorus. Rhyme whistled, and someone else cheered. A boom of jovial activity came from outside where tonight's events were still being broadcasted.

Lexia squeezed at the same time Axis made eye contact with his father. Valve was not clapping. He was smiling most unpleasantly. Axis shuddered, and his lover squeezed him tighter.

Against his jaw, Lexia whispered, "I love you, and I'm so proud of you. Just wait until I get you alone." It was something to look forward to, and Axis knew she'd intended it that way. If only they could get through the ocean of congratulations first before they found harbor in each other.

A hand clapped Axis on the back, and, in his growing panic, he whirled on the attacker.

The Count.

Gauge, the man who would officiate their wedding ceremony, smiled knowingly into Axis' face. He squeezed his cane between his bicep and his chest to clap his gloved hands together, saying, "Congratulations, you two."

Axis narrowed his eyes. Gauge didn't look like the same man who'd just danced with Lexia, his desire naked in his eyes. No. He looked…

Had someone told Gauge about Axis' phobia? Because he looked impressed.

Lexia took over the public engagement by smiling up at Gauge. "Thank you, Count. It seems I've stolen the show from you twice in one evening." Her decorum was flawless for someone who'd never attended these events.

"You can have my spotlight anytime, Ms. Tempest." There was more than a hint of admiring flirtation, and it straightened Axis' spine. Before he could warn the Count off, Gauge said, "I look forward to the engagement counseling, Master Flicker."

Axis fought not to wince. It was a formal requirement to discuss any intended engagements with the officiator so Gauge could approve the match. Obviously, Axis had bypassed this formality, and the Count intended to see it through.

Strangely, for the second time that night, Gauge's intrusion filled Axis with an icy resolve. He slipped an arm around Lexia's waist, pulled her close against his side, and said, "You'll see me soon, Count Snow."

The man had the nerve to wink at Lexia before stepping aside for Dr. Tempest.

Lexia's father kissed his daughter's cheek and shook Axis' hand. "Congratulations! I knew you could do it, my boy." To Lexia, he said, "I wish your mother were here."

Axis felt Lexia's mood shift. It was in the lessening of her grip on him, and the stiffening of her shoulders. She was trying not to cry. "As do I."

A moment of silence fell over the crowd as Winter mourned its lost Diamond. Two years gone without Lya's presence was two years too long.

"Mrs. Tempest, can I help you make lemon cookies for Lexia?"

"Of course, Axis. You can measure the flour."

Axis tried his best with the scoop, but somehow he'd been too rough and scooted the bag all the way off the counter. It exploded in a plume of white powder.

Lya's immediate laughter filled him with joy, and Axis smiled up at Lexia's mother. She said, "C'mere, let's get you changed—"

No.

Axis tried to keep her from pulling off his shirt, but he was small and he didn't want to hurt her by fighting.

The shirt came off, and Lya went still.

Axis felt the first tear fall on his floured cheek.

Winter's Diamond.

"Well, *my* boy, are you planning this wedding before or after my funeral?" Valve interrupted the precious moment and coughed violently into his dark handkerchief.

Again, Lexia saved Axis from answering. "Per the laws of matrimony, we will wed six months from now. Perhaps, if you quit the cigars, you may live long enough to see it."

"My dear, men have so few joys in life. Most of which I can't list in polite company. So excuse me if I enjoy myself while I can." Valve missed Lexia rolling her eyes to Axis' amusement because he looked over at Dr. Tempest. "Leon, I expect to discuss expenses with you soon.

Be sure these two don't spend the night together or risk Winter's legal involvement. Everyone else, good night."

On the night of Axis' engagement, Valve Flicker turned his back on his son. He was likely off to some brothel. It wouldn't matter in six months when Axis married Lexia, and officially became a member of Dr. Tempest's family.

The congratulations carried on well into the night much to the detriment of Axis' nerves. Lexia, bless her, must've sensed it. She rubbed circles on his back or gently squeezed his hand. Once, she said into his ear, "Soon, my love," on the most arousing husky breath.

Yes, Axis couldn't wait to get her alone. They still had to have her home by curfew, but he promised to make their two hours together count.

When Valve reminded the newly engaged couple they still couldn't spend the night together, Gauge let him do so. There were obligations to consider when a couple married on Winter, and, after tonight, Gauge found himself invested in the Tempest-Flicker merger of houses. As in, there was no way he could let it happen. It wasn't all because of the imbalance of the triumvirate either.

The warm smile on Lexia's face when she agreed to meet with Gauge about union models lingered like the memory of sunlight on his back. She was gorgeous with a good head on her shoulders, and a wealth of kindness lived in her heart. It was obvious by how she acted as public relations on Axis' behalf, curbing his exposure to his phobia.

Every second in the same room with Lexia left Gauge more determined to win her over, but how could he do that while also sabotaging her marriage with Axis?

With a great deal of enthusiasm, the young couple excused themselves for an evening of indulgence—all pre-curfew of course. Meanwhile, Gauge tried not to imagine what Lexia would look like with her hair down and her back arched in ecstasy—All while he served as host until the last guest left his ballroom in the late hours of the night. He complimented Jan on a stellar evening before rushing away to his library where he bit his thumbnail and paced.

Gauge paced and paced until his legs begged him to stop, but he couldn't see a promising way around this dilemma. He didn't hate Axis. In fact, he rather respected the younger man, more so since learning some of what he'd endured as a child. But Axis was a rival for Lexia's attentions, not unlike when they'd been children.

A knife twisted in Gauge's chest. While he'd wanted Lexia's time, he'd also wanted Axis' approval. Even as a youth, Axis had outsized the older Gauge. He could pull himself up in the boughs of a tree and climb to the very top...

No.

This wouldn't do.

Gauge poured himself gracefully into the nearest chair and ran a gloved hand over his face. The feel of the black leather on his skin frustrated him further. Axis never had to wear gloves, and what would Lexia's skin feel like to Gauge's bare fingers? Silky, he imagined.

This was pointless.

Gauge reached over and rang for Jan. The butler appeared promptly and bowed to his master, who waved off the formalities. Gauge said, "At ease, soldier. I need your guidance, not your pretense."

Jan fell into his relaxed stance: feet apart and hands clasped behind his back. He never loosened his shoulders, not completely. "Sir."

"Tell me what you've gleaned from tonight's gossip." Everyone carefully measured their words around Gauge, making it difficult to learn anything useful from polite chatter. But Jan…

"Most everyone seemed curious how you thawed sector twelve enough to prepare the site for a new city without drawing attention to the project.

"There are questions about the cleanliness of the mines, namely how is all the rock dust collected and disposed of without respiratory exposure. Simple technical speculations, nothing to draw any suspicion.

"And Axis Flicker assaulted a loom foreman during routine inspection."

It paid to have a spy on the payroll.

Gauge asked, "Was it the same man Mrs. Tenz named?"

Jan nodded. "Indeed, sir. Our man inside said Walker tried to sexually assault a young female inspector, and Axis intercepted."

Interesting… "She was so fortunate our boy scout happened by in time to rescue her."

"The man inside agrees. The timing is suspicious."

Would Axis intentionally bait a predator with one of his own employees? Was that not exactly what Gauge would do? This didn't seem damning enough to drive a wedge between Axis and Lexia, but it was a start.

Gauge stood and went to a desk in the corner. On his signature stationery, he read aloud as he wrote, "Our mutual friend, Mrs. Tenz, is doing well as a forewoman here in the crater. She named you as a reference for her employment. Would you care to discuss her performance history over a friendly match? PostScript: Please extend my invitation to Ms. Tempest should she choose to spectate."

"Sir, if I may?" Jan rarely asked for permission to speak. The thirty-five-year-old former security agent seemed quite content to follow orders without question. Unless it endangered Gauge, of course.

He handed the missive to his favorite employee, saying, "Yes, Jan, go ahead."

The spy-turned-butler looked uncomfortable as he minced his words. Eventually, he blurted, "Axis is the leading champion in all of Winter not because of his station, but because of his athletic prowess. Are you certain you wish to challenge him in your... condition...?"

Gauge had spent all day in public view of Winter, unable to eat, and he was weakened from it. The three consecutive songs with Lexia proved rather taxing on his tendons and ligaments. Jan was right to ask. Gauge reached over and put his hand on the older man's shoulder. "Thank you, old friend, but I would like to try. You can deliver the adrenaline this time, eh? It should take you back to old times."

Jan shuddered, and Gauge almost laughed. Neither one of them enjoyed those memories. He said, "Do you mind having a servant bring me dinner while you personally deliver the missive?"

"Very good, sir." Jan seemed genuinely delighted Gauge was taking an interest in food.

Well, he ought to. Gauge would need all his strength to meet Axis on the mat tomorrow.

Before Jan could leave, Gauge said, "Oh, and have Walker arrested. He'll make a fine addition to the Wall of Pain."

The butler broke into a rare grin, "Yes, sir."

It warmed Gauge to see it.

"Are you sure you don't want to try?"

Lexia smirked playfully at Axis, surely with all her lipstick smeared across her face. Her carefully applied eye makeup was likely melted under her eyes. Her hair was the first thing to fall, tangled in his fingers during their passionate lovemaking.

Axis, the man Lexia would marry, peered curiously at the leather restraints in her hand. There was a hesitation—a caution—to the openness in his face which tugged at her heart. He said, "It's not that I don't want to…"

Lexia understood. She dropped the restraints and crawled naked on her hands and knees across the floor to Axis where he sat on the edge of the bed. No part of her wanted him to regret saying 'no.' Also gloriously naked, he watched her come to him, lust washing away the hesitation.

Good.

Lexia went to her knees between Axis' legs, and she kissed the side of one knee, then the other. He brushed his fingers through her hair again, and oh, how she longed for him to pull it. To arch her neck for him.

But Lexia was happy for the beautiful smile on Axis' face. She would make him feel good if only for the smile to stay. She kissed her way up the inside of his thighs, and he kept his eyes on hers with feverish desire. When she drew almost the entirety of him in her mouth, he looked toward the dome with his eyes rolled back. "Lexia," he breathed.

This was enough for her. Maybe after they were married, Axis would feel safer and more adventurous, but Lexia would never push his boundaries more than he was willing to stretch. They'd shared one another this way since their first time when she was seventeen, and neither had sought pleasurable company elsewhere. They were all each other needed.

After round four, a knock sounded on the door of Axis' apartments. He didn't employ any servants, so it was up to him to dress and answer the door. He did so clumsily, and Lexia laughed at how he tripped into his pants. Especially as Axis confessed, "I can't feel my legs, woman. What have you done to me?"

It was late evening, almost time for Lexia to go home, so she listened curiously as to who was at the door.

"Young Master Flicker."

Lexia sat up in the bed. That was Gauge's butler. The rest of their exchange was too soft for her to hear, and she was dying to know what was said. So much so that when Axis walked back into the room, she couldn't contain her curiosity.

"What is it?"

Axis peered down at an open envelope in his hand—a copper leaf envelope. He leaned in the doorway as he read it, saying, "It's a gambit, and a poorly chosen one at that." With little regard for the expensive paper, he tossed it on the bed for Lexia to read.

Which she did.

Eagerly.

"Will you go?"

Axis folded his arms and licked his lips, slowly, lost in his thoughts. With him shirtless, it was rather distracting. He said, "I've already told Jan I would. Do you wish to go, Lexi?"

She smiled. "I'll be in your corner the entire time, but what puzzles you so?"

Axis shook himself out of his thoughts. "I'm trying to understand him. It makes no sense for him to challenge me unless he's planned something to shake my footing." At the last, he finally met Lexia's eyes.

Oh.

"You've nothing to worry about. I'm sure he doesn't know about the incident at the factory."

"Oh, I'm sure he does. In fact, I'm counting on it."

As Lexia let Rhyme drive her home that night, she sat in the backseat of the steam-powered car and fiddled with the restraints in her dress pocket. She did so with the same hand bearing Axis' timepiece. It swallowed her petite forearm up past her elbow and made her think of sleeping in his sweater. Same experience; more significance.

Soon, they would be married and sharing a bed every night. No more of Gauge's silly curfew—

The second the Copper Count entered Lexia's thoughts, she reflected on the evening with her dance partner. Were his eyes as piercing as people said? Was it her imagination or had he held her tighter than required by etiquette? Why did his smile linger in her memory?

But more importantly, what game was Gauge playing?

Count Snow never came across as malicious or inappropriate, but he maneuvered people like pieces on a board—Just as Lexia's father had said. Politics. A delicate balance. Even though the music had stopped long ago, the dance was still on.

Lexia smiled to herself.

She kinda liked it.

Only then did she realize she'd forgotten to tell Axis about the union models. Lexia bit her lip. Would he approve of her spending time alone with Gauge? Would Gauge approve of her inviting Axis, certain he would be interested in the prospect? Could the three of them work together—It was so inevitable in their future. Valve would die, drowning in his own blood, as he deserved. And Leon would retire to a quiet life overlooking the fields, as *he* deserved. Axis, Lexia, and Gauge would oversee Winter together.

So why did they feel worlds apart?

Lexia wished she could talk to her mother. Her chest squeezed so tight at the thought that a small sound escaped her.

"Are you all right, Ms. Tempest?" Rhyme asked with a glance over his shoulder.

She lied. "I'm fine. Thank you."

"Very well, miss." He did *not* sound convinced.

Mother would've approved of Rhyme. And she'd loved Axis so much.

Lexia frowned as something tugged on the edge of her memory.

"Do something, Leon. That monster will kill the boy."

"We have no means to interfere. The best we can do is let him stay here out of Valve's way."

"That's not good enough."

Lexia stared out the car window as it trundled down Tempest Boulevard. She might not see eye-to-eye with Gauge about policy and intrigue, but she agreed there were some crimes only copper could remedy.

FIVE

Righteous Deceit

A FENCING MATCH BETWEEN RIVALS WAS A BRACING WAY TO START THE DAY.

Axis slipped his cobalt Tempest silk waistcoat over his white button-down. He felt comfortable enough at swordplay that silk pants should do. They were also a bright blue which matched his opponent's eyes. Even though Axis had only seen them on a handful of occasions, their penetrating effect was lasting. Would Gauge wear his glasses during combat? It made sense for the man to hide his eyes during social engagements, but it seemed like a disadvantage for a match.

These and other thoughts occurred to Axis as he prepared for the midmorning encounter. Lexia had said she would meet him at the Copper Cathedral, and Axis was in a hurry to arrive before she did and was left alone to entertain Count Snow.

On the way, Axis asked his driver, Bolt, "What have you heard?"

The only servant he employed shook his head. "It's been silent all morning, sir. Winter is holding its breath."

The onset of a new city would do that. Even so, Axis felt as if more was in store, and, knowing Gauge, there was.

As they pulled up, Axis cursed under his breath. Lexia was walking up. Emphasis on 'walking.' He disliked her cavalier disregard for her own safety, but there was no changing her mind about it. Lexia would walk whenever she felt like it, and Axis would marry her accepting that.

She'd pulled her hair back from her unmade-up face in a tousled ponytail, her lips and cheeks rosy from the crisp wind. Lexia had her hands in the pockets of her loose cream pants with brown pinstripes, and they hugged her hips in a way that was almost too flattering. The suspenders went over an oversized cream blouse which was tucked into her pants, giving her a boyish look aside from one last detail. A brown leather under-bust corset presented her breasts in an all too appealing manner. She topped all this off by openly displaying her excessive steam cannon on her hip holster.

Rhyme followed behind looking sullen about the entire affair.

Bolt said, "She's a sprite, that one."

Sprite.

It made Axis smile. "I like that." He shouldered his sword case, jumped out of the car, and grabbed Lexia to spin her in the air. His future wife's laughter lifted his spirits, and there was really nothing better in the world for it. In an uncharacteristic display of affection, Axis kissed Lexia there on the cobblestones. She melted against him with a purr, and it was enough to shake him out of the respite from his phobia.

When Axis set Lexia down, she didn't pout. In fact, she peered up at him with stars in her eyes. "Dear Prince, feel free to do that anytime."

"Yes, we wouldn't want Winter to run out of play-acting material, now would we?"

The couple whirled to find Gauge Snow standing on the steps to the Cathedral, leaning on the copper-topped balustrade. He looked ready to attend the most stylish funeral on Winter. The man dressed similarly to Axis—a silk waistcoat and button-down—but his silk pants were tucked into thigh-high boots, and everything was black. With his deep complexion and his black braids, it all blended into one seamless shadow. Even his lenses were black today, answering Axis' earlier questions.

It all suited the Count.

As if mesmerized, Lexia took the first step toward him. Still holding her hand in public, Axis pulled to stop her. The moment froze—the gentlemen at odds and the lady in the middle.

When Lexia looked back at Axis, she beamed, shattering the ice. "The winner gets to take me to dinner."

Someone barked out a laugh, and everyone turned stiltedly toward Rhyme. He was coughing into his fist in a terrible attempt at disguising his poor decorum.

Snow said, "I'll accept those terms, but perhaps Axis could join us. We wouldn't want him to lick his wounds alone."

It was Axis' turn to bark out a laugh, and he was surprised it felt good-natured. "I won't be as charitable, Count Snow."

Lexia muttered something, and Axis thought he heard her say, "Pity."

He never let go of her hand, even as she pulled him up the steps. After parking the car, Bolt appeared, doubling as bodyguard. Rhyme walked with him to the door behind the couple. And Jan waited at the Wall of Pain.

There was something different about it...

"There are refreshments in the courtyard," Gauge offered, ever the gracious host.

They followed him through the egregious foyer with its mirrored set of circular stairs leading to an open second and third floors. Beyond it, their party entered a courtyard filled with...

"Are those third generation heirloom black beauty tomatoes?" Lexia listed off the details of the plants in the raised beds as if they were rare gemstones.

Gauge smiled in a way Axis had never seen as he said, "Fourth, actually. They're even sweeter."

Lexia went to the next bed. "And Winter-native corn. This isn't even engineered. I thought the last of it died when..."

When Gauge saved Winter from the apocalypse.

Rows of raised beds lined the courtyard with exotic fruits and vegetables. It explained why no one could match his chefs. The ingredients were enriched.

Axis loved the wonder and awe in Lexia's black eyes as she studied all of them. Even Rhyme, Jan, and Bolt were entranced by her endearing behavior.

It was a shame Gauge ruined the moment by doing the same. In a voice so quiet Lexia couldn't hear it, he said, "It looks as though you're not the only one who can make her happy."

Axis gritted his teeth. It was time to teach the Count some manners.

———————————————

Gauge loved the heat rolling off Axis from his comment. Almost as much as he loved Lexia's jubilation over his plants. Surely some arrangement could be made to suit all three.

Axis' restrained seething ended when he turned around and set his sword case on the nearest surface, a concrete bench. Curious, Gauge watched on as the younger man treated the long, carved rosewood box with reverence. Like a professional, he quietly opened it and admired his weapon.

For good reason.

The elegant rapier was death encased in steel with a cup hilt of intricate gold and silver detail. It sparkled under the Flicker wicks. Axis slipped off his white gloves and exchanged them for soft black ones, similar to Gauge's. He did all this with almost ritualistic regard. And when he lifted the sword, he peered at his reflection in it.

Axis glimpsed Gauge watching and fixed him with a challenging look. "I'll be more polite than you and offer you a quiet surrender before Lexia witnesses your pitiful defeat."

Intensity darkened Axis' green eyes. The hair stood on Gauge's arms, and a chill shivered down his spine. In for a penny...

"Why, Master Flicker, are you afraid of a little healthy competition?"

Axis gave a short laugh, and it was filled with genuine humor, igniting the part of Gauge which enjoyed being the center of attention. Perhaps he could win the younger man over.

Axis said, "Get your weapon and prepare yourself."

Gauge wanted to laugh, but he wasn't looking forward to the preparation necessary to complete this fight. Off to the side, Jan appeared equally unamused. Gauge said, "Excuse me while I fetch my sword. Enjoy the refreshments." He left Axis suspicious and confused by stepping into the foyer with Jan trailing behind.

"Sir…"

Gauge said, "Your reticence is noted, soldier. Just do it."

Jan took the vial injector and ported it into Gauge's jugular. Fire filled his veins and burned his arteries. The Count ground his teeth and hissed through his nose as the adrenaline found its way into his heart. Jan carefully covered the mark with Gauge's cravat.

Thirty minutes, and the clock had already started ticking down.

"Thank you, Jan—"

"Go, sir. Wait! You'll need this."

Jan tossed Gauge his rapier. It was fancy with a copper cup hilt, more for ceremony than actual use. But hey, Gauge had been the one to initiate this match. He would go through with it.

They returned to the courtyard in time for Lexia to return from the gardens, glowing with delight. She peered at Gauge, possibly noticing he was flushed with the anti-inflammatories. With his sharpened vision, a halo appeared around her white hair, and angelic didn't cover it. She was ethereal.

"Shall we begin?" Axis asked, his voice carrying a hard edge.

The light around Axis moved differently, and Gauge tried not to stare at it lest he focus on the vein pulsing in Axis' neck. Gauge held up his sword, acknowledging his opponent.

Axis did the same, and Lexia said, "Go."

The Factory Master's son didn't waste time and lunged first thing.

Gauge dodged it and swiped.

Axis twirled away and jumped onto the concrete bench. It lent his height closer to seven feet, and he smirked at the advantage. Well, the bigger they are…

The combatants' attacks became furious, and without the adrenaline, Gauge would never have been able to counter and parry Axis' aggressive swordplay. He lost track of Jan, Rhyme, Bolt, and Lexia. It was all he could do to focus on Axis' left arm—

Left.

Wasn't Axis right-handed?

Breathy from exertion, Gauge said, "You speak of manners and politeness, but you're holding back. At least treat me with the respect of a worthy opponent."

Axis suddenly stopped, and he smirked so sly it took Gauge's breath away. Not that he had much left.

Sixteen minutes.

Parts of Gauge were shaking and not all of it was because of the devastatingly handsome look on Master Flicker's face.

Axis said, "Few people notice."

Gauge took the moment to breathe deep and prayed his bones didn't seize up. He said, "Well, I can see why, but I'm not most people, Axis Flicker. You will not insult me with poor sportsmanship."

That dried up the smile, and Gauge regretted saying it. Axis said, "It's not poor sportsmanship. It's mercy. But if you insist… " He switched hands.

Gauge lunged, and Axis flipped backward off the bench. He attacked so fast Gauge almost couldn't see it, but he was detecting a pattern in Master Flicker's style. The Count noticed his opponent liked to parry with a twirl, lunge, and then come in with a flurry of attacks. All Gauge had to do was evade and counter. Not much of an offensive, but it was repetitive enough to keep his head above water.

With a flip to the side, Gauge blocked an attack, and they found themselves in a stalemate. At least Axis was breathing just as heavily. He asked, "Why did you contact me about Mrs. Tenz?"

Gauge welcomed the diversion. "Mostly to ruffle your feathers a bit. Which you make so easy, I might add."

Axis pressed against Gauge's sword, and the Count was losing the contest of strength. He was simply too weak. So back to subterfuge. "Is young Ms. Tija all right?"

Axis stumbled into the impasse, and Gauge went to point his sword at the Young Master's throat. Before he could claim victory, Axis recovered and blocked it. He said, "I'd suspected she was your source, but I didn't want to believe it. I want your spies out of my factories."

"Ah, but you know they are allowed in our accord." Gauge stepped back and spun his sword.

Axis let him, saying, "I think we'll revisit the terms once I inherit the factories."

"You mean, *if* you inherit the factories."

The icy exterior returned to Axis' expression, and he swiped, followed up with an aggressive lunge.

Gauge spun out of the way, slamming his back against a courtyard wall.

Nine minutes.

Now, Lexia came into focus. She was keeping a respectable distance, but looked concerned with the direction of the conversation.

Gauge wanted to assure her there was no reason for that. "I *want* you to inherit them, Axis. I think you're a fair Factory Master, and I look forward to revisiting the accord with you. But you've become involved in some affairs which are outside of your jurisdiction."

Axis looked stunned with his mouth agape. He visibly shook himself and frowned, asking, "Which affairs?"

Grateful once again for a respite, Gauge said, "Your father's attempts to spoil your inheritance cannot go unpunished. An example needed to be made of someone."

Realization dawned on Axis' face, but Lexia wasn't there yet. She asked, "What do you mean?"

Axis wet his lips and shook his head. Gauge didn't like the way he did it, as though he were wiping something from his mind. Master Flicker said, "Walker...Lexia, the doors..."

Lexia's eyes widened, and she blinked at Gauge like she was seeing him for the first time.

Why were they looking at Gauge like that? Didn't they understand? "I had to. Rape and any attempt at such results in the same end."

Zero minutes.

The edges of the world became less bright and more fuzzy, especially with the tears. Gauge's limbs froze up, and he almost couldn't draw enough air to keep oxygen to his brain. He felt like he was dying.

Axis, angry now, lunged at Gauge. The Count crumpled, and Axis held his sword to his throat. He said, "I don't know what you are Gauge, savior or monster, but never meddle in my affairs again. Stay away from Lexia." The last he said so quietly she couldn't overhear it.

More tears brimmed in Gauge's lashes.

After all these years, Axis still didn't understand him.

"Why are we leaving, Axis? You didn't let me say goodbye."

Axis was pulling Lexia by the hand, dragging her out of the Copper Cathedral. She spared a glance at the doors, and noticed the copper monument was plus one more figure, trapped in an eternal scream. She shuddered.

But didn't Lexia agree?

Rhyme and Bolt joined them out on the cobblestones, where Axis dragged her to his parallel-parked car. He still wasn't answering her questions. Then he planted both hands on the roof of the car, leaned against it, and contended with the emotions warring in his eyes.

Lexia couldn't hide her concern as she said, "Please talk to me."

Bolt came around the car, sword returned to its case in his hands, and sat in the driver's seat. Rhyme joined him on the passenger side, leaving the couple alone.

Haunted, Axis said, "No man should have so much power."

Gauge had acted as judge, jury, and executioner. It's true, his might was terrifying to behold, especially as nonchalantly as he confessed to the judgment. However, Lexia was conflicted. How else should they punish a man caught in the act of rape? Perhaps the Count would be open to alternatives. Maybe they could all three talk about it over negotiating the accords.

Even though Lexia feared disappointing Axis, she said, "I believe Count Snow acts in the interest of the public."

Axis snapped up to her, shock in his eyes.

She staved him with her hands. "We can discuss methods of delivering justice. I completely understand that, but I also understand why Gauge takes such extreme measures. By allowing assault such as what Walker committed, it can spread like the cancer now metastasizing in your factories. Or are you more offended Gauge was the one to dole out the punishment and not you?"

Almost as if Axis meant to wipe away the shock, he swiped a gloved hand down his face and cupped it over his mouth. A tear brimmed his lashes, and Lexia feared she'd broken his heart after all. He dropped his hand and said, "I can't believe you think so little of me. No, I'm not upset Gauge 'delivered justice' in my place. I'm upset because I endangered a woman I suspected was Snow's spy *and* entrapped a man—ultimately condemning him to his death." He cut the air with both hands. "I don't want any of this, and I'm angry with my father for leaving me with this mess to clean up."

Lexia winced. "Forgive me, but Axis…Think of Mrs. Tenz. She would see both you *and* Gauge as heroes."

Axis slammed his hand on the roof of the car, startling Lexia. He said, "There has to be a better way than copper. What about rehabilitation and redemption?"

This was it. Lexia took his hand. "You're right. We can take your ideas to Gauge. He'll listen—"

"No. And, please forgive *me*, but I don't want you to go near him again."

That took Lexia aback. It wasn't at all like Axis to hinder her spontaneous nature. He'd said a thousand times how he loved her 'untethered way of being.' She breathed, "Axis…"

Despite its excessive size on her, suddenly his timepiece felt… confining.

Regret softened Axis' eyes. He took her other hand until he held both, saying, "I'm sorry. Ignore my foolish behavior under this stress. Never would I ever restrict you, my wild, chaotic sprite. I only fear his influence over you, but I want you to know I trust you completely. Do whatever you like."

Even though Lexia believed Axis' words were true, she wasn't entirely confident his distaste for Gauge wasn't also genuine. She said, "Ask me why I offered myself as a prize."

Axis' eyes narrowed, but he played along. "Why did you offer yourself as a prize?"

She tugged on his hands. "I want us to get along. No matter how you see our future, we work with Gauge. Wouldn't it be best if we did it together?"

Axis brought her hands together and kissed them. "Will you let me think on it?"

"Always."

They didn't spend the rest of the morning together. Instead, Lexia had lunch with her father. It was too cold for the veranda today, so they ate in the kitchen, much to the fuss of the servants. Father and daughter sat on barstools across the butcher block from one another eating salad.

"I understand Count Snow and our Axis had a match today. Was that as bracing as I'd imagine?"

Lexia laughed. "Well, you could say that."

She opened her mouth to tell Leon all about Gauge's exotic crops, but her father said, "I also understand there's been some trouble in the factories and Snow had to intervene."

This again. Lexia blew the air from her cheeks, puffing her bangs. "Father, it wasn't exactly like that. Gauge only adhered to the laws as they're currently written. Could they use some revising with rehabilitation in mind? Absolutely. But I don't think he'll be open to such discussion if everyone keeps treating him like a tyrant."

Leon blinked at her, mid-bite.

Lexia tired of this. "Why does everyone look at me like that when I say something nice about the man?"

With stiff movements, her father set down his fork, pushed his plate away, and touched his napkin to the corners of his mouth. Finished with the motions, he said, "Perhaps it's because you've only been around him a short time—a single evening—and you're speaking as if you know him intimately. As if you know him better than those of us who have dealt with him for years. Myself, for a decade."

Well, that didn't come across as condescending at all. Lexia considered herself an expert judge of character, and she'd never said she knew Gauge better than anyone else. Just that they should work with the Count instead of against themselves. But if she tried to communicate any of this, it would seem like petty defensiveness.

Lexia sulked.

"Daughter mine, you have always been an optimist. It's why Winter loves you, but Axis' suspicions of Snow aren't unfounded. The Count has played a careful game with our accords and his Founding Religion for a decade. If you think the parade is eerie, wait until you see the play tonight."

Lexia perked up. "A play?"

Leon passed her a copper leaf envelope along the countertop, saying, "These came this morning before you returned from the match. I'd heard this decennial there might be a new addition to the Season."

The two copper cards boasted a shooting star and Lexia and Leon's names.

Lexia took hers and stood, ready to prepare for the evening. But she stalled and bit her lip. After a second, she said, "Father, be honest. Did you consider hiding these from me?"

"Absolutely—" Leon held up his hand to stop Lexia from arguing. "You are a girl who has always needed to experience things for herself. I would never stand in the way of that, but as your father, I can only pray you don't get hurt in your constant pursuit of fairness."

Lexia nodded her understanding at him. "I'll be ready in an hour." After she considered the outfit she wanted to wear, she said, "Make that two."

Axis read Lexia's missive. He appreciated her telling him she would attend the Founding Play tonight, but he also dreaded the event. However, he had to admit to some curiosity. Even the parade didn't tell the story of *how* Snow saved Winter. All Axis could remember was how the young scientist at age seventeen warned the world of the electromagnetic pulse, and no one listened. It had something to do with his father's lack of credibility or some similar misfortune.

Axis dressed in a black velvet three-piece and a crimson silk button-down, hoping to distract Lexia from his earlier misbehavior. No part of him wanted to restrict any part of her. She could make her own judgments. But why did Axis still feel he was right for warning Snow away from her? There was a danger there from which Axis wanted to protect Lexia, and damn Snow if he ever hurt her.

Bolt waited outside in the car, but Axis paused on his steps. In the light of the Flicker wick street lamps, he made out fluffy white flakes.

It was snowing.

Under the dome.

How magical it was to see any kind of condensation result in precipitation within the cities. He couldn't contain his delight and grinned as he climbed into the car.

Bolt said, "It should make for a wonderful evening, Prince Flicker."

Yes. This was much better than how the day had started.

They arrived at the theater—the only theater in Winter's capital city—to find a red carpet for cars arriving at the grand double doors. Axis almost considered rolling his eyes, but the snow had done much to improve his mood. He went with it, exiting the car with a regal elegance.

People waved and whistled, crying out, "The Prince! It's the Prince!"

It was enough to make Axis blush and duck his eyes until a sudden silence blanketed the din. He turned to see his father's blacked out limousine pull up, and Axis recalled how many times he'd seen the sight. And how many times he had ran and hid from it.

He would sooner look forward to seeing a hearse.

It took two servants to help Valve's heft out of the car, especially with him coughing the entire time. Once Axis saw the red stain at the corner of his father's mouth, he took a moment and stared.

How much longer now?

And how would Axis take his father's passing?

As if Valve had heard his son's thoughts, he barked, "Why do you look at me as if you've seen a ghost, boy? I'm right as rain." When the two women, naked but for some strategically placed diamonds, followed Valve out of the car and onto his arm, Axis decided he was fine with the sow kicking the bucket.

He turned and frowned the rest of the way inside.

No mother.

Axis' mother died in childbirth. There'd been no one between him and his father for Axis' entire life aside from…

"Axis, would you like to stay with us another night?"

"Yes, Mrs. Tempest. I'd like that very much."

The visceral intensity of his sincere gratitude from the unbidden memory took Axis' breath away. As the playhouse employee swept Axis' coat off, he fought tears. Why had the universe seen fit to take Lya so soon and leave Valve on this Earth for so long?

At least it had been kind enough to leave Dr. Tempest on Winter for Lexia. She needed her father, and if Axis were honest with himself, so did he.

A little less moody, Axis approached the stairs to the Flicker's theater box. Yet, as he contemplated an entire evening near his father, Axis thought better of it and went into the first-floor crowd.

Where to sit…

Where to sit—

Someone flagged Axis down. It was Mrs. Tenz on the first row. The joyful middle-aged woman beamed as he made his way through the significant throng of people. Some brushed him places he'd rather them not touch, but eventually he made his way through it mostly unmolested.

"Good evening, Mrs. Tenz."

"Prince Axis, you look as though you need a place to sit?" Her warm grin was infectious, and Axis found himself returning the expression.

"Yes, ma'am."

Mrs. Tenz patted the modest wooden chair beside hers. On the other side, a young man kept peering at Axis.

The People's Prince waved and said, "Hello. You must be young Mr. Tenz." He held out his hand.

The young man blushed but shook it, anyway. "Hello." When Mrs. Tenz beamed further at the exchange, the son rolled his eyes. "Mom, you're so embarrassing me."

She changed the subject as they took their seats. "Count Snow was kind enough to send us some invitations for these remarkable seats. I'm happy to have you as my plus one, Prince Axis."

It was his turn to blush when she looped her arm through his and winked.

Snow *and* flirting.

The evening was off to a pleasant start.

Even as the unmistakable odor of his father's cigars—Snow's finest—made its way down into the floor seats, Axis would not let it ruin the night.

The next couple down the red carpet would.

Gauge made his way from the entry doors into the theater of purple velvet curtains and copper ornamentation. With Tija on his arm. The blue-eyed brunette looked dazzling in a glittery champagne dress clinging to her, shifting from silver to gold. It matched Gauge's waistcoat and top hat. The rest of his tuxedo was white, including his cane and gloves. Tonight, his glasses were amber, complementing the glitz of the evening.

Axis' mood soured with the entrance. He'd thought of Tija as a friend, but now he was questioning her judgment. He could forgive her acting as double agent between Snow and Flicker because it was hard to elevate beyond factory hand without getting into some trouble. But dating Snow?

As soon as Axis thought it, shame heated his face. There was nothing wrong with the woman trying to get ahead in the world, and whether or not she actually enjoyed the Count's company was really none of Axis' business.

What was happening to him?

Stress.

The factory's reputation was in jeopardy.

Valve was trying to spoil his inheritance.

And Axis had just overcome a major phobia by finally proposing to Lexia in public.

It was stress.

Mrs. Tenz patted his hand as if she'd sensed his tension, and Axis appreciated the woman's maternal instincts. Especially as Gauge and Tija walked by with a smile for the Prince in the crowd. The two climbed a set of ornate circular stairs to one side of the stage and stood in the middle of it.

Gauge said, "Welcome one and all to the first annual Founding Play."

Of course he would make it annual.

"I bet you're asking yourselves, 'How can Count Snow lay the groundwork for a new city, sponsor a new play, and keep it all a secret reveal for the decennial Founding Season?' Well, you shouldn't be. I couldn't do it without the wonderful people of Winter, equally dedicated to progress and spectacle. Here I am giving a special thanks to all those involved in these wonderful projects and for their extreme loyalty to keeping my secrets." He kissed Tija's cheek as if he was including her in those thanks. "Now, I hope everyone enjoys…"

Shuffling and whispering drew Axis' attention off the stage, and with a glance, he noticed everyone turning around to face the doors. Someone had just walked in and stolen the show.

Axis grinned because he had an inkling who it might be. When he turned around, he was not disappointed.

Lexia walked in wearing scarlet leather pants so soft they looked as though someone had poured silk over her long legs, a black corset-laced bustier, and a scarlet coat reaching her knees. She'd pinned her white mass of wavy hair back at the temples with golden butterflies and wore Axis' timepiece on her wrist. Black lipstick gave her sweet lips a poisonous look, tempting Axis to taste them in front of all these people.

Mrs. Tenz mused beside him, "She's hard to compete with."

Lexia ruined the grand entrance by giving the crowd a wave with a dorky smile. "Hello. Don't mind me. I'm just on my way upstairs. Sorry."

Axis beamed, and she noticed him in the crowd with another silly wave.

Beside her, Dr. Tempest looked proud as he escorted his daughter up to their theater box.

Now it was time to see how Gauge had taken the interruption.

Axis turned back to find the Count watching Lexia ascend with fascination and admiration open on his face. At first, it nearly riled Axis, but Lexia was beautiful and sweet. How could anyone not admire her?

As long as Gauge kept it to himself, Axis wouldn't embarrass himself or upset his fiance by making a ridiculous scene. Even if it was obvious that both men would rather spend the play at Lexia's side.

Tija tugged on her date, and Gauge cleared his throat to regain the audience's attention. "Please enjoy a story you've heard before but never like this." The two disappeared behind the curtain, thoroughly upstaged.

Axis glanced up at Lexia's box, and she waved down as if she'd been waiting for him to do so.

Oh, but how he loved her.

The lights dimmed, the orchestra in the pit played a tinkering chime, and the play began with a child in a laboratory. An older man walked onto the stage, saying, "Son, you should be in bed."

"But father, I want to finish this sequence."

"You're four years old. What do you know of genome sequencing?"

When the boy shifted, Axis could see a centrifuge on the table behind him. The boy said, "I think I've isolated what's wrong with mother."

The older man picked up the boy and stared down at his work, saying, "Your mother is very sick, and you're too young to understand how any of this equipment works."

"But father…"

Father kissed son, but ignored his almost feverish insistence by tucking him back into bed.

The curtain closed, and when it opened again, the scene had transitioned into a sight Axis knew well.

A funeral.

Gauge was only five when he'd lost his mother.

Axis supposed it was a loss he, Lexia, and Gauge shared in common.

The play carried on, showing the little boy's interest in medicine increasing, and from there it grew into chemistry, physics, and astronomy. Meanwhile, it'd seemed he'd inherited his mother's illness.

"Little Bones?" The older man called as he walked onto set.

The boy of six wore a labcoat tailor-fitted for him while he contemplated a mathematical equation on a whiteboard. He rolled his eyes at what apparently passed for a term of endearment. "Don't interrupt me, father. I'm on the verge of a breakthrough."

"I thought you would like to meet a colleague of mine. He's an agricultural scientist with a background in herbal biology."

Gauge's child actor knew how to light up his eyes. They sparkled as he turned. "Truly?"

The father actor smiled, saying, "Yes, son. But first, drink your tonic."

The boy made a face, and the audience laughed.

Except Mrs. Tenz. She wiped away a tear which interested Axis. Were all mothers so compassionate? Lya had been...

As Dr. Tempest's actor was introduced, the theater clapped. Some people cheered. He was well-loved, but it was the appearance of a fair-skinned young woman in a white wig which made the entire house stand in silence with their heads lowered.

Axis went along with the audience, but he glanced up at Lexia. She was standing, and it was obvious she felt emotional at the tribute.

Winter's Diamond.

Lya's actress met Gauge's. "Hello, little snow. Would you like to stay with the adults, or would you like to make some friends your own age?"

The boy looked interested and followed her to a little girl with another white wig and a little boy with a burgundy one. Axis could remember meeting Gauge, and he'd been much smaller than the boy on stage.

"Little Bones."

Something about the nickname bothered Axis. Why would a father taunt their ill child that way? Or perhaps Axis was projecting his own terrible childhood onto Gauge?

No matter.

A few scenes went on to cover one or two play dates before Gauge's dad discovered the Ignis crater when the boy was nine, and the play dates stopped. Now, the play made it appear there was causation and correlation between those events, but Axis remembered the truth.

"Get away from her, Gauge." Axis pulled Lexia's face, yellow with tears, into his chest and held her. "Don't come near us again."

Young Snow had never returned, choosing instead to return his focus onto his illness and the crater's resources.

A twinge tightened Axis' chest, and he tried not to draw parallels between the present and the past. He glanced up at Gauge's theater box to see it hidden behind a screen and wondered if the Count recalled the moment as vividly.

The play did not address whatever had sent Gauge's father into exile within the scientific community. Only that shortly after, he'd lost his job, fell into a steep decline, and died, leaving Gauge an orphan at seventeen.

In the next scene, they'd replaced the teenage actor playing Gauge with a more robust one, staring through a telescope and marking down some calculations. Then he ran to a terminal—something Axis hadn't seen in a decade—and made some more calculations. The youth dropped his pen and ran to a phone, dialing in a hurry to say, "I need to speak with Galactic Leader Yed. This is Gauge Snow, and don't waste time. This is an emergency."

A disembodied voice answered, listened to the emergency, and then laughed through the theater. "A solar EMP our scientists have missed? Boy, you're as mad as your father."

Spurred, the young man assured, "If you won't take action, I will."

Sets and actors moved across the stage in a montage of copper mining, smelting, and engineering. Steam pipes formed the functional foundation for the domes. Leon's actor introduced Gauge's actor to a rather fit man playing Axis' father.

The actor playing Valve said, "You really believe a pulse will take out our electronics, fail unprepared climate systems, and send our planet into an ice age? And you also buy into this Leon?"

Dr. Tempest's actor nodded.

The young man playing Gauge faced off with the bigger actor. "I do, and I want to protect as many people as I can."

Together, the triumvirate as Winter knew it developed the glass domes, but only enough of them to cover three cities. In an unprecedented feat of ingenuity, they used the last of their time with electronics to fashion the tunnels for the trains connecting the cities. Meanwhile, each faction weaned their people off electronics.

This made Axis wince. He could remember his father confiscating his phone, terminal, and projection screen as a teenager. But the old man hadn't cited a mechanized apocalypse. Instead, Valve said it was because Axis had misbehaved at Dr. Tempest's house so badly, Leon had demanded Valve do something about it. Fourteen at the time, Axis had cried thinking he'd disappointed the one man who'd been good to Axis his entire life. He'd only learned after the world as they knew it had ended that Valve had lied.

Lya had told Axis the truth.

The woman playing her and the girl playing Lexia appeared now and then, but mostly as supportive ornamentation to sponsor Leon's motivation for preparing against the eventual doomsday. Axis could remember Valve did it solely for profit, but the play didn't touch on this. In fact, it gave the Flicker household a wide berth, leaving Axis curious if it was out of respect or out of details to go on.

Either way, the day finally came.

Electronics went offline, the Founding Families raised the domes, and Winter began.

All thanks to Gauge.

Axis wasn't sure what Gauge had left out, but he'd always known the Founding story had never completely added up.

Snow was hiding something.

———————————————————

Standing ovation. The cast came out and gave a bow.

From behind the screen around his theater box, Gauge helped Tija get her clothes on. Sometime after the scene about his mother's funeral, Tija had straddled him in the luxurious seat, and he'd welcomed the distraction. He liked the warm scent of her, like cinnamon and lust. Her bright red lipstick was no doubt smeared across his face, and he used the reflection of her necklace to wipe it away. Gently, he used his thumbs to fix her melted eyeliner and combed his fingers through her fallen hair.

"You're so gorgeous, and I'm lucky to have shared even a moment in your company."

Tija's smile was radiant with a hint of gratitude. There was even a girlish flush to her cheeks, and Gauge kissed her.

Jan had melted into the shadows for their privacy, but Gauge could feel the butler's apprehension through the curtain. The old spy didn't enjoy leaving his charge alone. The Count only had to gesture with one finger, and Jan returned to the box as Gauge pulled back the screen. He stood at the balcony, and the cheering amplified into a roar.

Yes, the people adored Gauge, but no one understood him. There was one among the blur of faces with their over-enthusiastic clapping who'd given him hope.

Across the way, Lexia's theater box was empty. Gauge had noticed her during every scene of the play, including during the emotional tribute to Lya Tempest. Her tears had moved him, as everyday Gauge walked on this Winter, he thought of his own mother's declining health and his impotence to stop it.

But unlike Lexia, Gauge also thought of his seething hatred for his father, which festered like a canker in his mouth—

"Gauge? Shall we go?"

Ever the enticing distraction, Tija waited at the curtain, eager for the rest of their night to begin. Jan looked equally pleased with leaving the very public venue. Gauge gave a final wave to the people of Winter and followed his 'butler' through the curtain—

Running smack into Ms. Tempest.

While Gauge blinked at the unexpected intrusion, Lexia waved to Tija, saying, "That's a magnificent dress. You two make a stunning couple. Hello, Jan." She also waved to the old spy, who...

Was Jan blushing?

He nodded back, and Gauge finally found his tongue. "Thank you for the kind words, Ms. Tempest. I hope the evening was to your liking." When he held his arm out to Tija, clearly dismissing the younger woman, they all peered at him as if he'd sprouted a second head.

"I don't know what you are Gauge, savior or monster, but never meddle in my affairs again. Stay away from Lexia."

It hurt Gauge to be rude to anyone, let alone a young woman whose company he enjoyed immensely, but Axis had been clear. There was little choice in the matter. Tija took his arm, and Jan, who clearly disapproved of the rudeness judging by the scowling frown on his face, followed Gauge down the stairs.

Lexia, however, was hard to spurn. "It was a beautiful play. I'd never fully appreciate how young you were or how lonely."

Gauge stopped.

Froze to the spot.

Lonely.

Yes, that's what he was.

"There you are, child. Hello, Count Snow. I see my daughter came to wish you a good evening." Dr. Tempest looked ruffled enough to better Gauge's humor, and he smiled.

"Hello, doctor. Yes, Ms. Tempest, you are so kind."

Gauge wasn't sure what he'd meant to start when he met her eyes and emphasized 'kind,' but he certainly triggered a marvelous chain of events.

Lexia said, "I would like to discuss those unions with you. Tomorrow."

Tomorrow.

"Tomorrow?" Someone repeated sharply.

Axis.

He was waiting at the bottom of the stairs with Mrs. Tenz and her son.

Lexia, ethereal in her radiance, beamed. "The Count and I are meeting *tomorrow* to brainstorm some standardizations for the unions forming within the crops and mines."

Mrs. Tenz clapped her hands and said, "That's brilliant. It would give us a place to start."

Tija said, "Honestly, we could use those in the factories. It would help keep situations like Walker from repeating."

There was an olive branch here Gauge could extend, and there was a mischievous sparkle in Lexia's black eyes as if she'd realized it at the same time. Gauge turned to Axis and tried not to falter at the hardness in the green glass of his eyes as he said, "Now there's a fine idea. *Prince*

Flicker, would you care to join us?" He'd resisted the urge to call him 'Master.' No, teasing Axis was only appropriate when Gauge didn't want something from him.

"Mrs. Tempest, why doesn't Axis like me?"

"Oh, it's not that he doesn't, little Snow. It's that he wants Lexia's attention all to himself. He's a little boy, younger than you, and he needs more practice in sharing."

Please, share her, Axis…

But the young Prince shook his head. "I wouldn't want to intrude. I'll send my thoughts along with the usual quarterly proposals."

Mrs. Tenz, Tija, and Lexia shared the same disappointed pout.

It was rather remarkable really.

Dr. Tempest popped the bubble by saying, "Lexia, would you like to walk Axis home in the snow?"

The prospect perked her up enough to smile again, although it was half as gorgeous as the beam from earlier. "Of course." She kissed Leon's cheek before taking Axis' free arm. Flicker nodded good night before escorting Mrs. Tenz and his fiance out of the theater.

Gauge's spine hurt, and Jan sensed it.

The old spy indicated the exit. "Sir?"

Tija reasserted herself on Gauge's arm, and they made to leave when Dr. Tempest spoke up.

"Actually, Master Flicker and I would like a word with Count Snow. Can we speak in the conference room?"

Every major venue in the capital city sported at least one conference room because these impromptu meetings always happened when the

Founding Families shared a venue. It was almost enough to make Gauge roll his eyes. The pain had made him grumpy.

He kissed Tija's temple and whispered in her ear, "Go back with Jan to the Cathedral where you'll be safe. I'll follow shortly."

She left with her eyes lingering on Gauge.

Dr. Tempest took off his glasses to clean them, saying, "That was wise. I don't believe Valve is happy with her right now. Or with you, for that matter."

"Bite me, Leon." Gauge turned and walked into the conference room ready to get this over with. His cane clamored when he threw it on the table, and he let it. After tossing his top hat beside it, he rubbed a white gloved hand over his black braids and growled into a sigh. "This is ridiculous."

"Yes…" Valve walked into the room with more noise from his coughing than Gauge had just made. "Your sense of 'justice' *is* ridiculous." He cut off one end of a cigar as he took a seat at the far end of the table.

Gauge said, "Don't smoke that in here," knowing full well the man would do the opposite.

The flame of Valve's embossed lighter illuminated his fat cheeks in a most unflattering way before he puffed on the cigar and floated a ring into the air. Master Flicker said, "If I haven't thanked you recently, I will again. These cigars are your… finest…" He couldn't finish the sentence for all the coughing.

Gauge smirked. "I'm glad to see they're doing your health some good old man. You've got color to your cheeks." And a red stain on his mouth.

Dr. Tempest cut the air. "I think that's enough of the prerequisite banter. May we proceed?"

"Sure. Why the hell are we meeting?" Again, Gauge was grumpy. He couldn't sit for the painful contortion sensation in his spine, but he could barely stand any longer for the ache in his legs. The match with Axis earlier had cost him dearly. With both hands planted on the tabletop, he leaned forward less for dramatic effect and more for the support.

Physical therapy.

Gauge needed to perform it more regularly starting tomorrow.

Dr. Tempest seemed to notice and took pity by cutting to the chase. "Valve is upset you killed one of his foremen without discussing it with anyone, and I'm concerned about you spending time with my daughter."

Very to the chase. That was probably the most direct the doctor had ever been, and it raised Gauge's brows over his glasses.

Valve finally stopped coughing enough to say, "What he said. Although spend all the time you like with young Ms. Tempest. It's driving my son crazy."

Leon's head snapped around and glared at the hefty man.

Gauge hung his head and sighed.

This was stupid.

"I'll remind both of you once that Winter is mine. And that includes every citizen under these domes—" Gauge held up a finger to stave Tempest from arguing. "I have the utmost respect for your daughter, and I'm sorry to disappoint you Master Flicker, but I also respect her engagement to Axis as unfortunate as it is for me. We'll discuss the reasons they can't marry at the pre-engagement screening which," he pointed at Valve to say, "your *son* and your *protégé*," he pointed at Tempest, "skipped entirely without respect to me. Both of you knew he'd intended to propose, and both of you kept me in the dark. So I'd say the first slight goes to me."

Dr. Tempest stared for a long moment of silence before giving a curt nod.

Valve waved his cigar, the smoke trail forming a white flag, conceding.

Gauge swiped a hand down his face before disguising his collapse in the chair as a graceful plop. "Secondly, Walker committed the act of sexual assault, condemning himself to a coppery death. Those are the laws, and if you weren't encouraging such ugly behavior, Valve, I wouldn't have been forced to kill him."

"Ah. But there was another factor in his demise, was there not?" Somehow Valve got all of that out without a cough and while sounding sly and knowing. Then he coughed up a storm.

Gauge hoped he wasn't following the man's meaning, but...

Dr. Tempest filled in the blanks. "Tija. She is complicit in his death by entrapping him. She is almost as guilty of the crime as Walker was."

Gauge's mouth fell open. He couldn't begin to comprehend his own incredulity—his own disgust. How could they even equate the two?!

And what would Lexia think of her father's pronouncement?

Almost as if Leon knew the direction of Gauge's thoughts, he held up his hands, saying, "I don't necessarily agree with Valve, but since the man can't stop coughing, I thought I'd finish his trail of thought."

Necessarily.

When Valve took his handkerchief from his face, blood was smeared across his mouth. He pointed at Gauge and vehemently argued, "You know I'm right, Snow. That viper deserves to be in the wall right next to her victim."

Gauge had had enough. He straightened despite the pain, took off his glasses, and glared at the man across the table. The room went quiet, and Gauge fought to maintain the eye contact even as the soft candlelight pierced through his corneas. He said, "Entrapment is not the same as attempted rape. At most, *my* employee has deserved exile from the capital. At most."

Damn this penetrating halo.

Gauge's icy tone lost some of its effect as he hid his eyes once more behind the amber lenses.

Leon rapped his knuckles on the table. "Here, here. We have it then. You'll exile her from the city tonight."

Gauge wasn't finished. "But... Neither of you have evidence of entrapment."

Valve gargled in fury.

Leon pinched the bridge of his nose and sighed. He said, "The entire city knows."

The old Factory Master croaked, "Exile her tonight."

"And if I don't?" Gauge asked it quietly, softly. Almost not loud enough for them to hear.

But both men heard, and they blinked at him. Even Valve's errant lungs gave the moment its due silence.

In truth, the accords mattered very little between the three men. This so called 'balance of power' was only an illusion to keep up appearances for the sake of public opinion. At the core—at the heart—these men owed everything to Gauge. And not often, but on occasion, they forced him to remind them of it.

Gauge's mind, body, and soul ached and longed for bed. "Gentlemen, if you don't wish your dirty laundry aired to a people perfectly content with tearing you apart, limb from limb, then don't make demands of me. You've soured my evening, and now the only salve for it, Tija, is your new mark. For her own safety, I will sequester her off where she'll stay out of trouble. Are we in agreement?"

Leon nodded. "I think that's best for her." He flicked a quick glance at Valve regarding her safety.

The Factory Master also nodded into his handkerchief, once again at a loss for breath.

Gauge put on his top hat and grabbed his cane with a curse. "All this for a fucking rapist."

Outside, the snow came down heavily. Heavier than Winter had seen since Lya's funeral. Gauge wondered how Lexia was faring with the memory and hoped she was too busy enjoying herself with Axis to notice.

Tija greeted Gauge naked in his conservatory, both improving and further exhausting his evening. He was almost in too much pain to enjoy the surprise. Not to mention, he didn't feel right accepting her pleasurable offerings without first telling her the bad news.

"Exile?" Tija breathed, grasping her throat.

Gauge took her hand down and kissed it, saying, "I think we can hide you as an employee in my mines, if you would prefer that instead.

But you would need to dye your hair or wear tinted glasses—Something to hide your distinct beauty."

Which was impossible. Her cheekbones alone were a giveaway.

Never mind, it would make for a miserable life—hiding in seclusion and dodging bounty hunters.

Tija must've shared Gauge's thoughts because she shook her head, swallowed, and held her chin high. "I can move to another city and find my way."

Brave girl.

Gauge pulled her into an embrace, and when Tija sniffled, he vowed to spit on Valve's grave.

$\mathcal{S}$IX

Lapsed Fortitude

LEXIA WOKE THE NEXT MORNING TO FIND THE GARDENS BLANKETED IN SNOW, A FITTING REMINDER OF THE DAY AHEAD. A day in the company of her lover's enemy, but what if Lexia could make them friends? She didn't buy into the Founding Religion. There was more to it, and that was obvious to her, but…

Was the Copper Count as despicable as Axis and her father wanted her to believe? Or was there more to the man than a history of pinned butterflies?

After seeing the tribute of her mother in the Founding Play, Lexia decided not to cover the blue freckles at her temples as she dressed. Instead, she wore a loose cobalt button-down to emphasize the spattering of color at her temples. Next went on black leather pants. Because duel. That's why. She even strapped into her shoulder holster for both steam cannons, rigging them over the blouse before tucking it into her pants.

She donned another pair of black over-the-knee boots. Her long black duster completed the snow-ready ensemble. Pun intended.

With her waves left loose to flow behind her, Lexia set off on her walk to the Copper Cathedral. And, yes. She might have cheekily left the house before her father rose for breakfast, but she was tired of everyone trying to influence her opinion of the Count. It was time to give Gauge a fair chance.

Rhyme cursed behind Lexia.

She peered back to find him almost sprawled out on the snow-covered cobbles. His prosthetic didn't like the lightened traction.

After tousling her hair, Lexia said, "You can get the car. Just this once."

"Oh, your charity knows no bounds, Heiress." The rust of Rhyme's voice and its iron sarcasm made her giggle.

As they approached in the car, Lexia admired the Copper Cathedral shining amid all the fluffy white. The clocktower chimed to the hour, resounding the capital with a cheerful regard for the time. She said, "It's a beautiful day for an outing." She patted the folio beside her in the backseat.

Rhyme humphed and muttered something to the effect of, "My joints say otherwise."

He was fortunate they lived under the dome, protected from the ice hurricanes outside the domes. It hardly snowed within, and Lexia tried not to let the memory of Winter's last snowfall dampen this beautiful wonderland.

Someone had shoveled the snow off the cobbles and steps leading to the Wall of Pain, stemming Rhyme from complaining further.

Meanwhile, Lexia tried to ignore the copper doors and their gruesome monument.

Jan answered, "Good morning, Ms. Tempest. The Count awaits you in the conservatory. Follow me."

"Thank you, and good morning to you."

They followed the butler into a round room of glass with a view of the crater beyond. Snow covered all that black rock veined with copper ore until it was hardly recognizable. A grand piano took up the center of the room, tempting Lexia to try its keys. Sat at a long table off to the side of the room, Gauge stared out at the view so deep in thought he hadn't noticed their arrival until Jan cleared his throat.

The Count startled and turned in his chair to face them.

Jan half bowed. "Sir. Ms. Tempest."

Exhaustion cast dark shadows beneath the rim of Gauge's copper glasses. Today, the lenses were an azure so light they were almost translucent, and for the first time since they were children, Lexia could see the blue of Gauge's eyes. Sad as they were. Something had occurred overnight to age the Count of Copper. With his shirt wrinkled and the sleeves rolled back, he looked positively disheveled. Stubble further darkened his already deep complexion.

Withered.

That's how Gauge looked.

"Would you like me to come by another time?" Lexia offered out of kindness despite her own curiosity. Meanwhile, Rhyme found an armchair out of the way, sinking into the decor. She realized Jan had done the same only far more convincingly.

Gauge wiped a hand down his face, stifled a yawn, and said, "Not at all. You're a perfectly welcome sight, Ms. Tempest. A persistent one at that. You want to discuss those unions, and here we are. Please, have a seat." He stood and gestured at the one closest to him.

"Mommy, why is the Snow boy so small? Axis is half his age and twice his size."

"Little Snow is sick, sweetheart, but both he and Axis could do with more hugs."

Lexia smiled and took the seat.

Gauge looked once then twice at her. As he sat, he mused, "Do you fear I would dare challenge Dr. Tempest's daughter to a duel?"

She patted one of the steam cannons. "It's better to be prepared than caught unawares."

He laughed, and the rich warmth of it melted some of the snow outside. This room suited him, surrounded by greenery he helped preserve. Was that a succulent—

Lexia almost pinched herself. Focus. She said, "Your home gets more beautiful the more I see of it."

"I think you just admire my green thumb." Gauge smiled, leaned back in his chair, and laced his fingers over his stomach.

With him relaxed and a little mussed, Lexia could appreciate what Tija and, she supposed, other partners saw in him. She wanted to see his eyes without the glasses, and she had to stop herself from reaching over and taking them off.

"Ms. Tempest, have my horticulture skills rendered you speechless?" Gauge's words held an edge of laughter, but also something else. Almost as if he'd figured out the direction of Lexia's thoughts.

She shook herself. "No. Sorry." Try for half-honesty. "It's just been a decade since I've seen your eyes this clearly."

Gauge chuckled, and again the genuine warmth touched Lexia. He said, "Well, it's best you not see them. I only take the glasses off when I'm right mad or…Heh. Ahem." He clapped his gloved hands and sat back up in his chair to change the subject. "Let's discuss those unions models. I'd like to keep things professional between us."

Lexia took his meaning and appreciated the change of subject. The warmth in the room wasn't only because of his laughter. She took out the papers from her folio and spread them across the tabletop. With an irritated swipe of her bangs, she flattened her hands on the table and leaned over to point at the documents. "Here's what I had mind. The combine machines require a certain expertise in steam-powered machinery. It's more of a skilled labor, so I think their unions should be separate from say the seeders, whose hands are worked almost to the point of bleeding. Their needs are different, and their benefits should reflect that. And looking at this gave me an idea about our current shifts. There aren't enough of them, for instance, here and here." She pointed at the graphs. "We could easily create twice as many jobs and reduce unhappiness among the overworked employees—Sorry, I know this is off topic from the unions, but I only realized this opportunity because I got caught in the weeds."

Gauge was watching her from his seat, staring at her and glancing down at the documents when she pointed. He nodded along, but there was some emotion or regard in his eyes that she couldn't interpret. He stood and looked at the graphs, playing with the stubble on his chin as he stared. "Hmm. I see what you mean here about the shifts lacking in manpower. It's a good catch which I'm sure your father will value. I appreciate your idea of manual versus skilled labor, but I'd like to know more about how you mean their benefits are not the same."

Lexia went on to say the laborers needed more time off to rest, while the machine operators needed more employees to support them. They shouldn't do their own mechanic work, for instance, and by dividing those positions, it created a new wave of jobs.

All the while, Gauge kept looking at her in that indiscernible way. He would nod along, agree or challenge her, and smile here and there. But beneath it all, he was keeping his true thoughts hidden.

Lexia grew more curious and even desperate to decipher it.

The next thing she knew, they were peering at one another across the spread of papers. Only a breath separated them.

Gauge's eyes fell to Lexia's lips and back up to her eyes again. That's when she realized what the look was. He wanted her.

And Lexia was surprised to find she reciprocated the interest. It was a curiosity buried in her growing respect and admiration for him.

But…

Axis.

Lexia went silent and straightened. Gauge watched her do it and backed away a step, hands in his pockets to appear neutral. The second she'd separated herself from the moment, he knew what she was thinking. He respected it by giving her space. Why did that make her want him more?

Lexia bit her lip, and Gauge's eyes devoured the habitual movement, filling her with warmth until she was flushed with it.

The Count's expression darkened before he rushed around the table and reached out his hand. Eternity help her, Lexia took it, and Gauge pulled her toward another room.

Jan made to follow, but Gauge shook his head.

Rhyme stood, and Lexia...

Oh, Lexia waved him off. The man looked so unhappy about it, and she wasn't really sure if it was the best idea either. But sometimes chances had to be taken.

Gauge led her into a library of rosewood casings and hundreds of books. He slammed the double doors shut and pressed his forehead to the wood.

Lexia, breathless, took a few uncertain steps backward into the room.

What was happening?

What was she doing?

"Lexia."

What would her father think? Or Axis?!

"Lexia..." Gauge's hand...

Lexia peered down at the fingers entwined in hers. Compared to the stark white of her skin, his was a beautiful gray, but his hands were still paler than the rest of him. She looked up into startling blue eyes with no barrier between them. There was a world inside them, and the heat from his hands was an invitation to explore it.

Lexia breathed, "What do you want from me, Gauge?"

He leaned down, saying, "I just want to taste you."

Axis laid in bed, not ready to leave it just yet. With an arm thrown over his head, he tried to relax and consider the day ahead. This review and revision of policy across the factories' standards was vital to prevent another Walker situation, but it wouldn't be simple work. Especially with him thinking about Lexia all day.

Was she already at the Cathedral? Would Gauge heed a word Axis had said during their match? And above all that, had Axis been wrong to turn down the invitation?

Working with the two of them might have proven more fruitful than working on factory policy all on his own.

With a groan, Axis rolled out of bed and went to check his mail. More Founding invitations and a few resumes—

A linen envelope with a plain seal and no address captured his attention. He opened to find a lengthy letter and…

A kiss imprinted in red lipstick.

Dearest Prince,

At my request, I am writing you from our Count's desk for I'm afraid I won't have the opportunity to speak to you again. The mighty Triumvirate has deemed me unworthy as a citizen to our capital city—

No, that's not fair. Forgive my bitterness.

Your father all but threatened my life if I weren't exiled after the execution of his toxic employee, Walker. Dr. Tempest advised Count Snow it was in my best interest to flee, and under the circumstances, I agreed.

But I couldn't leave without telling you *none* of this is your fault. Do you understand me, Prince Axis? You are a good man, and Winter is better for your leadership. I fear your conscience won't relieve you of the guilt of my departure, so here's a kiss to reaffirm that I am all right.

One day, I will return, though Gauge believes the city won't be safe for me while Valve yet lives. He said after the Factory Master dies, and you ascend, I can come back with your permission. In that case, I would like to remain employed to you and to Gauge as an official mediator between the mines and the factories. For half a decade now, I've served as such in an unofficial capacity. I think the time for coyness has passed, don't you?

In such a fortunate position, I've learned some truly unfortunate things. Your father is indeed spoiling your inheritance, but worse than you may know. He's exploited discrepancies in factory policies to abuse employees, yes you know. But there are positions held by specialists without intentions to pass on their knowledge to ensure their own job security. There are quotas on hold to prepare for union strikes along every line but the Flicker wicks. Those linemen and their foreman are exceptional and hold loyalty only to you, Prince Axis. Expand on this virtue, thread it throughout the rest of the lines, and you will have no need to worry about your inheritance.

Begin with the linemen.

Beware your father's intentional negligence.

Work with Gauge to start the standardized unions before you break ground on the new city's factories, and you should have a cornerstone on which to build your foundation.

Regarding our Count Snow…

Many years ago, I was his father's student. Gauge walked in on Prof. Snow propositioning me for a higher grade. After I refused the professor's advances, he failed me from university. Gauge hired me straight after to coordinate efforts for the steam domes. I was his employee long before I was yours, and I meant what I said when I agreed to entrap Walker. I enjoyed it. Consider it a little female revenge.

Perhaps with too steep a price as I have loved this city since its Founding much as I have loved you since the moment we met.

Take care of Lexia, Axis. She's lucky to have a dark knight like Gauge and a white knight like you to look after her.

Yours truly,

Tija Cloud.

Axis wasted no time dressing in a simple suit. He crushed fruits and vegetables together for a shake on the go as he rushed to his car in the snow. Once inside, he said, "Bolt, take me to the Avenue."

"Good morning to you, too, Prince Flicker."

Axis snorted into his breakfast. Flicker Avenue looked serene in the snowy landscape with no smoke from the stacks. It was enough to lift his spirits as he traversed the unshoveled cobbles into the Factory Master's offices. Bolt parked the car and followed Axis inside. Together, they were otherwise alone in the front building.

Bolt asked, "What has you in such a state?"

Axis went through the filing cabinets, saying, "Tija. She was banished from the city last night, but she's left me with a place to start."

"How kind of her." Bolt sounded solemn, and it fit with Axis' mood.

Yes. Tija's letter was kindness in short and a lifesaver in essence.

Axis pulled out the current policies for employee conduct, quotas and backlog, and a very dusty treaty on unions. Some time had passed since this issue was last reviewed.

New factories; new policies.

Axis waved at the seat across his desk, "Bolt, get comfortable. This will take a while."

"I just want to taste you."

Lexia was driving Gauge crazy. The entire time they'd worked on the unions, he couldn't help but admire how her blue blouse accentuated the freckles she was no longer hiding. How those pants hugged her ass and drew entirely too much attention to the length of her shapely legs. Here and there, through the gape in her blouse, Gauge had glimpsed her breasts straining against a lacy black bra.

Lexia surprised Gauge when she closed the distance and pressed her lips to his. Without hesitation, he opened his mouth to draw on her bottom lip and drew out the sensation in a languid caress.

Soft. Easy.

Lexia moaned into the kiss, and a dam broke, opening her mouth thirsting for more.

Gauge used both hands to cup her nape in the waves of her hair and gave her what she wanted. She smelled of rain in the summer and tasted sweet like berries—both only memories now to Gauge.

When Lexia licked his bottom lip, Gauge lost all composure and did what he'd wanted to do since the first night he saw her. He reached down and lifted one of her legs to his hip, beckoning her to wrap them around him. This way, she could make no mistake of how much he wanted her—

Lexia broke the kiss, took a step back, and touched her fingers to her lips. Her eyes were yellow-rimmed and brimming with tears. Shame and guilt had left the black of her irises like reflecting mirrors, and Gauge saw himself in her.

Of course. How could he not realize it before?

Axis had been Lexia's first and only lover.

She had so much to lose. Her fiance. Her father's approval. The sweet girl image she'd upheld with the public, inheritor to Winter's Diamond. Cubic zirconium just wouldn't do.

Gauge quit the room lest he do something he regret. As he passed the conservatory, he said, "Jan, see her out." He was surprised to articulate even that much, he was so overcome.

It would be the work of a moment to seduce Lexia into more, and every fiber of his torn being wanted it. He wanted to push her over the edge, and it wasn't beyond her desires. He'd tasted it in the passion of her kiss, but damn it—

Gauge wouldn't have her shamed over him. It was likely she wouldn't forgive herself for the kiss, let alone a night in his bed.

Leon would know, too. Rhyme would tell him—*Everyone* would know if the Crop Heiress had spent a night at the Copper Cathedral.

The scandal.

Axis would challenge Gauge to a duel and kill him legal and proper.

A kiss worth dying for.

Once in his bedroom, he stared at his bed, imagining Lexia's hair in disarray all over it while her nails tugged at his braids as Gauge dedicated some time to pleasuring her. Again, with her legs wrapped around his neck. The yellow flush of her skin as she bit her lip with each swell.

Fuck Gauge, Axis was going to kill him.

Gauge stared at his bare hands. He'd left his gloves in the library. Ten years… Why had he taken his gloves off to touch her? A decade he'd deprived himself, and now he was craving the silky softness of her hair and the textured goosebumps along her skin.

With a swipe of his hands, Gauge pulled on his braids.

What had he done?

Because of Valve, Gauge couldn't confide in Tija for her usual relationship advice. He'd seen her off only hours ago, and he was already missing her brand of friendliness. Tija was the only person who wouldn't balk at the physical contact without his gloves. She *would*, however, berate him for getting so close to a woman who was already spoken for. And she'd be right…

Gauge peered out the windows of the front stairs to see Lexia getting into her car. She clutched Axis' timepiece against her chest and stared out at the white scenery with an awful look in her eyes.

Lost.

Forlorn.

The intensity of Lexia's regret twisted a knife in Gauge's heart.

"Little Snow, aren't you lonely around all these adults? Why don't you go outside and play with Lexia and Axis? Did something happen?"

"We're not the same, Mrs. Tempest. But I'm not lonely, I promise."

Gauge had lied to Lya. The woman always could see right through him, and for an instant at the play last night, he'd thought Lexia could, too.

"It was a beautiful play. I'd never fully appreciate how young you were or how lonely."

Could Lexia understand Gauge?

As the car pulled away, the separation felt final. If she could be the one person to see into Gauge, he'd just let his only chance drive off. Let her escape.

For her sake.

For Winter's.

Nothing could come between the Heiress and the Prince.

Not even the Count.

Lexia stared out of the car, worrying her lip as Rhyme drove her home in stern silence. The air in the car, breathing into her lungs, judged her. Every molecule consumed her with guilt.

"I trust you completely."

Axis...

What had Lexia done?

She'd kissed Gauge. That's what she'd done. A searing, promising kiss which she'd felt in her toes among other places. When he'd lifted her leg, Lexia had wanted him to slam her back against a bank of bookshelves and make her scream his name.

This...

Couldn't...

Happen.

Lexia had never—*ever*—wanted anyone other than Axis. He was her partner in everything but business, and she'd hoped to bridge that gap once their two houses became one. She'd never once considered another person in her bed or saw herself in another's as in this scenario. Lexia would've let Gauge lead her to his room and do whatever he wanted to her there.

Axis deserved better.

The thought was pure and true, so much so it drew an involuntary sound from Lexia's heart, and she had to bite down on her lip to suppress it. She was curled up against the door in the car, hugging her knees to her chest, and trying with everything in her not to cry.

Twice the guilt.

Twice the shame.

Lexia owed Gauge an apology as well. He'd done the right thing and exited the situation before it had gotten out of hand. In truth, he'd spared her from further ruin. Someone who'd experienced the kind of solitude as he had in his life deserved better than Lexia's fickle and childish antics.

A tear escaped Lexia's defenses and trailed down her cheek. The first of many.

Rhyme would tell Leon she'd gone into a room alone with Gauge before the Count burst from it upset demanding the butler see

Lexia out. It did not look good, and truth be told, she *did* care how it looked.

To her father.

To Winter.

But most of all to Axis.

When the car pulled through the gates and up to the portico, Lexia burst from it and ran up the five stories to her bedroom. She didn't stop running until she hit the bed and curled into a ball of messy tears.

It took some time to cry her soul out, but eventually Lexia felt up to changing into some pajamas and wiping off her makeup. She stared at her freckles in the mirror, trying to ignore the mess of her nude lipstick.

Rhyme would've noticed it, including if any had been smeared on Gauge's mouth.

The scandal.

A soft knock sounded from the door, and Leon called through the oak, "Sweetheart, please talk to me."

Lexia didn't respond. She wasn't ready to face her father or anyone because she knew how this would play out. Why of course the villainous Count Snow had tried to mar the perfection of Winter's Diamond Heiress, but the heroine escaped his clutches without falling into his bed and ran back to her valiant Prince.

And Gauge would let it perpetuate. Lexia knew he would. All the plays and songs would get the story wrong. He was the hero, and she was the villain.

How could she face this?

By not facing it.

Lexia hugged Axis' timepiece to her chest and settled in for another round of tears. Amid this latest fit, she did one thing differently. She opened a drawer in her desk and pulled out the most curious of gifts.

A board with butterflies pinned to it in alphabetical order according to the genus and species displayed on the labels. Lexia blew off the dust and set it on the desk. She stared at it while tears, plump and hot, breached her lashes.

Their childhoods had been so different. Gauge was lonely. Axis was abused. And Lexia was privileged to have parents who loved her. They'd given her so much love that she'd found plenty of it to spare for the boys, but Gauge had been so small. And Axis so protective. Abnormally so on both accounts.

Why couldn't they have found a way to play with each other?

All because of butterflies...

"What do you think, Bolt? Should I take these to Gauge and Lexia?"

Axis awaited the man's opinions of the diagrams and text Axis had spent the last hour laying out. He'd organized all the lines and their management into sustainable union models and looked forward to showing it to Lexia. She would approve.

As a retired foreman, Bolt's opinion was credible. So it warmed Axis to see his friend's smile. "This should work excellently, sir. I like what you've done with the foremen's benefits increases relying on the evaluations of their linemen. That'll teach anyone from becoming another Walker."

Axis said, "Yes! That was my thought exactly. I think Tempest crops and Snow mines could also benefit from the same strategy."

With a grin, Bolt offered, "Shall I get the car and prepare it for Snow Plaza?"

Axis nodded. "I think it's time we join Lexia at the meeting."

"Lexia has already left the meeting."

Valve.

Axis' father hulked his great heft through the doorway with an entourage of vicious-looking company. One burly man was picking his teeth with a rather large knife, while a slender woman in a hiked-up skirt sported a steam pistol on both hips.

The future inheritor of Flicker's Factories frowned, saying, "I wasn't aware you needed an armed escort, father."

"With vipers like that Cloud woman around one, can't be too careful," Valve jeered and then coughed to pay for it.

Axis talked over the phlegmy ruckus. "Why are you at work during Founding Season? You don't normally take part in the inspections."

With a great gulp of air, Valve asked, "Well, what kind of father would I be if I didn't warn my son of his fiance's indiscretions?"

What on Winter was the Factory Master on about? Axis narrowed his eyes and said, "Explain."

Valve peered at the woman, who said, "Ms. Tempest was seen exiting the Copper Cathedral in quite a state. Flushed. Lipstick smeared. Hair messy. Then she ran into her home without a word to her father and locked herself in her bedroom. She won't let anyone inside."

The man with the knife added, "Oh, and the Count isn't in much better straits. This all took place after they spent some time in his library alone together. Some *quality* time."

Ice froze Axis' veins and made it impossible to breathe. He heard their words, but had stopped listening to their meaning. All he took from their instigation was that Lexia was upset and in need of consoling. Everything else was simply venom from his father's fangs.

Valve choked out the words, "Of course, what do I know? Perhaps Snow took out his displeasure at how you ignored his betrothal laws by shaming Lexia. You know he won't reverse the sterility unless you follow pre-marital protocols, not that I think you should be allowed to have any children—"

"Get out."

The room grew quiet as everyone stared at Axis. He stood, and the desk nudged back with the abruptness of the movement. With a gesture, he indicated the people in the room. "Everyone but my father leave this room. Now."

Valve's entourage looked to him before they accepted his nod as permission to leave. Bolt didn't need telling twice. Once alone, Axis watched his father clip the end off another cigar and light it in his son's smoke-free office.

Valve said, "You know I'm right, boy. Lexia… She would make a wonderful wife and mother, but you…"

"You rank, abusive bastard. Come for my inheritance, but don't you dare come near Lexia again. I don't care what 'indiscretions' you'll claim to protect me from. She's as much an angel as her mother, and you know it. Leave my engagement alone." Axis tried hard to maintain calm, but he couldn't keep the edge of a threat from his voice.

Valve said, "But son. She's fucking Snow—"

Axis leaped over the table and grabbed his father by the lapels of his jacket. Startled, the old man crumbled into the chair behind him, and Axis used the surprise to wrench Valve's wrist until the son pressed the cigar toward his father's eye.

"What the hell do you think you're doing—"

Valve glimpsed Axis' eyes and went silent.

Axis asked, "Do you know what happens when a cigar meets flesh? First the hair fibers burn away, in this case your eyelashes. Then your cornea will melt back until the fluid beneath it blisters and pops, oozing down your face. But the cherry is hot enough to sear it into a coin-sized mound of scar tissue. Everyone who sees it will know it's the exact size of a cigar and know what happened. You'll be blind, and you'll learn to hate the smell of smoke. Are you ready to know how it feels, father? Because I'm ready to show you."

A tear spilled from Valve's eye, the heat coaxing moisture to the surface. Hoarse, he said, "Axis, you're better than me, and you always have been. I'm not long for this world, and I'll die with many regrets. This ice in your voice will make the top of that list. I'm sorry, son. Please, don't blind your old man."

"I don't care if Lexia stripped naked for Snow in the street. Stay out of my business. When we attend the pre-engagement meeting with Gauge, you'll nod along with everything I say. And that's the last I want to see of you. Do you understand? No surprise visits to the

Factory. No outings or dinners together. Nod so I know you're hearing me loud and clear."

Valve nodded emphatically.

It hurt to pull away. To let Valve go. A dark appetite craved the man's agony, and Axis was obliged to feed it. Instead, he straightened his clothes and combed through his hair, remembering how to breathe. Valve watched him, too smart to make any sudden movements or to say a word.

Axis pointed at the door. "Now get the fuck out of my office."

Valve turned with a cough and left.

Only after the old man vacated the premises did Axis allow his thoughts to stray to Lexia. Whatever had happened between her and Gauge, Axis would be there for her. To forgive or to console—He didn't care.

Axis loved Lexia too much to let anything come between them. Now if only she would give him the chance to tell her so.

SEVEN

Captive Game

Concern for Lexia occupied Gauge's thoughts. It had been a week since their encounter in the Cathedral, and word from Tempest Manor was she still refused to leave her bedroom. Not even for one of her infamous walks. Rumors had circulated immediately, ranging from a feud between Gauge and Lexia to a toss in the sheets so passionate it had broken her. In all the scenarios, he'd bullied her. There was even a cruel nursery rhyme about it.

Snow claimed Winter and all/

Even the Diamond who came to call/

But the Heiress escaped in time/

Before the Count committed his crime/

And now they both await/

Judgment at the copper gate/

Who will end up in the Wall?/

Gauge allowed it. Let Lexia be the victim or the brave heroine who escaped his villainous clutches. It was no worse than the old rumors that he'd secreted a fantastic machine which transmitted the electromagnetic pulse in the first place. Wild stories.

Early in the morning, Gauge stared out over his three-dimensional model of the new city's plans. He was working to prepare the new city's infrastructure for inclement weather as a blizzard had rendered the capital city immobile at the height of the Founding Season. The snow had forced Gauge to postpone several events and hire an emergency crew to thaw the train tracks and shovel the streets.

"Gauge, wake up. It's snowing."

"Really, mother?"

"Let's go outside."

"But what about you?"

"I'll bring my cane. Trust me. It'll be worth it."

Truth be told, Gauge loved the snow. It was the only time he could remember his mother being happy. As he leaned on his own cane, he tried to ignore how the cold seeping in through the walls stiffened his bones. The lenses in his glasses today were black to match his mood.

No Tija. No Lexia. No smiles or warmth.

Gauge stared out at the sprawling masterpiece of architecture and ingenuity and sighed.

Why the fuck was he always alone?

Jan entered the library with a handful of envelopes. "Sir, today's missives."

What timing.

Gauge smiled for his old friend and tried to remember his house was, in fact, filled with warm smiles. "Thank you, Jan."

As Jan handed Gauge the envelopes, the old spy peered around at the empty library before asking, "Would you like me to send the tailor's little boy up to play chess? Eternity knows you could use a proper beating."

Silly company. Perfect. "Yes, please. Thank you."

As the old man left, Gauge sorted through his mail. A burgundy envelope piqued his interest immediately. He opened it to find a letter sealed with a single flame.

Count Snow,

Despite the weather, I would like to meet for the pre-engagement screening. Dr. Tempest and Master Flicker have agreed to this afternoon. If you can make arrangements on such short notice, we would be much obliged. As you know, I'm eager to marry my fiance. We can begin planning for the wedding once you approve our request.

Regards,

Axis Flicker.

The young Factory Master and the crop Heiress could keep their relationship, but the wicked Count couldn't let them marry. Not without impacting the accords.

But how to break this to Axis without the younger man jumping straight to a conclusion based on foul play. He would certainly accuse Gauge of wanting Lexia for himself. And he would be half wrong. Gauge would easily share her with Axis, but also, the imbalance of power had nothing to do with the Count's interest in the girl.

A merger of those two houses would leave the mines at a disadvantage. With their resources combined, they could drive up trade prices. Or lower the value of mining ores.

And, unfortunately but not unexpectedly, Gauge's spies had never turned up with blackmail material on Axis. The worst thing he'd done was entrap Walker, and Gauge approved of the gambit.

What about persuasion material on Lexia?

Gauge laughed bitterly into his coffee mug. Lexia's only sin was taking an interest in Gauge, and well…

All of Winter had opinions on that. Surely by now Axis knew the rumors, yet he insisted he still wanted to marry her.

Gauge was both relieved and discouraged at the Prince's persistence. Still…

He went to his desk and lit his ink pad. After a quick scribble, he signed with his seal, musing that no one ever noticed the Count didn't wear a timepiece. It was such a small thing, but one even Tija never remarked on.

"Jan?"

The 'butler' appeared immediately. "Sir."

Gauge said, "Please see that Axis receives this promptly. Be careful in the snow."

Jan accepted the missive, saying, "Yes, sir. The Plaza, Boulevard, and Avenue were all cleared in the last hour."

Gauge stamped his cane on the parquet flooring. "Excellent. Thanks again."

Jan paused in the doorway. "Sir, if I may?"

With a curious lilt of his brow, Gauge said, "Go ahead."

The older man smiled warmly. "You were never cruel, but recently you've been even more kind. I think Ms. Tempest is a good influence on you."

Hmm...

Gauge considered this with a twirl of his cane. He said, "I appreciate the insight, old friend. Even if I don't know what to do with it."

Jan said the next with the utmost confidence. "You will."

Who will end up in the Wall?/

Seven days without visitors.

Seven days without mail.

Leon Tempest was starving his daughter of contact until Lexia talked to him. She understood why. He was concerned, and he should be. She wasn't eating, and she wasn't sleeping. But Lexia also knew one other thing...

Lya wouldn't approve of Leon's technique.

Lexia shoved her legs and their wool leggings into a pair of thigh-high boots. Without regard for propriety, she donned Axis' stolen sweater and soaked in its warmth as it swallowed her. It still smelled of his aftershave—woodsy and sweet. She left her waves cascading down her shoulders to protect her ears from the cold.

This would be a long walk, but first Lexia had to make it through her house. A gauntlet of curious faces and judgmental presumptions.

Sure, the people who worked for her had loved her once, but how could they now with all the rumors flying around?

Stupid nursery rhyme.

Lexia would do this one way and one way only. She held her chin high, straightened her shoulders, and glided down the first flight of steps. When no one came down the landing to attack her with accusations, she went down the next. And the next. One step at a time, she kept her eyes straight ahead even as servants paused in their duties to stare at her. Some flitted off to no doubt notify Leon that his daughter was loose in the world.

After Lexia exited the front door without a hitch, she relaxed and grew confident in her task, marching down the long drive. No one could stop her. She would make this right.

"Where do you think you're going?"

Fuck.

Lexia stamped her boot in a half a meter of snow. Without turning around, she said, "Rhyme. Please."

From behind, the intrusive bodyguard snorted. "No fucking way, Heiress. Your father has been worried sick about you, and if you think for one second I'll let you slip away on my watch on some fool's errand—Stop! Where are you going?"

Lexia ran like a wild woman for the gate. Behind her, Rhyme cussed and struggled, unable to keep up with his prosthetic in the snow. She was going to hell for taking advantage of his handicap, but there was nothing for it.

The guardsman at the gate looked ready to argue, but Lexia pointed a stern finger at him. "I've been teaching your little boy how to play tuba for years with a wealth of patience for the tone-deafness he inherited from you. Don't you dare betray me now."

The gate opened, and Lexia ran through it to find the cobbles were cleared. It wasn't exactly in her favor right now. She probably had a five-minute lead against Rhyme before he grabbed the car and chased her down. Possibly with father in tow.

Lexia shuddered and ran. She heard the car peel onto the road about the same time she reached the apex of Tempest Boulevard and Flicker Avenue. Only a few more steps. Axis' apartments came into view right at the same time Lexia heard Rhyme give the car some real steam and floor it. She looked over her shoulder to judge the distance—

"Ow!" Lexia ran into a brick wall that wasn't there before.

"Lexia?"

It wasn't brick. It was muscle.

"Axis!" Lexia jumped into his arms and buried her face in his neck.

He squeezed her so tightly it melted away all of her anxieties. Whatever he'd heard, he either didn't believe or didn't care. However…

Lexia regrettably pulled them apart, ignored the sound of the car pulling up, and blurted, "I kissed Gauge. Not the other way around. I hope you can find it in your heart to forgive me, but I completely understand if—"

"I forgive you."

Lexia stopped apologizing and gaped at Axis.

He took her hands, saying, "I'd already guessed something along those lines had happened. You're so passionate about everything, Lexia. It doesn't surprise me Snow would take advantage of that."

She shook her head and tugged on his hands. "No, you don't understand. It was my fault. Gauge didn't take advantage. He spared me—"

"Lexia Alya Tempest."

Lexia froze mid-sentence and winced against the weight of her full name. Her father must be furious with her to invoke it. She turned to find him standing in the street, not fuming, not seething, but frowning in abject disappointment. Leon's eyes were even a little glassy with unshed tears.

How could Lexia have done so much wrong trying to make something right?

"Father, I—"

Leon looked away, distressed by her misbehavior. While staring at the cobbles, he said, "I have spent the last week thinking about nothing other than your suffering. All I wanted was to help you. If your mother were here…"

Lexia gasped and let Axis go to cup a hand over her mouth. Tears stung her eyes. She'd thought many times over the last week about how much she wished her mother were here to help. Lya would've sat outside Lexia's door and sang until her daughter opened it. Then they would talk about the virtues of love and friendship, and how sometimes the two couldn't coexist. Lya would give Lexia advice on how to manage her love life and reputation without causing her guilt.

Leon wasn't exactly living up to his former wife's expectations either. And perhaps that's why his icy exterior melted, and he opened his arms. "Forgive me."

While Axis and Rhyme watched, Lexia went into her father's embrace and wiped her tears on his shoulder.

Leon murmured, "I'm so sorry."

Lexia said, "Me, too."

"I know it's not fair we don't have her in moments like this. I didn't know what to do, and I've been beside myself with worry. Tell me, how can I be a better father for you?" Leon kissed Lexia's freckled temple.

She pulled them apart to meet his eyes, trying to ignore her audience as she shamed herself publicly once again. "We can talk about it later. I want to do things in my own time." Not because he was icing her out.

Leon smiled weakly and squeezed her hand. "Of course." He looked over Lexia's shoulder at Axis, asking, "Are we on?"

Lexia stepped to the side to put all three men in her sights.

Axis said, "Yes. The Count is expecting us. Father will join us there."

The Count.

Lexia tried to remain neutral at the mention of Gauge, but her cheeks tried to betray her by warming in the chilled air.

Rhyme said, "I'll see Ms. Tempest gets home."

"Wait." Axis stepped off the sidewalk and put his arms around Lexia again. He whispered against her ear, "I know you're curious and afraid to ask. We're heading to the pre-engagement meeting. It's all formalities and ceremony. There's nothing to worry about."

Lexia couldn't hold back any longer. "Axis, it wasn't Gauge's fault. It was mine."

He kissed her cheek, saying, "We'll talk about it. Tonight. Sneak out if you have to. I've gone a week without my bed smelling of summer rain, and I won't have it another night."

"Yes."

Tonight.

Bolt pulled up to the curb and let Axis and Leon into the car. Meanwhile, Lexia faced her irate bodyguard.

Rhyme already had a finger out and pointed sternly at her. His rugged features suited the snowy backdrop like a lumberjack in the mountains. The censure in his whiskey eyes did not.

With the air cleared between Lexia and Axis, she felt light enough to smile and asked, "Have I ever told you how handsome you are, Rhyme?"

The man shook his head. "No flattery will work on me, young lady."

Lexia went around to the back of the car and pressed, "But you really are quite the catch. Do you know Sami in the kitchens?" Sami was the most buxom of the kitchen hands.

"No, ma'am. This is not working." But when Rhyme got in the car, his cheeks were red and not from the chilly air.

Piece of cake. "She talks about you all the time, and she's single. I can make some arrangements…"

———————————

"Axis, it wasn't Gauge's fault. It was mine."

A kiss.

Axis could forgive a kiss. He knew what Lexia was like in the heat of the moment. In their own relationship, she'd initiated all of their firsts. Axis loved her passion, but he also knew what Snow was like. The Count enjoyed making every moment about him. It only made sense the two of them alone together would turn into this.

One day, Axis would take it up with the man, but not today. The pre-engagement screening was such a juvenile way to control everyone's lives, and Axis did not look forward to asking for permission to marry Lexia from a man who'd preyed on her spontaneous ways. No, looking Gauge in the face would take some serious control of Axis' temper, but he would do it for the sake of marrying Lexia.

Valve, doubled-over his handkerchief in a coughing fit, joined Leon and Axis on the steps to the Copper Cathedral. There was no armed guard in sight.

Jan opened the door and said, "Welcome, gentlemen," before leading them to the conservatory.

Notes from a finely tuned piano greeted them, and Axis wanted to roll his eyes and groan.

Valve muttered to Dr. Tempest, "Snow must be in one of *those* moods, eh?"

Leon just shook his head.

This day would be long.

With Jan as escort, the three men arrived in the conservatory to find the Count furiously coaxing the keys with his slender gloved fingers. He swayed with the movements and rocked his foot on the pedal to the demands of the tune. It was angry.

Gauge was angry.

And when the Count was in one of these tempers, he wanted all of Winter to know it.

Nimble and meticulous, Gauge didn't miss a note as he quickly traversed the keys, and Axis had to admit to some impress. No one played like Snow. Lexia could match his tempo, but not his fury. The man's eyes weren't even open behind those black lenses.

"You.

"Are.

"Late."

No one questioned what Gauge meant. He wasn't referring to this meeting at all. He was referring to Axis' disrespect toward Winter's honored customs.

When Gauge slammed on the keys and hopped abruptly off the bench, Valve flinched. Gauge's sleeves were rolled back, his collar undone, and the jacket which matched his gray houndstooth slacks was nowhere to be found. The man even sported the beginnings of a beard.

Unkempt suited the Count and his infamous smolder.

At two in the afternoon, Gauge knocked back the off-colored whiskey in his crystal tumbler and finally faced his guests.

Rudely, Axis ignored the man's temper, gestured toward the conference table, and said, "Shall we proceed?" After all, in the last seven days, only one of them could say they'd kissed Axis' fiance.

Gauge went to the head of the table. Leon and Valve followed, taking seats on his left and right. Axis, feeling bold and not at all in a pleasant mood himself, sat at the opposite end of the table. He propped his elbows on the rosewood surface and laced his fingers together against his chin, waiting.

Valve peered between the younger men, and Leon looked ready to get this over with so he could reconcile with his daughter. All fair points—Wait. There was a sag to the doctor's shoulders. Was that defeatism—

"Prince Axis, I think we should start with your apology." Those words came out of Gauge Snow's mouth and went immediately to the engravers for his tombstone.

"You think what?" Axis glared at him in disbelief and teeming anger.

Leon shook his head.

Valve chewed on the butt of his cigar—Snow's finest—his jaw working nervously.

But Gauge...

Gauge smiled. A bitter, angry smile with a dark edge of smoke to it thanks to his deep complexion. This was Snow seething at Axis. He said, "We both know you didn't 'overlook' a formality. You simply ignored it. So, you owe the grace of the marital laws an apology and as their litigator, you owe that apology to me."

A whirlwind of emotions assaulted Axis all at once. He wanted to shout at Gauge for kissing Lexia, but how could he after she'd insisted it was her instigation? How could he be this upset with Snow if he wasn't upset at all with her? But then, over the course of the last week, Snow had done nothing to absolve Lexia of her shame, costing Axis precious time with her. Even dividing a wedge between father and daughter.

The Diamond Heiress deserved better.

So did Tija.

"And if I don't apologize, Count Snow?"

Gauge quirked a brow over his glasses, and a quiet settled over the room. Everyone waited for his reply. Which he gave after careful consideration. "Then the meeting doesn't happen."

Axis gritted his teeth to bite back his swearing.

The gall of this man.

Lexia's sweet smile flashed before his eyes, and Axis said, "I apologize for insulting the traditions, however young, of our dear Winter."

Would Gauge insist Axis apologize to him directly? Because that might be the end of his engagement to Lexia—

"Apology accepted. Now, state your case." Gauge sounded instantly less angry, down right congenial almost. He leaned back in his chair and laced his hands together over his stomach.

Axis nodded at Leon, who returned in kind. He glanced at his father, who also nodded as he was told to do. It was really up to Axis to argue for his engagement to Lexia and for the children they wanted to have.

For their future…

Axis said, "Mine and Lexia's friendship predates Winter's Founding. It evolved into stronger feelings, organically, and led to our eventual romance. We love and respect each other deeply and want to extend that love and respect into our futures. To cement it in time." He rolled his wrist on the table where Lexia's signature butterfly from her timepiece pressed into the back of Axis' hand. "We want to combine our two houses into its natural union and marry as one does when they're in love."

Gauge glanced at Leon, asking, "What do you say as the intended's father?"

Leon peered down the table at Axis, and the respect in his gray eyes warmed the younger man's heart. "Lexia is a sound judge of character and a bright young woman. She's also very determined to get what she wants when she wants it without a doubt of knowing what that is. In this case, Axis has grown into a fine young man with nothing but the best for her in his heart. They've abided by the courtship laws and have never broken curfew, which has brought me great relief over the years but also immense respect for Axis. Despite his ill regard for the particular formality of this meeting, he has upheld all the others as only an upstanding gentleman would do. Not to mention, a merger of our houses is in Winter's best interests and was inevitable with this young couple's future."

Axis' chest swelled with pride.

Gauge pressed his hands together like a prayer and tapped his fingers against his lips. Why Axis had noticed how the bottom was fuller than the top escaped Axis, but there it was.

The Count nodded toward Valve. "What about you?"

The Factory Master's fervent glance at Axis spoke volumes of the man's cowardice. Valve said, "Lexia and Axis are a perfect match, equal in every way. Their children will be the jewels of Winter, though I would never get to see them."

Axis blinked at his father, incredulous.

Gauge also blinked and shook his head as if to erase whatever thoughts had sprung to mind. He faced Axis once more down the length of the rosewood table and frowned. "Axis, you brought up the word 'organically.' Is that how you believe this took shape?"

The direction of this interrogation was not heading for an easy approval. Axis said, "I don't know what else you would call a childhood friendship budding into a romantic relationship."

"I would call it convenient. . . Yes. Awfully convenient. Maybe even contrived. You at no point felt you and Lexia were pressed together in the hopes of this very outcome between two such powerful families?" Gauge shot a glare at Leon and another at Valve. Then finally settled on Axis, not with ire, but with pity. Almost as if Gauge believed Axis were naïve.

The Prince didn't like this at all. "Are you saying our families arranged my relationship with Lexia?"

The Count said, "Either that, or you are complicit in this violation of the accords. What do you say to that?"

"You're fucking insane. That's what I say to that."

Gauge almost laughed. He derived entirely too much entertainment from keying Axis up. Fortunately, the dark tint of his lenses kept the humor in his eyes from showing.

Dr. Tempest blinked at Axis, but Master Flicker shrank away.

Interesting.

Had the son confronted his abusive father?

Regardless, Gauge stared down the table at the People's Prince and tried to decide what to do with him. The vein pounding in Axis' neck was a good indicator of the younger man's temper. Was he on the verge of challenging Gauge to a duel? Was it wise to continue needling Axis? And what exactly did Gauge hope to gain?

"Young Master Flicker—"

Axis clenched his jaw so loudly Gauge could hear it across the conference table.

"—You're treading in treacherous waters. I would be careful if I were you."

Some of the Prince's fury abated, enough for him to ask, "Are you accusing the honorable Dr. Tempest of agreeing to manipulate my relationship with Lexia?"

Carefully constructed words, and he neglected to say he didn't believe such things of his father. Just Leon. Well, if Axis only knew the secrets in Gauge's vault.

The Count said, "Not only am I accusing him of encouraging your marriage, but I'm almost certain everyone at this table besides you can see why."

To Gauge's right, Leon shut his eyes like he was praying or counting to ten. On Gauge's left, Valve coughed with a shaking hand itching for his lighter. Axis was the only one at the table who looked sincerely clueless with his narrowed eyes and dissenting frown.

Eventually, the People's Prince cut a hand through the air, saying, "It doesn't really matter how we came to be in love. Although I see a long talk ahead of me with my future father-in-law, the result is the same. Lexia and I want to marry and have children, but first we must go through you, *Count*." He bit out the last as if Gauge's title was worse than swearing.

Gauge flexed his fist, appearing angry when in truth his fingers hurt from their earlier exercise on the piano. How he longed for the glossy surface of the keys beneath his actual fingertips almost as much as he craved the silk of Lexia's hair. But no. Simple pleasures were denied him thanks to this fucking malady.

Bitter.

That's how Gauge felt, but not toward anyone in this room. Just at life in general.

Axis, the protector, must share similar frustrations, and perhaps Gauge was a bastard for antagonizing him further. He'd try another approach.

Gauge sat forward and tapped his fingers together over the rosewood tabletop. He looked between the two older men beside him and admired their commitment to this arrangement though neither said anything. Gauge gave Axis the full weight of his gaze and said, "I want you to understand my position, because I fully appreciate yours. I am not against your relationship with Lexia. In fact, I wish you both all the best. But I can't ignore the risk this levees at my business—a union of Flicker and Tempest. Can you not see that?"

Axis straightened his tie like it was strangling him and he wanted to lose it. "Dr. Tempest. Father. Would you please excuse us for a moment?"

For a man of such girth, Valve sure hopped out of his seat quickly. He peered down at Gauge. "Is the veranda suitable for smoking?"

"Be my guest, Master Flicker. Don't forget to take your co-conspirator with you."

Leon actually rolled his eyes with a click of his tongue but followed Valve out without a word of denial.

Alone.

With Axis.

The younger man wasted no time in standing and making his way down the length of the table. Gauge stood to face him, fifty percent amused and one hundred percent enticed. There was something about the way Axis moved when he was angry. More fluid where others became rigid. Like a great cat stalking his prey.

It was enough to send a shiver down Gauge's spine, one he barely concealed by grabbing his cane. Unsure he could trust himself, Gauge let Axis speak first.

"I don't look forward to telling Lexia." What an odd thing for Axis to say.

Gauge tilted his head, trying to figure the other man out. "Telling her what?"

Axis said, "That I was right. That the magnanimous and misunderstood Count Snow can't let one thing happen on this planet without making it about him. Including our relationship. After the last few weeks of her trying to convince me there was more to you, she'll be so disappointed to hear about this."

Exasperated, Gauge stamped his cane and let it take the weight of his bones. Reason. Logic. Where had they fled to? "Axis, I look forward to a future with Lexia heading the crops and you mastering the factories, but Winter cannot afford an imbalance of power."

"You look forward to a future where you can work closer with Lexia, you mean."

Now all sense had flown out the window.

Gauge took another step and put himself in Axis' personal space. They glared at each other from a breath away, and Gauge tried desperately to find the brilliance he knew lived behind those soft green eyes. "Say what you want to say, Prince. Let us no longer dance around the issue."

Axis was an inch taller, and he assumed every bit of it as he said, "You kissed her, and that gives me every right to challenge you to a duel."

All the cards were on the table now, and truth be told, Axis had the better hand.

Gauge, Winter's savior and Founder of their new way of life, would lose to Axis in a fair fight. Even now, the twenty-nine-year-old Count scanned the twenty-four-year-old Prince's stronger build. The man's shoulders were nearly twice as wide as Gauge's, and the older man would kill for the strength in the younger man's legs. No, there would be no winning this through violence.

Honesty.

It was the best tactic with a man like Axis. Gauge said, "You're right. You have every right to kill me, and if that's what Winter requires for my transgression, then I will pay that cost in blood. But only at your hand. No one else would do."

Axis narrowed his eyes, taken aback. His face softened as he searched Gauge's eyes. "Why are we always at odds, Gauge? Winter doesn't call for your blood, and I believe it needs you more than the lethal restitution over one transgression. Apologize to Lexia and grant us permission to marry. Is it not so simple?"

The Prince held out his hand to the Count.

Gauge lifted his gloved hand to take it, but he held up a finger with the other. "Under one condition."

Axis clicked his tongue, rolled his eyes, and ran a hand through his hair in a frustrated gesture. "What is it?"

"You present me with a proposal outlining how this won't disrupt the accords, and then we'll renegotiate when you take over the Factories. Convince me, and you'll have my permission."

Axis beamed, and it was quite the attractive grin. It warmed Gauge to his toes. The Prince said, "Deal," and put his hand back out.

Gauge took it, and they shook, smiling at one another.

How promising…

It was too bad Gauge couldn't behave himself. "Be sure to tell Lexia I said, 'Hello.'"

Axis dropped the Count's hand and stormed out of the room, leaving Gauge snickering into his second tumbler of whiskey. He went to the veranda and called out to his business partners, "He's gone. You may go."

"Thank the angels of Winter," Valve grumbled between coughs as they made their way back inside. "My eyelashes were freezing shut."

Dr. Tempest blinked at Valve, incredulous. He stopped and turned to Gauge. "Will you let them marry?"

Gauge folded his arms with his cane tucked into his elbow. He glared at the two of them. After a moment of censured silence, he said, "Clever work putting them together against me, but I think you'll find I'm far too charming for mortal enemies. They will marry, but only after Axis commits to a plan which ensures the triumvirate remains a triad. The next time you two underhanded bishops make rooks of your children, think about what you might lose by endangering them. While Axis took the news of your manipulations like a noble martyr, Lexia may not be so forgiving. I'll let you leave with that on your conscience, Dr. Tempest. And you, Valve…"

Gauge held up a finger as he walked away to pick up a box from the bar. He brought it back over to the choking Factory Master. "Another box of Snow's Finest. If only because you never fail to be consistent in your ways."

Valve accepted it with an appreciative nod, unable to gather enough air to speak.

"Good night, sirs."

Jan appeared to show a despondent doctor and a dying man out the door.

If they weren't careful, they might soon find themselves in it.

———————————

Lexia sat on the steps, waiting for her father to get home as she'd done when she was a child. Perhaps seeing her this way would lessen his disappointment in her. Although, it wasn't doing much to lessen her disappointment in him.

"You're too strict on her, Leon. Let her play with the boys."

"Lya, today it's play. Tomorrow, it's heartbreak. We have to shelter her from certain things."

"You're only saying that because she's a girl. If Lexia were a boy, you wouldn't care how much she got around or who she played with. If you don't let her experience things for herself, you will push her away."

"Let's agree to judge it on a case-by-case basis. She can play with the boys, but only if we watch closely."

Lexia would have to sneak out tonight. There was no way Leon would let her leave after this anticipated heart-to-heart. Around her, servants peered and whispered in their gossip. Sami in the kitchens kept ducking her eyes rather than talking to Lexia.

One little kiss.

One *amazing* kiss.

Lexia almost slapped herself. She'd managed to brood fine over her guilt and her angst, but every now and again, she'd thought of Gauge's soft lips and the proof of his undeniable desire when he'd lifted her leg. It was passionate in a way that differed from her and Axis. There was a reckless abandon to it which some part of her craved—

Leon walked through the door looking forlorn until his eyes fell on Lexia. He smiled, but it wasn't completely happy.

Had the pre-engagement meeting gone badly?

"Lexia, dear, let's have a cup of tea."

They sat down at the counter in the kitchen again with two porcelain cups of earl gray between them. Neither of them looked eager to talk, so the silence stretched on between them. With the servants gone from the kitchen, there wasn't even the comforting background noise of cooking and organizing. Just quiet.

After Lexia had had enough, she said, "I suppose I received a lot of mail over the last week."

Leon winced, and she wished she'd gone with something less harsh, but he nodded. "Mostly from Axis."

Nothing from Gauge?

He continued, "I'll forward it to you as soon as we finish here."

"Father, I don't think we handled this well." Lexia meant it as much on her side as his.

After a sip of his tea, Leon shook his head. "No, I expected more maturity out of you, and I'm sure you expected more understanding out of me. We should learn from this and come away better people for it. Forgive me for withholding your messages and visitors—"

Visitors…

"I'm not proud of my actions, no matter how much you concerned me."

Lexia reached a hand across the counter, and Leon took it. But really she wanted to ask about the visitors. A segue was needed, but first… "I'm sorry I behaved like a child. Every one of my actions is heavily scrutinized, and that's a lot of pressure. I made a mistake and felt the weight of it immediately. It was hard to face those consequences."

Leon peered at their hands, keeping his eyes ducked away from her. He looked ready to ask if the rumors were true, but seemed to think better of it. "You picked a good week for it. All of the capital was shut down from the snow. I suppose now we can return to our social obligations, and you can return to Axis."

That's exactly what Lexia wanted to hear, and she couldn't keep herself from beaming. "Really?!"

Her father nodded, saying, "He wrote you multiple times a day and dropped by once per day at the least. And with Snow mostly approving your engagement, I see no reason to hold you back from Axis." He pointed a finger at her. "But mind the curfew laws. It's still in effect until your wedding."

Gauge had approved of it...

Mostly?

Despite her questions, Lexia hopped up and ran around the counter to hug her father. "Thank you!"

Leon muttered against her hair, "It's not like you wouldn't sneak out tonight to see him, anyway. At least this way Rhyme doesn't have to chase you down. Your stunt earlier really hurt him, you know?"

"I know. I've already apologized, and, since he has a date with Sami, I think he's forgiven me."

Leon barked out a laugh, and Lexia soaked it in. They were okay. They would be okay. This one week of them not at their best didn't have to ruin their relationship.

Visitors...

Lexia pulled back enough to ask, "Uhm, father. Did I have any other visitors?" Her white hair slipped past her ear and fell in her face.

Leon reached up and brushed it back behind her ear. As he grazed her freckled temple, sadness darkened the gray of his eyes. "You are so much like your mother. Intelligent, curious, and perhaps a little too kind for this world. Jan came by with a message directly from Snow, and I sent him back to the Copper Cathedral after receiving it in your place."

Lexia's brows popped high as she blinked at her father, unsure to what to say. Well, sure what to say, but a little reticent to say it. "Father..."

But Leon was already nodding. He said, "I know. I know... Not my best."

"What was the message?" She tried to conceal her unbridled curiosity, but the question came out a little breathy.

Leon sighed. "'You are always welcome at the Cathedral even without invitation. Do not hesitate to call regardless of etiquette or protocol.'" After he recited the message, he searched his daughter's eyes a little too deeply to ascertain the meaning.

Lexia looked away.

One little kiss.

Lexia took the long way to Flicker Avenue through Snow Plaza. She stared at the front of the Cathedral while Rhyme stood behind her in judgmental silence. Snow blanketed the gables, and icicles teemed from their copper peaks. She could go in right now, and Gauge would welcome her.

After a while, Lexia hugged Axis' sweater around her and went on her way. This seemed to satisfy Rhyme as she no longer felt his eyes boring in between her shoulder blades. When she arrived at Axis' apartments, the glow of the lights from the inside made her smile. He was waiting for her.

Lexia knocked on the door, and Axis answered within seconds with his arms open for her, completely unaware of her treacherous detour.

He chuckled, saying, "I guess if Rhyme's waiting outside that means your father gave you permission to come here tonight."

Lexia smiled and nodded against his warm strength. "We made up."

There was a wincing sound, and Lexia pulled away to see Axis pained. He said, "Did he talk to you about the pre-engagement meeting?"

"Just that the Count 'mostly' approved of it." At Axis's silence, Lexia pressed, "Why? Is there more?"

Some time went by where Axis sat Lexia down on his sofa and told her of Gauge's accusations, but he gave proper weight to the fact that their fathers didn't deny they had encouraged the young couple's relationship.

Arranged.

Lexia's romance with Axis had been arranged by their fathers to join their houses and overthrow the Copper Count.

"Can you believe Snow made it about him? After all those kind things you said about him, he made our engagement about his mines." Axis sounded so naïve.

Lexia frowned at the incredulous look on his face until it transformed into concern. He asked, "What's wrong?"

It took her a moment to realize she was shaking in his arms.

"Leon, I said let her play with the boys. Why are you toying with her future like this?"

"Because I want what's best for her."

"What's best for you, you mean?"

"Lya, please. Let's talk about this later. Lexia is only pretending to be asleep."

"If you don't stop, I'll have to do something about it."

"Why are we arguing, dear? It's only a little encouragement."

Only a little encouragement.

Lexia wanted to break down in tears. Instead, she threw her arms around Axis' neck and held on for everything he meant to her, arranged or not.

She loved him.

She loved him.

But maybe Lexia could've loved Gauge, too.

EIGHT
Fiery Obstacle

THE NEXT MORNING, AXIS STARED AT HIS SCARS IN THE MIRROR THROUGH THE STEAM. Each one reminded him of a time he'd thought he would surely die, yet here he was, preparing to marry the love his life and revolutionize his family's business for the better. But how could he forget where he'd come from with so many small reminders?

"Boy, stand up. This'll be a long night if I have to keep picking you up off the ground."

"Please. No more."

"I invited the fellas over tonight. You know what that means."

Yes. Axis had known what it meant. He couldn't remember what was worse. The searing agony or the smell of Snow's Finest melting through the skin on his chest. Stomach. Back...

Axis had scars everywhere except for where people could see, and his father's friends had laughed. They'd brought their own children for the traumatic entertainment. Axis had often wondered how they'd turned out, and sometimes he fantasized about challenging each one of their fathers to a duel. Or worse...

Sometimes...

When the scar tissue ached in the cold, Axis thought about telling Gauge and letting him smelt the bastards into the Wall of Pain.

That's where they belonged.

Axis shivered in the room as it cooled, and the steam dissipated. He dressed in blue, the same color as Snow's eyes, and went to work with Bolt for the day. A surprise awaited him in the office. Right in the center of the room stood a massive three-dimensional model of the new city. There was a note attached on copper leaf.

Prince Axis,

Welcome to sector twelve. Here are my rough estimates of the locations for our industries and Tempest's crops. Put some consideration into what you'd like to see, would you? To scale, this city is twice the size of the capital, so plan with room in mind to grow.

Yours truly, as always,

Count Snow.

PostScript: Don't let this distract you too much from your engagement proposal.

Axis didn't know what to make of the Count. The man infuriated him, but also intrigued him. Right now, staring out at this sprawling city, it was overwhelming. What didn't Gauge think of?

Bolt pointed at the train tracks, asking, "Are those double-insulated?"

Axis hiked up his pants at the thighs to crouch down and place his eyes level with the model. He smiled. "Yes, they are. It's such a clever response to this year's weather. And look here, Snow set the factories away from the city instead of centered in it to help keep the pollution down." Instead, a vista lived at the heart of the city. One Dr. Tempest would be most interested to see.

Had Gauge also sent one to the Tempests' offices on the Boulevard? The question had barely entered his mind before the answer followed.

Of course he had.

Axis stared at the iron and gold mines, realizing Gauge had discovered the ore before thawing the sector. He'd planned the city so that the mines skirted the factories. This meant fewer transport resources were necessary to ship ore to the lines, reducing costs. It was smart, but there was still something about all three industries butting up against each other.

"What do you make of it, Bolt?" Axis leaned his ass against his desk, took another sip of his espresso, and pondered at the marvel in front of him.

Bolt said, "Our city is quite the gem, but it's not without its flaws, coming from the electronic era and all. These new plans, however, keep in mind how we use steam and how it affects our surroundings. I wouldn't mind living there." He gestured toward a set of townhouses, rowed alongside the vista. "For instance."

Axis peered down at the crops bordering the factories in the southernmost point and wondered what Leon and Lexia would make of the model. Line after line of train tracks converged on these working locations, but was it really best to mix the industries?

The courier bell took Axis from his thoughts.

Bolt waved him back. "I'll get it." The older man left to fetch the mail while Axis tried to tear his eyes away from the thoroughness of the city's design—

"Sir. It's red," Bolt said as he handed over the scarlet envelope.

No.

Axis ripped it open and frowned at the message inside. It was from the Flicker wicks' foreman.

Prince,

I regret to inform you all other lines are refusing to return once this Founding Season is over. We, at Flicker wicks, are always on your side and will return at first whistle. But the others are already collecting their demands before officially commencing the strike. I thought I'd warn you. Their demands are high.

If there's anything I can do to help, call on me anytime.

Phoro.

Well, it wasn't news of his father's death, and Axis wasn't sure if that was reassuring or not. Instead, he found himself lost in one of his father's lessons.

"People only understand force and control, son. You know exactly what I'm talking about, don't you?"

Axis shuddered and dropped the letter.

Bolt picked it up and read it without being asked. He clicked his tongue before saying, "And here you were trying to give them more benefits."

Axis wiped a hand down his face and paced around his desk. It was smart of them to use the free time during Founding Season to plan their strike, and he couldn't fault them for it. Not with how Valve had let the foremen mistreat everyone.

But how to stem this artery from bleeding?

The unions.

Phoro.

Those linemen and their foreman are exceptional and hold loyalty only to you, Prince Axis. Expand on this virtue, thread it throughout the rest of the lines, and you will have no need to worry about your inheritance.

Tija's message...

"Bolt, I need a courier and some red envelopes." Axis' burgundy ones simply wouldn't do.

"Right away, Prince Flicker."

"Sir, they've finished attaching the railcar."

"Perfect. Thank you, Jan."

Gauge finished up an invitation and handed it over to the courier. He grabbed his coat, top hat, and cane before stepping out onto the veranda. Only a few steps away, the copper-plated railcar glimmered on the train, ready for a day trip.

There was no doubt Gauge enjoyed the spectacle of the shiny car traveling the railways, and the unmistakable destination would be a slap in Valve's face.

How delightful.

The luxurious car boasted comfortable leather banquets and booths, a bar, small kitchen, and through the door further in the back, an obscenely enormous bed dressed in silk linens. What more could a Count ask for? Jan and a few other employees boarded and got to work while Gauge fell gracefully into a banquet, sorting through this morning's mail.

An invitation to a new school opening.

Would attend.

A petition and proposal for a vaster theater.

Would review.

A burgundy envelope slipped into Gauge's fingers next. Valve or Axis. He checked the seal. It was a single flame, enticing Gauge to open it immediately.

Count Snow,

While it pains me to admit it, I can't deny the genius in the new city's design. However, there is something I don't fully appreciate about it. I believe Dr. Tempest or Ms. Tempest will put a finger on it. After feedback from a trusted adviser, I can honestly say I am looking forward to working with you on this new endeavor.

Despite myself.

Sincerely,

Axis Flicker.

PostScript: Don't worry. You'll get your proposal once you return to the capital.

Ah…

Axis' spies were on top of their game. Gauge had told no one but his closest people about this trip into sector ten. His paranoia demanded he ferret out the traitor, but truly the young Master Flicker wasn't a threat to Gauge. He could keep his spies. It was honestly flattering that the People's Prince would keep tabs on the Count.

The train took off and hit the first corkscrew spiral into the ascent, glinting the copper for everyone to see. If not for the seat's straps and the furniture bolted down, everything would go flying. But there Gauge sat, comfortably secured in his seat. His hat, however, went on a journey of its own. It would go on like this for some time until they went into the underground tunnel.

Once inside, Gauge continued to sort through his mail until he came across a black envelope with a gilded butterfly seal.

Lexia.

He opened it a little too hurriedly to read what the Heiress had to say. Some part of Gauge fully expected her to renounce their kiss and deny their chemistry. Deny the dreams she'd surely experienced as Gauge had experienced almost every night since their passionate encounter.

Count Snow,

Thank you for your kind invitation to the Copper Cathedral. I'm sure you understand that I'm of two minds about it, and the conflict keeps me awake at night. There's no denying a spark between us, which is why I can't accept your kind offer. Any contact with you would only accelerate it, and I can't trust myself with you.

I love Axis. I want to marry him. Please don't let this affect your decision on my engagement to him. I'm twenty-three, and I dream of the day I can sleep overnight in my fiance's bed. You're the only person with the power to grant me that, and I know you'll be fair in your determination.

In the meantime, I enjoyed working with you, and I would like to continue to do so. But only with a chaperon present. Someone with more force than Jan or Rhyme. Please tell me you understand.

I hope you can forgive me.

Sincerely,

Lexia Tempest.

PostScript: I just woke from a dream, and you were in it. What I've recently learned about my father and my relationship with Axis makes me wonder if things were different then maybe you and I...

I love Axis.

But sometimes I think of your incredibly infuriating flare for the dramatic and smile.

What do you think that means?

Gauge needed to decide if he would ignore the thrill from Lexia's confessions and stem his on the softness of her skin. Or...

Pursuing Lexia would ruin Gauge's rapport with Axis. But the Count didn't even need to ask if it was worth it. All he had to do was close his eyes and think of Lexia's thigh wrapped around his hip to answer that question.

Tija.

Tija would know what to do.

Hence, Gauge's little outing.

The tracks straightened and dove into the underground tunnel. It would do him some good to see how sector ten was faring. It was the weakest of the city designs. After all, it had been an emergency rush job. Initially, Gauge had only wanted to fashion the capital city, but after more people came on board with his supposed 'doomsday plan,' it became obvious more cities were needed.

Sector ten was the smallest, therefore the most crowded. People commuted from here to do the jobs no one else wanted to do for the most benefits. Bigger townhouses and apartments, but with the space cramped so everyone knew everyone's business.

It made sense why Tija would relocate here. She could gather the most intel in this sector.

Despite that one advantage, Gauge expected most of the people living in this sector would move to the new lodgings in sector twelve. Once sector ten was empty, he could begin improving it by broadening the space a little. All in the name of progress.

The train surfaced in a spiraling arc, and even through his blue lenses, the sight of sector ten blinded Gauge. So much polished marble. Columns in every touch of architecture. This was an homage to civilizations in stories of old. A planet not unlike Winter with philosophers and astronomers privileged enough to spend all their days talking about their favorite subjects.

It was something Gauge's father had taught: theoretical history. Oh, how Gauge had hated listening to Prof. Snow's lectures, but here Gauge was. In a city dedicated to the man. Maybe that's why he wanted to revamp it at the first opportunity.

"Little Bones, drink your tonic."

"I don't want to, father. It tastes bitter."

"If you don't do it, you won't recover from your malady."

"Mother drank it, and now she never wakes."

Gauge was seventeen when his father had died. It was the age when Gauge had stopped drinking the tonic. And it was the age when he could first get out of bed without any help.

Gauge gripped the jewel on his cane, ground his teeth, and tried to ignore the pain in his gloved fingers. He looked at his wrist, absent of a timepiece and mused to himself. No genes in the pool. The name 'Snow' wasn't worth passing on, yet it was the most well-known name in all of Winter.

Gauge shook his head and tsked. Hopefully, some time with Tija would deter the unfortunate direction of his thoughts. There were still Founding events to host, and the Copper Count must always be at his best.

The train pulled into the station, and Gauge tried to hide his bitter smile.

Tija would help.

If only to substitute for a sweeter smile for the day. One coated in burgundy or black. One with a happy childhood behind it. Lya. Leon. Axis.

Lexia was privileged in ways she couldn't understand, but she tried. And that's what intrigued Gauge.

There was nothing subtle about the Count traveling into the city, and a parade of people followed his car to an apartment complex close to the station. They gaped and pointed as Gauge entered the domicile.

Tija answered on the first ring in a tight pencil dress. She took one look at him and rushed his entourage inside, asking, "What happened?"

Gauge took in the room furnished with a leather sofa, loveseat, and coffee table. A wood-burning fireplace crackled beside them. He gestured for Tija to sit across from him, and she only looked more concerned. Jan melted into the kitchen for the illusion of privacy, and the Count appreciated it.

With a sigh, he admitted, "I've made a terrible mistake."

"What did you do?" Tija's beautiful blue eyes searched his through the glasses.

It hurt to confess it to her, but..."I touched Lexia Tempest without my gloves."

"Oh, Gauge. No."

That's about how Gauge had expected Tija to react.

<hr>

Lexia peered at the three-dimensional model of sector twelve's new city, and admiration for the brilliant man who'd created it occupied her thoughts. So much so that she'd missed what her father was saying.

"And then we can discuss the transit stations for the workers—Lexia are you listening, dear?"

Caught, Lexia straightened and smiled at Leon. "Of course, father, but don't you see the model isn't quite…"

Dr. Tempest gestured for her to continue. "What is it? What do you see?"

Lexia checked the southernmost region where Gauge had grouped the factories, mines, and crops. She pointed out what was obvious to her. "You can't have the factories polluting the fields. We'll need to move them to the northernmost region and spread into the east and west for crops with different moisture needs. Like see here? The eastern most region is swampier than the rest. That's the best place for rice paddies. You know we couldn't get them to grow here in the capital. It's too dry."

Leon's gray eyes sparkled with pride as he said, "My brilliant daughter, that's exactly it."

"I can't wait until we present this to Count Snow." Lexia had almost called Gauge by his name, but that would surely ruin the moment. She'd heard the servants in a fuss over the copper railcar leaving the center of the city, and it had left Lexia wondering what Gauge was up to in sector ten.

But that was none of her business.

Father and daughter stood inside Lexia's rose-tinted office where someone had installed the model. So far, Leon had said nothing about the location of it, and she was grateful.

They'd both worn pantsuits today, brown—almost matching. Only hers was fastened with a burgundy corset.

Leon took his hands out of his pockets to clean his glasses, saying, "We will. Together. It's only fair you get to demonstrate your findings in person." On the last, he reseated his glasses and peered at Lexia through them with a gentle smile.

They were working it out.

"Thank you, father." Lexia ducked her eyes, feigning deeper interest in the model as she asked, "Do you know when the Count will return?"

Leon was staring at her. She could feel his eyes pressuring her to look up for contact, but she couldn't face him while talking about Gauge. It was an admission of guilt.

Eventually, her father said, "I suppose when he's tired of the attention. There's no telling how long the Count will be up to his pleasures whenever he makes these trips."

There was no doubt Gauge enjoyed being the center of attention, but Lexia suspected it stemmed from his loneliness—

The courier bell rang.

Leon said, "I'll get it," before heading down the hall.

Would Gauge respond to her missive here or at home? Lexia was worried her father was screening her mail still, and there was no way around it. It left her feeling confined.

"Lexia." Her father looked distressed as he came around the corner. "This is from Axis addressed to both of us."

It was red. Not burgundy.

Lexia hugged Axis' timepiece to her chest and crossed the room around the model to read the letter with her father.

Tempest & Tempest,

It seems my father's plans to ruin my factories have come to fruition. I've discussed the situation with you both, so there's no need to keep this from one another. I need help to dissuade the strikes, and the only way I know to do that is through the union models.

Ms. Tempest, can you please share with me what you discussed with Count Snow on the matter?

And Dr. Tempest, I would take any council with exceptional gratitude.

Thank you both for everything,

Axis Flicker.

PostScript: I suppose you've also received a model in your offices, and I was wondering if Ms. Tempest had put her finger on why I don't agree with the factories, crops, and mines bordering one another. I'm sure she figured it out rather quickly. She's just that bright.

Lexia beamed, but Leon frowned. He said, "It may take more than standardized unions to placate the factory workers."

This was another moment to shine. Lexia said, "Not with the standards I discussed with Count Snow, and I'm sure Axis has his own ideas which will further enrich them. It's a matter of awarding benefits to skilled and manual labor accordingly. Support, time off, housing vouchers—Everything needs improvement. I think Gau—Count Snow had all of it in mind when he designed the city."

Leon caught the slip, but mercifully let it go. Instead, he gestured at her folio. "Are these the union models you designed with him?"

Lexia smiled and took out the papers to spread them across her desk. "I was hoping to revise them with feedback from Axis, but maybe you should take a look at them first."

With a smile in return, Leon sat down and dove into the documents.

Was now a good time to ask about Gauge's accusations about her and Axis' relationship being arranged? Would there ever be a better time than now? Of course, by asking about it, she risked burning this bridge they'd only recently built between them. But if Lexia didn't ask, she may never get her answers.

Axis' naïve expression as he broke the news to Lexia, incredulous at Gauge's accusation, flashed before her eyes. The image of Gauge followed it, staring at her across the library after she'd backed away from him. The thirst in his bright blue eyes...

Could someone feel for more than one person at a time?

Lexia wished she could ask her mother. If only Lya were still with them.

"These are excellent standards, Lexia. With these benefits, no one should feel an imbalance between their work and their lives. And this support system you have in place—backups for each position— guarantees if someone's ill or simply wants to stay home for the day that we don't go without work in their place."

Now was not the time to ask about arranged marriages.

Lexia smiled at her father, and for the first time in her life, it felt like a lie.

Axis was finishing the ridiculous proposal to satisfy Snow's ego. He filled it with promises to uphold the triumvirate and Winter's current balance of power. No mergers of Tempest and Flicker would cause the devaluing of Snow's mines. The People's Prince had meant what he'd begrudgingly confessed to in his letter to Gauge: he was looking forward to building Winter's future with the man.

While Axis worked on the proposal, he listened out for the afternoon courier, hoping to hear from Dr. Tempest and Lexia before he left for the day. How could Axis sleep tonight without a clear trajectory for the strike solution?

"Force and control, son. Force and control."

Valve was wrong. It was that line of thinking which had brought on the strikes.

"Sir," Bolt said, interrupting Axis' thoughts. "The courier is here."

"Perfect." Axis slipped the proposal into an envelope and exchanged it for a black envelope from the courier. The gilded butterfly stamped on the front was an instant relief.

Lexia.

Dearest Mr. Flicker,

I hope you are well with all of this on your shoulders. Fear not, for father and I are planning a trip to the Copper Cathedral tomorrow. We would like you to join us for this unappointed visit, as Count Snow may have some input into your situation. We all care for you, Axis. Let us help.

Yours forever and always,

Lexia Tempest.

We.

Us.

Obviously she meant Dr. Tempest and herself, but did Lexia also mean Gauge cared for Axis? The man did nothing but drive Axis crazy. If only she knew how much Snow tormented him.

Calm.

Axis set the letter down and tried for calm. She was right. Snow could contribute some ideas, and everything else was just Lexia being herself. He loved that about her.

"Bolt, we've put in a hard day's work. City planning. A proposal. And a strike on our hands. Let's turn in for the night and go home."

Bolt had spent the last hour bent over the model adjusting the train traffic ways for better transit. He straightened with an audible creak from his back, saying, "Yes, sir," with much gusto.

On the drive home, Axis considered Lexia's timepiece on his wrist. It was intricate and beautiful like her. He should ask how she enjoyed wearing his clunky thing. The thought made him smile as they pulled up to his apartments.

Soon, they would marry and start a family of their own. Once Gauge granted them permission, of course. Then he could reverse Axis' sterility. It wasn't a puzzle why Snow had sterilized all the men—it was safer and easier to reverse—but it was a rather interesting choice to enforce sterility at all. Sure, young couples took advantage of it—Axis and Lexia certainly had—but was that Gauge's only reason? Or was there something else…

"Sir."

For the second time tonight, Bolt snapped Axis out of his thoughts. He peered ahead of the car to a most welcome sight. Lexia was waiting on his front steps with Rhyme leaned against the exterior wall to the building.

Axis exited the car and scooped Lexia up in his arms. Her brown suede duster wasn't nearly as soft as the skin of her neck, which he nuzzled for comfort.

This.

This was exactly what Axis needed after the strike news.

Lexia kissed his cheek, separated them, and held up a bag of groceries. "I thought I'd cook for you."

No, this.

This was exactly what Axis needed.

An hour later, Axis sat back on his barstool and beamed at Lexia. She was in the only apron he owned, and even with her height, it swallowed her, adding to her cuteness. As she cleaned the kitchen, he appreciated the view of her reaching to put dishes away or bending over to put a pot in the lower cabinets.

Axis smiled as he realized this could be the rest of their lives together. Them taking turns cooking and cleaning, existing in their home. Lexia was used to servants, but they'd talk over the idea of caring for themselves soon.

She slapped her hands together, saying, "All done, and I don't think I broke anything."

With a crook of his finger, Axis called her over. "I think I owe you some gratitude."

Lexia came around the counter, and he picked her up onto it. She 'yipped' with an excited smile, sweetened by how her lashes fluttered closed for their kiss.

Axis liked to treat her slowly to let the passion build between them, and Lexia moaned into his lips, opening for more—

Someone knocked at his door, and Axis laughed incredulously. "What terrible timing."

Lexia smiled and pushed him toward the living room.

He went, calling over his shoulder, "Hold that thought."

Bolt stood outside the door with the Flicker wicks' foreman, Phoro. The foreman held up a red envelope. "I came as you asked, sir."

An anxiety, which had itched at Axis throughout the day, eased. He held out his hand and Phoro took it. Axis said, "Thank you so much for coming," and he meant it. After they shook, he gestured through the door. "Please come in. Lexia, I have a guest."

She came around the corner, still in the apron. "Hello."

When Lexia held her hand out to the foreman, Phoro took off his hat and shook her hand with a blush. "Ma'am."

Axis said, "Please have a seat."

Phoro obliged, and Axis followed suit. Lexia sat on the arm of Axis' chair, and he put an arm around her. Bolt stayed standing, leaning back against the wall per his job description.

Axis said, "I appreciate your warning, and I must admit, I've been expecting the strikes for a few days now. But thanks to your help, I could prepare for them more directly. Thank you."

Phoro worried his hat in his hands, saying, "Yes, sir. I'd hate to speak ill of your father, but we'll continue on the line for you, Prince Axis."

The man's confidence in Axis warmed his heart, and he let it show on his face as he rocked Lexia a bit. "Ms. Tempest and I are working with the Count on some union models. Once we have the standards down, I'd like to run them by you as the pilot line. Would you be willing to do that for me?"

Phoro's eyes widened a touch. "Tempest, Snow, and Flicker working together? On the lines?"

Lexia said, "We believe we can match benefits to the labor position better than they are now and provide more support for each one. That way if you want to take a personal day, the entire line doesn't shut down because you'll have a second-in-command to take your place as needed. For instance."

Again, Phoro blushed at Lexia's direct attention on him. He murmured, "Yes, ma'am." For Axis, he could make eye contact and say, "The Flicker wicks' line will support you any way we can, sir."

"Excellent, so here's what I had in mind."

As Axis explained their strategy, his smile broadened.

Everything would work out.

"Tija, speak freely with me. I want to hear what you have to say."

She shook her head. "No, you don't, Gauge. You can't know what you're asking me to do."

Maybe she was right, but Gauge had to know, anyway. "Please. You're my friend."

Tija raked both hands through her thick black hair and stared at him, incredulous. She said, "You're asking me to call Winter's Savior, the Copper Count, a fool."

Gauge didn't wince. She was right.

Abruptly, Tija stood with a hand cupped over her mouth. Her blue eyes shifted off into the distance as she shook her head once again. "I mean...Axis alone is reason enough not to touch Lexia Tempest, but then there's her father—" Tija's eyes focused on Gauge once more. "And are you serious? Did you truly touch her without a glove?"

Again, Gauge only nodded without wincing.

Tija went to her knees at his feet and peered up at him, asking, "How many times had I asked you to take your gloves off for me? Why, Gauge?"

He'd expected this question, and the hurt in Tija's eyes didn't surprise him. Gauge pushed a strand of her hair behind her ear and kissed her forehead. With his lips pressed against her skin, he said,

"You've told me many times before you can't feel for me that way, Tija, and we've never wanted to be exclusive. So please try to understand…"

She sat back on her heels with her eyes more grave than hurt. "Axis will kill you in a duel if you don't practice caution, my friend."

"I can't stop thinking about the softness of Lexia's skin or the silkiness of her hair." Gauge hated to confess this to a regular lover of his, but Tija was the only person from which he could seek council.

Well, Jan.

But Jan had made his position on Lexia clear. In fact, Gauge was surprised the old spy hadn't offered to assassinate Axis, yet.

Tija reached out and brushed her knuckles against Gauge's cheek. She asked, "Do you think you could love Lexia?"

"Mrs. Tempest?"

"Yes, Little Snow?"

"How can I make Lexia like me?"

"That's easy. Be her friend. Find out what she likes and like it, too."

"But I already like Axis."

Gauge would never forget Lya's rich laughter. Lexia sounded so much like her mother, but more unfettered. Less reserved. No, Lexia committed to everything with a freeness only granted to someone with a wholesome childhood, and her enthusiasm for life was infectious—Something Gauge hadn't felt since the first Founding Season. Maybe even before. Or never?

"Yes. I think I could love Lexia."

Tija clicked her tongue and stood with her arms folded. She said, "Well, fuck."

Gauge barked out a laugh. That summed up the situation quite succinctly. "Now, do you see why I came all this way to seek your council?"

Tija looked through the threshold of the kitchen at Jan, saying, "And you're letting this carry on?"

Jan shrugged. "I can only hope for my Count's happiness, Ms. Cloud."

Gauge took off his top hat and brushed it across his thighs, saying, "It gets worse."

Tija groaned. "How?"

"Axis recently petitioned me for approval of his engagement to Lexia."

Her laughter was incredulous and earned. "Oh, the drama play this will make. This may even deserve an opera."

Gauge quirked a brow. "Actually, I like that idea."

Tija climbed onto her sofa so that her ass sat on the back of it and her feet pressed into the cushions. She said, "You know, when I'd heard you were in our sector, I was hoping you were coming to speak to me about the factory strike."

Gauge blinked at her.

Both her brows shot up. "You mean the Count doesn't know all the lines but Flicker wicks are striking once the Founding Season ends? I do enjoy knowing things before you hear about them, but I was sure with me being all the way over in this sector you would've heard of it first. I guess you *do* need me around."

"My needing you, Tija, is never in question." Gauge gave her a wink, but his mind was on the strikes.

Would Axis ask for help this time? From Tempest? Absolutely. But would he ask for Gauge's help?

Gauge would give it and maybe without teasing him.

Maybe.

"What was it like?" Tija's voice was soft while she stared out a window into the window of a neighboring house only a few meters away.

Gauge stared up at her, gently pressing, "What was 'what' like?"

With a sigh, Tija breathed, "Touching someone after so long."

Ah…

Tija didn't know why Gauge wore the gloves. The only person who did was long dead, but it was all related—the weak corneas, the aching bones, and the lowered stamina. The malady had left the nerve endings in Gauge's fingers extra sensitive. Texture overstimulated him. Mostly, anyway.

Gauge's hands on Lexia had given her the most enticing goosebumps, and it was a sensation he wouldn't soon forget. To answer Tija's question, he said, "I was aware of everything I felt to an almost painful acuteness. I think if it weren't for Lexia's disarming demeanor, I might've been overwhelmed. As it was, I drowned in her without ever feeling the need to breathe."

Tija hopped off the couch and held out her hand. Gauge trusted her enough to take it and let her pull him to standing. She pressed her fingers and palm against his gloved one and stared at the contact.

"Be careful, Gauge. I'd heard the rumors about you and her, of course, but I never thought…"

Tija went on her tiptoes to kiss him, and he accepted what she offered. She fell back on the sofa and pulled Gauge on top of her. He acquiesced, shrugging out of his jacket and shirt. She reached for his pants, and he slipped off her panties.

Gauge understood what Tija wanted. Assurance. Acknowledgment. No matter how much he wanted Lexia in his bed, there would always be a place for Tija in it. This was his promise, and Gauge intended to keep it.

NINE

Mortal Conundrum

"What about Lexia, Lya? What about our daughter?"

"You don't understand. I can't stay here with you."

"I won't let you go."

Lexia startled awake alone in her bed the next morning.

Again.

She held her head in her hands and tried not to cry. Every memory and dream of her mother felt like a sucking wound in her chest.

And what were these arguments? Lexia couldn't remember her parents fighting much when she was a child, but lately she was recalling what she'd rather remain forgotten.

No crying.

The day ahead was far too exciting for tears, and Lexia needed to prepare accordingly. She slipped into a tight black blouse made of silk, and she strapped into a suede burgundy corset. For Axis. The shirttails went to the backs of her knees, so burgundy leggings would do for pants. Black suede ankle boots complemented the outfit. Next was the hip holsters for her steam cannons. She painted black on her lips and dusted gray over her eyes, emphasizing her personal signature. Axis' timepiece with its burgundy leather straps completed the ensemble.

No, wait.

Lexia braided her thick white waves and capped her hair with a top hat. For Gauge.

There.

Downstairs, Leon waited with Rhyme, who blinked at Lexia as she came down. She said, "Good morning, gentlemen. It's such a lovely day for a walk—"

Rhyme shook his head, and Leon chuckled. "Come along, daughter. We're taking the car."

Lexia caved only because her stomach was too full of butterflies to argue. The fluttering worsened as they pulled up to the curb on Snow Plaza with Axis waiting at the bottom of the Copper Cathedral's steps. He went for a more casual look today in brown leather pants, a cream shirt strapped with buckles, and a matching leather jacket thrown over his shoulder.

He was all smiles until Lexia stepped out of the car. Axis' soft green stare assessed her, and when he made eye contact, the heat in his gaze said he approved.

Lexia's cheeks warmed, and she ducked her eyes before her father made it around the car to see their interaction.

Even so, Leon said, "Love birds, get your minds on work. Remember propriety."

Axis held out his arm, and Lexia looped hers through it. There'd been no snowfall for days, but what had accumulated didn't want to melt, much to her delight. It bordered the Cathedral into a scene from a snow globe, beautiful and unreal. Amid all the splendor, their group made their way up to the Wall of Pain where Jan answered the door with a dutiful expression on his face.

Lexia beamed at him. "Good morning, Jan."

The butler brightened and smiled. "Ms. Tempest, it's always a pleasure to have you at the Cathedral."

Axis bristled a bit, but Leon noticed and took the lead, saying, "We've come to call on the Count."

Jan's smile lessened into more of an apology. "I'm afraid Count Snow only returned from sector ten early this morning, and he won't be having any visitors—"

"Let them in, Jan. Remember? Ms. Tempest is always welcome, including whatever riffraff she's brought with her."

Jan opened the doors, framing Gauge with the horrifying copper monument. Disheveled again, his black linen suit was wrinkled, and he sported the scruffy shadow of a beard as before.

Lexia nearly blushed remembering the roughness of it during their kiss.

Likewise, Gauge's glasses traveled over her in a brief appraisal. One she couldn't see the result of for the deep blue lenses—

Why did he draw out licking his lips like that?

"I just want to taste you."

Axis cleared his throat, and only then did Lexia realize she'd been staring at Gauge.

Dr. Tempest further interrupted the moment by saying, "Count Snow, we'd like to discuss those union models with you."

Gauge blinked as if he'd just noticed the man was in the foyer. "Yes. Of course. Let's move this into the conservatory." He walked into the brightly lit room, continuing to talk over his shoulder. "Have you had breakfast, yet? Jan, do we have any buns left?"

Knots twisted in Lexia's stomach, robbing her of an appetite, but still… "I would love some, Jan."

"Yes, Ms. Tempest. Right away." The butler went off somewhere in the vast Cathedral, presumably the kitchen.

Dr. Tempest called after him, "And some tea, please, if you would."

As they made their way to a set of sofas and armchairs, Lexia couldn't help but notice Gauge's carriage. Not that she was an expert on all things Snow, but he seemed to walk differently today. Like his bones were heavy—

Where was his cane? And was it more than a mere fashion accessory?

Almost as if Gauge had heard her thoughts, he said, "Forgive my appearance. It was a late night in sector ten, and I haven't been to sleep yet. But by all accounts, I'm eager to discuss the unions with you. Here." He gestured for them to have a seat on the sofa across from the armchair he practically draped himself in. "Shall we start with the factory line strikes?"

Axis was halfway seated when Gauge dropped this little bomb, but he handled it with impressive decorum. "Yes. Now, that the news of it is out of the way, let's get down to business."

The three discussed their ideas for standardizing the unions based on labor types and skill level, backup support, time off, and Axis' wonderful idea about foremen benefits depending on linemen evaluations. The two younger men got along, mostly. However, Lexia couldn't shake this feeling it wasn't because Gauge didn't want to needle Axis, but more because he lacked the energy. Some of his usual bombastic behavior was toned down.

Well, until…

Gauge smirked into his coffee and said, "Ms. Tempest truly is a genius for initializing these standards. Would you consider sharing her more often, Master Flicker?" There was no mistaking the innuendo in 'sharing.' It was in the challenging arch of his brow as he sipped from his teacup.

Axis tugged Lexia closer on what she knew was instinct, but it was her father who said, "Now, Snow. There's appropriate banter and then there's just instigation—"

"Master Flicker, you can't enter this Cathedral by force—"

Jan.

"Just watch me, old man, or do you plan to lay a hand on me?"

The shouts came from the foyer, followed by the sound of a steam gun cocking and a coughing ruckus.

Valve.

Gauge hopped out of the armchair and went to the conservatory's threshold. "What's the meaning of this, Flicker?!"

The entire party stood and followed him to the uproar.

Lexia muttered to Axis, "Were you expecting your father?"

"Not at all." The deep frown and the clench of his jaw added to the fury in Axis' voice.

Dr. Tempest rounded the corner first, trying for peace. "Master Flicker. Count Snow. Let's listen to reason and talk as civilized people—"

"Fuck you, Leon. You've sided with my son after everything I've done for you. And Snow." Valve pointed a thick finger in Gauge's face and coughed out, "Don't think for one second I don't see how you benefit from this."

All the while, Valve's armed entourage kept steam pistols trained on Gauge and Axis.

Gauge didn't seem frightened at all. He said, "I think it's transparent how I benefit from this. The factory, the mines, and the crops make for a symbiotic relationship. You're the only one who was ever too foolish to never see it that way."

But Valve wasn't listening. He'd doubled over, spraying blood through his handkerchief onto the parquet floors. Concerned about their paychecks, the armed man and woman lowered their guns to check on him.

Finally.

Lexia drew her steam cannons and aimed them at the mercenaries.

Gauge's eyes widened, and his brows popped high.

Jan smiled approvingly.

Dr. Tempest looked horrified, but dubious.

Axis was the only one not looking at her. Both of his hands were on Valve's shoulders, and he was saying, "Father. Father, breathe. Take a breath—"

Then Valve collapsed to the floor.

Silent.

———————————

"Father?!"

No.

Axis knelt and rolled his father's great heft onto his back. "Father—"

Valve's soft green eyes stared at the vaulted ceiling.

Quiet.

So quiet.

So still.

Axis couldn't breathe, and his heart stopped pumping blood to his body. "Father?"

Leon fell to his knees beside him and put his ear to Valve's mouth. He muttered something, but Axis couldn't hear it. When the older man pushed Axis aside to begin chest compressions, the future son-in-law let him.

There was a window in the next room—a dining room—with stained glass in prismatic color. Blue. Violet. Green. It took Axis a long time of staring at it before he realized the colors formed a shape.

A butterfly.

"Axis?"

Lexia's voice came to him, and it sounded like she'd been trying for a while. "Axis?"

"Yes?" Why did his answer sound so distant?

There was a rhythmic percussive noise and only after the bubble popped did Axis see Leon trying to save Valve's life with CPR.

Thud.

Thud.

Thud.

Check for air.

Thud.

Didn't the doctor know? Valve would never breathe again.

Somewhere outside of Axis field of caring, Gauge ordered, "Jan," and the butler produced ties from nowhere to apprehend the man and woman Lexia was holding at cannon point.

"You killed him."

Axis wasn't expecting the three words to come out of his mouth, and neither had the others. They stared down at him, blinking, but he turned and glared at Gauge. He repeated, "You killed him."

Gauge gave an incredulous and a long blink before shaking his head of the notion. He held his hands out in a staving gesture, saying, "You're in shock."

"No." Axis stood and got in Gauge's face before Jan could stop him. "Those fucking cigars. You may as well have killed him yourself."

Gauge looked like Axis had slapped him.

Lexia's voice was gentle and kind amid all this horror. A dream in his nightmare. "Axis, please. Father, stop."

Axis turned to find her reaching out to him, and he let Lexia pull him in for a hug.

She smoothed a circle on his back. The touch felt separate from him and lost. Her words came to him through the wool in his ears. "Your father was ill of his own vices, and he knew his time was short. It's difficult to imagine how hard and conflicting this is for you. I, of all people, with as much as I know, still can't imagine it. I'm sorry he died in front of you."

But Lexia wasn't sorry Valve was gone.

That about summed up how Axis felt. When he squeezed her, it loosened his purchase until a tear rolled down his cheek and another.

The abuse.

The lies.

Every ugly sneer.

All the undermining schemes.

No.

The worst thing Valve ever did to Axis was dying in front of him, because now the young man would never stop believing he could've done something about it.

A hand brushed Axis' shoulder, and he turned to find Dr. Tempest staring down at him with so much sorrow in the lines at the corner of his eyes. The older man held open his arms, and Axis left Lexia for the embrace.

He squeezed his eyes shut and whispered, "I can't look at him."

"It's okay, son. You don't have to." Leon nodded against Axis' shoulder and movement happened around them.

When Axis next opened his eyes, a sheet covered his father's body. It was strange for cloth to do so much, but it helped.

It helped.

Lexia and Leon stayed close, and Axis truly needed them as he croaked, "Count Snow, may I trouble you for some red envelopes and a glass of water?" He couldn't meet Gauge's eyes, so he stared at the Count's shiny shoes.

"Of course, Prince Axis. Of course. I think you should take a seat…"

Axis sat down on one of the sweeping staircases, and when Jan brought the paper, he wrote several messages against his lap. The first was to the mortuary. The second was to the Flicker mansion's butler. And the third was to the papers.

Valve Flicker's obituary was three lines long.

Master flicker died during the tenth Founding Season.

He is survived by his son, Axis Flicker, and a house full of loyal servants.

The funeral is in two days.

Axis didn't have to ask Gauge for a courier. They arrived within moments, and no one said a word as they took the red envelopes from Axis. As the courier left, Bolt appeared in the doorway.

"Sir…" He sat by Axis' side and kindly left it at that.

In fact, everyone in the room was kind. When the coroner came to collect Valve's body, no one forced Axis to interact. Gauge directed the entire event. Jan brought coffees and teas for all. Lexia kissed Axis here or squeezed him there. Dr. Tempest kept a solemn hand for Axis' shoulder every now and again—

It was all so mundane.

How much time had passed?

Hours?

Seconds?

Did it matter?

Sure, eventually Gauge would expect his guests to depart, but right now Axis couldn't think about that. It was all he could to sit right here on this step and sip some truly luxurious dark roast with just the right amount of cream.

"Jan, your beverage skills are excellent..." was Axis' first sentence since the courier left.

The butler gave a half bow. "Thank you, Prince Flicker."

Wait.

Something was different about the room.

Axis glanced around until he zeroed in on the change.

Gauge's cane.

Sometime during the passing of this haze, Jan had brought Gauge the cane, and the Count was leaning on it—Completely. As if his legs couldn't support him anymore without the aid of the bejeweled walking tool.

Gauge was exhausted, and he was letting Axis sit through his shock. *Helping* him through it, even.

"Let's go home." Axis stood and took a moment to appreciate the beautiful room swirling around him. After a second, he managed to take a full step without vomiting.

Lexia steadied him with an arm around his waist. She kissed his cheek, and it helped revive him.

Dr. Tempest muttered some farewells to Gauge who said, "Just make sure Prince Axis knows if he needs anything, he shouldn't hesitate to call on me."

They followed Bolt to Axis' car, but he wasn't sure where he wanted to go.

"Son, stay with us. I'll act as chaperon, so you won't violate the pre-marital laws. I don't like the idea of you alone in that apartment tonight."

Dr. Tempest's offer sounded fair.

"Yes. Let's do that."

Gauge couldn't feel his toes for the tingling numbness in his legs. The tiny needles of pain had finally coalesced into a full-on assault on his nerve endings for which there was no cure. Only rest.

"Drink your tonic, Little Snow."

Fuck off.

Gauge waited for the door to close behind Axis, Lexia, and Leon before calling, "Jan!"

The older man was right there with an arm around Gauge's waist. He threw his ward's arm around his shoulders, supporting the Count as they made their way up the stairs. They'd left the cane in the foyer for now.

Gauge groaned with each upward movement and hissed with each step of half his weight. It had been stupid to let Axis and the rest into the house when Gauge had gone all night without sleep. No doubt Jan was thinking the same, silently chastising his Count all the way to his bedroom.

Further, Jan led Gauge to the bath, where he started the taps on high heat. Equipped with the best pipes in Winter, steam immediately consumed the black granite-slabbed room. Without being asked, Jan stripped Gauge of his clothes in a clinical manner which the younger man had learned to resent all his life.

Aids.

Nurses.

Doctors.

The only one he'd tolerate was this old spy here, and still, Gauge gnashed his teeth from it. Yet Eternity knew he couldn't do it himself.

In seconds, Jan submerged Gauge with as much dignity as possible into the almost scalding hot water. And instantly, the Count felt the relief in his aching bones. Unfortunately, with his nerve endings in recovery, all the numbness subsided and let the pain inside.

Gauge howled and gripped the edges of the tub. To fight from screaming, he clenched his teeth and sucked air through them in shallow breaths.

Jan didn't offer platitudes or soothing words. Instead, he waited. The old man waited for words Gauge didn't want to say.

And yet...

"Pills. Please. My pills."

Without hesitation, the butler went to fetch medicine for Gauge. Not the dreaded tonic, but still a measure he wished he didn't have to take.

Seconds, but an eternity later, Jan emerged with two pills, a glass of water, and Gauge's test kit. Despite the heat of the tub, Gauge's teeth chattered together, and he thrashed uncontrollably.

Jan held out the pills. "Please, sir."

Despite the convulsions, Gauge shook his head. He managed to say, "The kit."

The old spy looked hurt as he opened the kit and dusted powder onto the two tablets. There was nothing for it, and Gauge was in too much agony to sooth his oldest caretaker. When the powder didn't react, he opened his mouth and let Jan feed him the morphine. It tasted tangy from the powder.

In a familiar routine, one Gauge wished was less frequent, they cycled hot water through the tub. Opening the drain, while running the pipes until the morphine finally kicked in allowed Gauge's body to relax. Jan dismissed himself, leaving the younger man alone with his thoughts.

Axis had come to Gauge for help.

The Wall of Pain would soon collect two fresh additions.

And Valve was dead.

At last, Gauge could stop manufacturing the cigars.

He'd learned so much about the people in his house from such a brief ordeal. Dr. Tempest had lived up to his title. Lexia had impressed Gauge to no end with her quick draw and tactical thinking. And Axis...

After learning Valve had abused the young Prince, Gauge had never expected Axis to respond to his father's death so deeply. But then again, Gauge was sure the younger man hadn't expected his father to die right in front of his eyes.

It was all so tragic.

Gauge would give Axis space or support or whatever the Prince needed in this time. Including the approval for his proposal. Although

Gauge had wished many times for his own father's death, afterward the world felt…

Untouchable. Unreachable. And untethered.

No more 'Little Bones.' No more tonic. But no more parents as well.

These melancholy thoughts were caused by the morphine and only postponed Gauge from leaving the warmth of the tub for the naked exposure of the cold granite room. He would do this without Jan.

It only took three tries.

The fur-lined silk bathrobe and fur-lined slippers helped with the chill, and eventually Gauge made it into the bedroom. As much as he'd like to climb naked into his bed, tasks required his attention in the vault. With Valve's death, chapters must be closed.

Gauge grabbed a cane from the caddy and made the slow journey back down the stairs. When Jan intercepted, Gauge stopped the older man with a grim shake of his head. He walked into the library, climbed a spiral staircase, and dialed the combination into this most sacred place.

Inside, Gauge went straight to the Flicker's slots. The drawers on Valve's blackmail material were thick with vice and abandon. Whereas, Axis' files lacked any material of the kind and contained mostly testimony of his merit.

How would the son cope with the father's death? Sometimes losing the abuser was as traumatizing as the abuse itself. Gauge hoped for Axis' and Lexia's sake this wasn't the case.

Either way, Snow's Finest had done the trick.

Now, it was time to make way for the Prince's reign.

Gauge opened up Axis' file to a copy of the engagement proposal he'd sent. This should cheer him up at least a little now that Axis had convinced the Count a merger between Tempest and Flicker wouldn't take place. Yes, they would marry, but they would keep their business separate as not to threaten the mines. If any such merger took place after Gauge granted approval, he reserved the right to retaliate with any force in his arsenal, including, but not limited to, public execution.

Hopefully, it wouldn't come to that.

Gauge glanced over at the Tempest slots and recalled Leon performing CPR to save Valve's life. A bitter chuckle escaped Gauge. Leon Tempest was no saint, no matter what he wanted his daughter to believe, and these files were proof positive of that. But telling her the truth would make no friend of Gauge, so he'd keep the old doctor's secrets.

Unless Leon became as cumbersome as Valve, that is.

Tempest Manor housed ten guest rooms amid its five floors. Axis was on the second floor, the furthest from Lexia, but no one could stop her from delivering this tray of tea. While Leon acted as chaperon for propriety's sake, he understood today differed from any other day.

Lexia knocked on the door, and when no answer came, she let herself in.

Axis was sitting in an armchair by the window, staring out of the panes, with a thumbnail to his lips. He didn't seem to notice her entry as the lost look in his eyes never faded.

Determined to bring him some measure of comfort, Lexia set the tea aside, poured him a cup, and sat across from him. She asked, "Is there anything I can do for you?"

"You went through this two years ago with your mother, and I felt so incapable of consoling you because I didn't understand." Axis' voice sounded haunted, a pale ghost of his usual optimism. "I understand now."

Lexia leaned forward and kissed his cheek. There was no helping him with the loss so fresh. She could only be here for him and wait for the grief to process. If he would let her, she would plan the funeral to shoulder some of the burden. She'd had practice, after all.

With a sigh, Axis sat back and faced her. A tear rolled down his cheek as he asked, "What am I supposed to do?"

Lexia took his hand and squeezed it. "You go through the motions and smile when you can. Time will help. It's really the only answer for it. You'll inherit the factories, and when the Founding Season is over, you'll throw yourself into the work. That will help as well."

Axis nodded along as if he heard Lexia's words, but not as if he could absorb them right now. He stood so abruptly that Lexia nearly dropped the teacup. With a wipe of a hand down his face, he muttered something she couldn't hear before he left her to walk onto the balcony outside.

This reminded Lexia of when they were children, and Axis' dog had died from 'mysterious circumstances.' Another crime she would gladly blame on his father. Axis had been in a state for days and had refused to come outside and play.

"But, mother, how can I cheer him up?"

"There is no replacing true loss, but after a time, there is space to move on. We could find him a new puppy when he's ready."

But Lexia knew firsthand losing a parent wasn't the same. No new puppies would fix it.

Perhaps...

Lexia went out onto the balcony and grabbed Axis by the hand, saying, "You and I are going outside. Right now."

He didn't argue. In fact, he seemed too dazed to protest.

Lexia dragged Axis down the two stories, through the kitchens, and across the veranda. She said, "Here is a perfect patch of snow."

Axis blinked at her.

Lexia rolled a ball of snow, smaller at first until it accumulated more snow and grew to three times the size of her head. While Axis watched, his eyes became more focused. Eventually, he crouched down and rolled a second ball, smaller and rounder. When he stacked it on top of hers, Lexia gave him a winning smile.

Even though the one Axis gave her in return was small and a little forced, Lexia appreciated that he was taking her advice seriously.

In the dusk of this exhausting day, they built the smallest snowball together, and Axis plopped it on top. Lexia dressed it in her top hat, and Axis gave it his scarf. They stole some smooth rocks from the shore of a reflecting pool and fashioned their snowman some eyes. The mouth and buttons followed.

Lexia pointed at a bough on one of their oak trees, asking, "Can you break us off some sticks? He needs arms."

As Axis stomped through the snow, an awful idea came to Lexia's mind. When he stretched to reach the branches, she rolled a snowball and threw it at him.

Right in the face.

Axis froze mid-reach and blinked at her with snow falling from his lashes, but his eyes were no longer lost.

No.

There was retaliation in the spread of Axis' grin.

Lexia turned to run for cover, but it was far too late. Axis tackled her into a drift and pinned her wrists beside her head in the snow. They stared at each other, panting their breath in bursts of white fog.

Axis wasn't smiling anymore. Instead, his eyes hungered for more diverting sport. Lexia could feel how much so through their coats, and she spread her thighs to welcome him.

Starving for distraction, Axis kissed Lexia as if only she would satisfy. Sadly, he let her wrists go to plant his hands to take his weight and broke their kiss. With a plea in his eyes, he said, "Not in view of the house."

Lexia understood. When he stood, she took the hand he offered, and they returned to building their snowman. The distinguished gentleman possessed arms, a face, and double-breasted buttons. Lexia examined him with a tilt of her head and an ironic twist to her smile.

"Uhm. Axis?"

"Yes?"

Lexia couldn't keep the laughter out of her voice as she asked, "Did we just build Gauge?"

Axis squinted and scrutinized their creation. After another moment, he chuckled, and it warmed Lexia through. He said, "I suppose we did…Count Snow."

The humor was such a relief at the end of this arduous day, but Lexia could see the dark circles under Axis' eyes in the Flicker wicks of the landscape lights.

Rest.

Time.

Even though Lexia couldn't hold Axis in her arms tonight, he would be all right.

"Do you think Gauge will murder them?"

The words fell from Axis' lips before his brain even considered their impact on the moment.

Lexia peered at him with her mouth open for a second until she registered his question enough to ask, "Who?"

Axis stared at the snowman, seeing the Copper Count instead. "My father's mercenaries. The ones who trained their guns on us."

There.

For one fraction of an instant, Lexia's eyes flashed with understanding and...

Disdain.

How could this be?

"Do you think they deserve death, Lexia?" Axis couldn't feel shock, but its next of kin, disbelief, had left his voice incredulous.

Hurt passed over Lexia's face, and Axis immediately regretted starting this conversation. Softly, she said, "Not death, but something. They meant to kill you, and if they'd raised their guns again, *I* would've been the one to see that they didn't."

The snowman's cheery expression mocked the severity of their conversation, and Axis didn't know how much more he could take. "Forgive me for mentioning it—"

"No. You're right." Lexia took him by the arm before Axis could turn away. Tears shone in her eyes as she said, "If you think rehabilitation is the way, then reach out to Gauge before it's too late. I want nothing else to burden your conscience."

Axis looked back at the snowman. "Do you think he'll listen?"

Lexia tugged his arm, insisting, "I think he values your opinion a great deal. Yes, he'll listen. C'mon. I'll walk you back to your room unless you want to stop in the dining room? Father will be sitting down to dinner."

Axis shook his head. "No. I need to send this message before it's too late." He cupped Lexia's nape to kiss her forehead and said, "But you go. Give your father my apologies for taking dinner in my room."

They parted, holding hands stretched across the distance. Lexia asked, "Are you sure?"

"I'm sure. Good night, Lexia." Axis glanced back at the snowman and the drift they'd ruined. "Thank you for this."

"I love you."

"I love you, too."

They dropped their hands and set about their separate tasks. Axis all but ran up to the room Leon was kind enough to open for the Prince, and he set about writing to Gauge with no small amount of urgency. As quickly as the Count had 'disposed' of Walker, Axis was cutting it close with the mercenaries.

Count Snow,

Thank you for your altruism earlier.

Regarding my father's mercenaries, consider rehabilitation over execution.

Please.

If you've no ideas in mind as to how, I could brainstorm some methods with you.

Sincerely and gratefully,

Axis Flicker.

Axis asked the manor's butler for red envelopes and a courier. Both arrived within minutes, and the letter went off to the Copper Cathedral. From his window on the second floor, Axis could make out the metallic peaks through the various trees on the Tempests' property, and he wondered if Gauge was sitting down to dinner just now.

It was odd how Axis' brain kept trying to escape itself. For the life of him, he'd never once considered the habits and routines of Gauge Snow until this very moment, but yes…

After seeing Gauge in pain, Axis wondered if the man had slept any. Wondered how Gauge ever managed to hold his own in a match with Axis. And wondered if there was genuine kindness in someone like the Count as evidenced by today's events.

"Why don't you like to play with Little Snow, Axis?"

Axis hesitated to say, "He scares me, Mrs. Tempest."

Lya knelt to make herself the same height as the little boy and asked, "Is it because he's so small?"

"No. It's because he doesn't smile."

Children could be so cruel, and Axis had been no exception. If one removed every action Gauge took the day after the pinned butterflies, Axis would be the villain in the story. A bully, even.

Perhaps one day Axis should apologize to Gauge.

And perhaps Axis' mind was spinning out of control to avoid thinking about the guilt and anger and sorrow and—

He gripped his hair and squeezed his eyes shut.

Why couldn't Valve have the decency to die somewhere far away from Axis? Why did he have to leave his stupid bodyguards on the Prince's conscience? And who did Axis blame for the failing of the factories now—

A knock sounded at the door.

Dinner.

Without looking away from the Cathedral, Axis said, "Come in."

"Special delivery."

Lexia.

Axis turned to find her in the door with a silver tray piled high with food. He blinked at her, and she smiled.

"I may have gotten a little carried away with the leftovers. Also..."

Lexia stepped out of the way to reveal Leon in the doorway. He said, "Hello, son."

Son.

Son.

A pang twisted Axis' insides, and he didn't even know why. No, he did know. He simply didn't want to. Axis said, "Sir."

Dr. Tempest walked in behind Lexia, who left the tray at the desk in front of Axis. The smell of roasted meat and sauteed vegetables turned his stomach. The only appetite he wanted to slake reared its inappropriate head as Lexia bent over to set Axis boots out the door. Her ass in those leather pants was a cure for almost any ailment. Except Axis' mind couldn't focus on it. Instead, he wondered why she was doing it in the first place—Oh. For a morning polish.

Servants.

That was a conversation for another time.

Leon said, "Axis, I hate to bring up the mundane at a time like this, but I wanted to offer some help. I can arrange everything for your father's service if it would help relieve you of the burden."

Yes.

So many burdens.

And did Axis really care to add his personal touch to such a procession in memorial of the bastard who'd abused him? However...

Axis said, "I'd appreciate that. The only contribution I know for certain is he wanted it at the factories."

Leon gave a curt nod. "Leave it to me."

A bit of the weight in Axis' chest lifted, and he found it in him to smile as Lexia had advised. "Thank you, sir." He glanced over at the clock. It was later in the evening than he'd thought, and soon the manor would turn down for sleep.

But Axis knew better.

The moment Lexia and Leon left, the dark spiral would begin anew.

Almost as if Dr. Tempest had sensed Axis' thoughts, he said to Lexia, "I find the marital laws a little archaic, but we'll honor them to keep Snow happy. So good night, dear, and I'll escort you out." He held up a stern finger at her. "No sneaking about the place. I've asked a detail of watchful eyes to guard over this door. There'll be no illegal activities in this house tonight. But tomorrow, I would like you and Axis to finish discussing those union models." There was a charitable and very astute cast to Leon's eyes.

Lexia smiled and said, "Yes, father," before crossing the room and kissing Axis' cheek. "I'll be with you first thing in the morning."

Axis couldn't wait for the sort of distraction he had in mind. "Tomorrow, then."

Tomorrow was another day, but in two of them Axis would bury his past.

Of course, he'd have to find a way to make it through the next eight hours alone.

Stupid Snow.

Snuffed Flame

Two days had passed since Valve died in Gauge's foyer, and news from Tempest Manor said the Prince and the Heiress were abiding by the marital laws. Meanwhile, Gauge had received Axis' missive and found himself in an interesting conundrum.

Brainstorming.

With Axis.

What a notion.

Gauge wasn't sure about all this 'rehabilitation' business. He quite liked the current model of 'if you don't aim a gun at the Count, you don't end up in the Wall of Pain,' but perhaps that was a little old-fashioned. So in the meantime...

"Please let us go, Count Snow!"

"We'll leave for sector ten and never return!"

Gauge peered up at the ceiling of the dungeon beneath the Copper Cathedral and wondered how long was too long to hang upside-down. The purple faces above him with their watering eyes indicated perhaps an hour was too long. He said, "Let them down, Jan."

Jan, who'd employed this method all on his own, frowned, but did as he was told.

The woman cried out in relief as the mechanism lowered them to the icy stone floor. There was no heat down here, and even Gauge had wrapped himself in a fur-lined coat before checking in on their progress. He asked his butler, "What do you think?"

Jan didn't take kindly to people aiming a gun at his ward. His chocolate brown eyes had hardened into merciless glass as he peered over at the prisoners. "We can do the water again."

A pained cry from the cell indicated their prisoners had overheard him.

Gauge tsked and said, "No. We need to keep asking ourselves, 'What would Lexia think?'"

Jan's expression broke into a warm smile. "I was most impressed with our Ms. Tempest. She trained those cannons on them at the first opportunity."

"Yes. She was magnificent, wasn't she—No. Stop changing the subject, Jan. We can't torment them needlessly without an aim."

"Please, no more," the man begged this time. He was on his knees in the cell with his hands clasped together. While the blood drained from his face, his complexion was transforming from purple to the brightest red.

Jan offered, "I can try to gain more information from them regarding the late Master Flicker."

Gauge rolled his eyes. "I'm not sure I want to hear any more brothel stories. As it is, I almost want to write those ladies and gents an apology for ever having to entertain the old hog."

The woman said, "That's right. He was a nightmare to work for. We only did it for the money to support our families. Please let us go."

Jan wasn't having it. "Quiet in there."

'Or else' was implied, and the mercenaries fell silent instantly.

Rehabilitation.

Lexia's opinion.

Axis' conscience.

Gauge muttered, "Let's be off for the funeral. In the meantime, these two can starve. I wonder how long it will take one to consider eating the other."

"Yes, sir." Jan sounded a little too delighted, but decades in the service of unjust warmongers would do that to a person.

They left their prisoners in their shared cell, ascended the dreary stone steps, and stepped through the iron-banded door into the kitchens. There, the servants scattered about their tasks.

Gauge didn't mind their eavesdropping. It wasn't often one could overhear the sounds of torture without finding themselves in danger. He took a moment to peer at the dinner preparations.

When Leon had asked Gauge to host the wake, he'd accepted immediately. Despite how much Gauge wanted Lexia, he didn't see Axis as a rival. Not truly. He wanted to make an ally out of the new

Master Flicker. And what better way to ingratiate oneself to another than to provide a little support here and there?

Gauge and Jan exited the Cathedral to find snow falling like small pillows to the cobbles. Gauge clicked his tongue before saying, "That's the third time this year." He regretted not wearing a top hat, but a funeral was hardly the place for one. Instead, he tucked his cane in and lifted the hood of his coat over his braids while Jan got the car.

They arrived at the factory offices on Flicker Avenue to the entertainment of an enormous crowd. Despite the lack of morale which led to the strikes, thousands waited to attend Valve Flicker's funeral even in the freezing cold. A security detail hired for the event kept the crowd off Gauge as he and Jan made their way inside, with a few waves for the people.

Inside was more organized with an auditorium reserved for those more intimately acquainted to the Tempests and Flickers. Gauge zeroed-in on Axis. He was sitting on the stage as far from the podium as possible with Lexia at his side.

Leon was welcoming the guests at the door. "Count Snow, thank you again for the reception."

"My Cathedral is always happy to host an event, doctor." Gauge shook his hand and ignored the extra sensitivity in his gloved fingertips. Quieter, he said, "Truth be told, if it wasn't in poor taste, I would encourage dancing tonight." To celebrate Valve's passing appropriately.

Dr. Tempest shared a look with Gauge that said he understood and appreciated the Count's humor. He said, "You and me both."

No one would miss Valve.

Gauge left the doctor to walk onto the stage without permission. Lexia looked up and noticed him first. A flicker of something passed in her eyes, and he couldn't help but appreciate the plain black pantsuit. Although, he lamented the lack of a corset. She wore those very well.

But Axis never looked up. His eyes stayed on the stage's simple wood floor without even seeing it.

Gauge mouthed to Lexia, "How. Is. He?"

She shook her head and smoothed a hand over Axis' back.

Perhaps now was not the best time to tell him Gauge approved of their engagement. Later at the Cathedral may be better suited for this discussion. Instead, Gauge bowed to Lexia with his head and left the stage for the most centered seat in the front row. Jan sat behind him.

With Gauge's arrival, the funeral began.

Lexia had hated Valve. Hated him for abusing Axis and hated him more for trying to ruin what little legacy the old bastard would leave his son. He deserved to die more slowly and somewhere far colder than Winter.

Alone.

Watching Axis suffer through this internal conflict was even more reason to hate the man.

Dr. Tempest went to the podium, postponing Axis' public phobia for as long as propriety would allow. But eventually, the people expected to hear from the son.

It would surprise Lexia if Axis spoke at all.

Leon said, "Thanks to everyone for joining us today. We've lost a pillar of the community and cornerstone of Winter's industry..."

Lexia couldn't listen to the rest. Her father was quite the diplomat, but some words were simply too hard to swallow. Instead, she rubbed circles on Axis' back and glanced around the crowd.

People from all walks of life attended the funeral. It wasn't every day one of the mighty triumvirate fell, and Lexia supposed, at least it was this one who'd brought the people some relief. Even if Axis was poisoned with grief.

Closest to this side of the stage, Bolt waved to Lexia, and she nodded back. Axis' valet looked worried sick over his charge. Then there were the head foremen from each of the lines. Phoro met her eyes with the barest of nods. She wondered how many of them were still considering striking now that their primary concern was dead and burnt to a crisp.

There were no burials on Winter as there wasn't enough space. Rather than that, the Tempests opted for the fertilizer route, and the Flickers voted for cremation. And the Snows? Well, Gauge seemed to refuse the notion of death. Even so, people in his camp opted to be pressurized into a gemstone. Wasn't it all so predictable?

Once Gauge had entered Lexia's thoughts, she couldn't keep herself from looking at him. Like the rest of the audience, he peered up at Leon. But unlike the rest, he didn't seem to buy it any more than Lexia had—

Gauge glanced over at Lexia, and their eyes met. Her breath caught in her throat, and she swallowed it with an audible gulp.

Had he felt her staring? What did he think of Valve's death? Lexia wanted to know everything on Gauge's mind as he slowly licked his lips before breaking the spell by looking forward once again.

All the sound returned to the room with a deafening pop in Lexia's ears.

"Now Prince Axis will say a few words."

Beside her, Axis stood and met Leon halfway on the stage. The two men hugged in the middle before Axis went to the podium. Creaks resounded as the audience went to the edge of their seats.

Lexia kept her eyes on her lover where they belonged, and it took every ounce of restraint in her not to glance at Gauge again during this inappropriate time.

Axis faced the people and said, "Not everyone will miss Valve Flicker."

The crowd went still, and Lexia straightened in her seat. Leon shifted uncomfortably beside her, but Axis continued.

"He was a smart businessman, but a tyrant. A dedicated servant of Winter, but a glutton. He believed in the future where others were blind to its inevitability, and through that faith, the strongest of bonds was formed. Count Snow."

Axis nodded toward Gauge in the crowd; he responded in kind.

"Dr. Tempest." Axis did the same for Leon, who followed suit.

"If Valve hadn't fought for Winter, none of us would be here today. And that counts for something. So, in respect to his love for the future, I dedicate this in Valve's name."

The curtain behind Axis pulled open to reveal a massive grayscale mural of the new city. Lexia recognized it from Gauge's three-dimensional models, but there was something about the painting—

Oh.

It wasn't paint at all.

Ash.

Axis had used Valve's ashes to paint the future.

Someone clapped.

Lexia turned to see Bolt standing in the crowd clapping slowly. Another joined him. It was Gauge. Others followed until the entire assembly stood and clapped to celebrate what little good Valve had done in this life. Eventually, Lexia, too, gave in. She supposed, in this one respect, it was deserved.

Thousands poured into the factory offices to witness the mural which Axis promised to move outside on the Avenue in full view of the onlookers, but Lexia had tired of this tribute. She dragged her father and fiance to Snow Plaza where Gauge had already opened the doors for the wake. They both came readily, also tired of the gathering. Hopefully, the repast wouldn't take long as Lexia wanted the time to lie in bed with Axis before curfew demanded she return to her room.

"Welcome, Prince Axis. Dr. Tempest, Ms. Tempest," Jan said as they entered the Cathedral. "The buffet is in the ballroom. Please come to me if there is anything you require."

Lexia went on tiptoe, which said a lot given her height, to kiss the old butler's cheek. "Thank you, Jan."

His face reddened as he bowed deeply.

"Are you trying to steal my butler, Ms. Tempest? Because this is how you steal my butler."

Gauge.

Lexia couldn't keep the smile from her face as she turned to face the Count. Axis squeezed her hand where he held it, and when she met his soft green eyes, he tried to smile before reaching a hand out to Gauge.

Axis said, "Thank you, Count Snow, for the kind reception."

"You're most welcome, Prince Axis. And before you come to dread repayment for the favor, this one's on the house." Gauge smiled, eliciting a more genuine one from Axis.

He said, "I appreciate that. As for my missive..."

Gauge looked as if he'd suddenly remembered it. "Oh, yes. Right. Of course, we can brainstorm some ideas. Until then, our errant citizens are under arrest, and they can stay safely that way until such time you feel up to the task."

When Axis' shoulders loosened, Lexia almost sighed with relief. One less burden.

Now to remove only a million more...

Axis didn't recognize most of the faces in the Copper Cathedral's ballroom. They whirled by him in a blur of anxiety and confusion. Public events were already too much for him, but one where everyone kept shaking his hand and offering condolences would surely shatter Axis into pieces.

"Not much longer, love," Lexia said the exact thing he needed to hear against his ear.

It soothed some of Axis' anxiety for now. It wasn't all about the crowds.

Gauge was acting suspiciously courteous. In fact, Axis found himself looking through the faces for the Count—Not because Axis wanted to glare at him across the room. But because now and again, Gauge gave Axis a nod.

A simple nod.

And yet it meant a world of reassurance to Axis.

Gauge would take care of things or field this or that, postpone whatever needed pushed back. There would be no unpleasantness during this time, and Axis reveled in it while mistrusting every second it.

Was the Count up to something? Was grief making Axis paranoid?

Or perhaps not, seeing as Gauge was making his way through the crowd to Axis, Lexia, and Dr. Tempest.

Axis tensed, preparing for battle, and Lexia noticed. She peered at him before seeing Gauge approach. When she did, Axis couldn't help but notice a brightening to her. It was curiosity and something more.

Axis couldn't fault Lexia for her interest. Even to someone who'd spent regular time across a conference table from the Count, Gauge was still mysterious. Always immaculately dressed, he was handsome and irritatingly charming. It was easy to see the appeal, but even in Axis' current mental state, he didn't see Gauge as a threat. More of a fantasy.

The flesh and blood Count reached their party with a dip of his head at Axis. He said, "I know I don't have much of a grasp for the most appropriate timing, but it seems there won't be a better opportunity during this mourning period. So I'll cut to the chase. Prince Axis, I've approved your proposal, and I grant you permission to marry Ms. Tempest."

Lexia gave a little cheer of delight. Dr. Tempest smiled and shook Gauge's hand.

Axis malfunctioned.

His hearing shorted out, and he couldn't draw in enough air to breathe.

The wedding was on. The *public* wedding.

Lexia in a glorious gown of her own unique design, and the night which followed when Axis could release her from it. And everyone would know, wouldn't they?

Then children would follow, and everyone would know that. Their every move as Winter's royal couple would make headlines and literature, plays and operas. Not one detail would go unnoticed.

No privacy.

Ever.

And here Axis was grieving the loss of his father in public, when all he wanted to do was scream at the old bastard for dying in front of him. For leaving him the biggest mess to clean up.

Axis tipped over.

To the sound of gasps all around, someone caught him in their arms. Someone with gloved hands.

"Damn, he's heavier than he looks."

It was Gauge.

Someone else lifted one of Axis' arms over their shoulder. "Let me help."

Lexia.

Another's hand went to his forehead and checked his cheeks. "He's burning up."

Dr. Tempest.

It was all rather distant, and within a heartbeat, Axis found himself in another room.

The library.

Gauge said, "Let's set him down here. Prince Axis, can you hear us?"

"What's happened?" That was Bolt. He sounded half-angry. "What have you done to our Prince?"

Lexia jumped to Gauge's defense, saying, "Nothing. He's fainted."

Dr. Tempest added, "I believe he's become physically ill from the grief."

Sure.

Axis liked this sofa. It was plush.

As Lexia and Gauge left his weight on the black suede, Axis let the couch have him and fell over on his side onto it.

Leon's face appeared level to Axis' field of vision. He flashed a Flicker wick's lighter in Axis' eyes and said, "His pupils aren't reacting. He's in shock again."

"I wasn't expecting the news to undo the man." Gauge sounded genuinely remorseful.

Lexia asked, "Bolt, can you please help us get him to the Manor? You're welcome to stay in the room next to his."

"Of course, Ms. Tempest."

Dr. Tempest said, "Don't move him, yet. Wait until he comes back around."

Gauge said, "He's welcome to stay here as long as it takes."

Soft suede.

Plush cushions.

Was Axis broken? He wanted to think of nothing but the textures under his fingertips. Anything else brought on a wash of anxiety, flooding his entire body in toxic anguish. Well, not entirely.

Lexia's beautiful freckles as she smiled at Axis from where she sat on the floor.

Further in the room, Gauge glanced over through dark lenses at Axis while speaking to Dr. Tempest.

The tightness in Bolt's throat as he suggested clearing the Cathedral with his voice thick from emotion.

Those were checks in the positive column. And truthfully, the negative was manageable, wasn't it?

Cope with losing Valve.

Employ union models on the Flicker wicks' line.

Marry Lexia in a public ceremony.

Exist…

The last one was proving difficult at the moment.

"Axis, what's wrong?"

He didn't answer, and from his silence, Mrs. Tempest derived the answer. She said, "C'mere, child."

Lya enveloped Axis in a warm embrace unlike anything else in his life. It was safe and solid. Warm and bright. Axis cried in her arms, not because he was sad, but because the hug was exactly what he'd needed.

Motherly comfort did not exist in Axis' life aside from his time with Winter's Diamond, and that was the crux of it. There was no one else to share the acute loss of Valve. No wife left behind or aunts and uncles. Just Axis.

Alone.

But the four people in this room were substitute enough, were they not?

"I'm ready to go home."

Dr. Tempest said, "Very well, son," and Axis felt a little better.

A bit at a time.

An hour had passed since Gauge saw Axis, Leon, and Lexia out. The rest of the crowd remained, taking their fill of the Copper Cathedral's offerings. Gauge didn't mind because the buffet wouldn't eat itself, but his head wasn't in the space to host tonight.

Instead, Gauge asked Jan to take him for a drive. The Count's head was full of so many thoughts.

Axis had subconsciously trusted Gauge to carry him.

What a momentous occasion, and for once things transpired between them without a hitch. Sure, it had taken a great deal of restraint on the Count's part not to rib Axis over it, but not as much as Gauge would've thought given the state of the Prince.

Axis was truly heartbroken.

And what a heart to break...

To watch the younger man's soft green eyes hollow out, and to catch Axis as he fell over...

Whatever it meant, it meant something *true* to Gauge. He would protect Axis from whatever came their way for as long as the Prince would allow. That included not broaching the topic of Tija's return until Axis was himself again.

Gauge remembered it took some time to recover from his own father's death, but it would take the Prince longer. They had more in common than Gauge had originally thought, and he wondered if Axis had ever wished for Valve's death. Gauge had certainly wished for Prof. Snow's.

Immobile, lying in bed, a teenage Gauge fumed at his father in impotent rage. "Mother died because you refused to help her."

"I'm afraid, Little Bones, it is more complicated than that." Prof. Snow held up a new bottle of his homemade concoction.

"I won't drink your disgusting medicine anymore. None of the research supports it as a treatment!"

Prof. Snow nodded along as if he expected this protest, but afterward, he said, "Yes, you will. Jan?"

The old spy sounded reticent. "Sir?"

"Hold him down."

Why did it look as though Prof. Snow was suppressing a smile while he drowned his son with the useless tonic?

Yes.

Axis would recover slower than Gauge in mourning his paternal loss—

"Sir?"

Jan interrupted Gauge's thoughts, who took in their surroundings. The Tempests had lined their Boulevard with crabapple trees, their red berries adorning otherwise naked branches. They were only a few meters from the gates to Tempest Manor. And...

Lexia Tempest was climbing out of a tree over their wrought-iron fence onto the cobbles.

Oh, what diverting mischief.

Gauge said, "Follow her, Jan." He leaned forward on his cane where he held in front of him in the car to keep his eyes on Lexia as she walked toward Flicker Avenue.

Gone was the respectable black pantsuit. She'd replaced it with a tight burgundy double-breasted blazer over black tights. The blazer was mostly long enough to cover her assets as she kept up a brisk pace.

Jan said, "Rhyme is nowhere to be seen."

Gauge smiled. "Lexia's escaped. I wonder why…" As soon as he said it, he knew the answer.

Lexia was a sprite—a creature of untamed spontaneity. Tending to Axis in his grief was in her heart, but it must also suffocate her need to act on every impulse.

So here they were. Chasing freedom.

When Lexia stopped in front of the factory offices, Jan pulled up to the curb. She stared up at the mural, hung only moments ago, at what remained of Valve Flicker.

Inspired by her impulsiveness, Gauge left the car and wandered over to her. He kept his pace casual as not to alarm her.

Without taking her eyes off the truly generous memorial, Lexia said, "I don't suppose you finding me here is a coincidence."

Gauge smiled at her. "I happened by the Manor as you made your daring escape."

"Please don't tell my father," Lexia said as she continued staring at the mural. Her black eyes roved over the plans for the new city in all its grayscaled splendor. Snow fell in her white waves, left exposed to the chilled air.

Gauge removed his hood, exposing his black braids to the white fluff surrounding them. He assured, "I wouldn't dream of it, dear Ms. Tempest. I understand the need to get away now and then." Now he peered up at the work of art, standing beside her.

Lexia interrupted a long stretch of silence by blurting, "I hated the man."

With a half-laugh, Gauge commiserated. "Who didn't?"

She swallowed audibly. "I think Axis loved him. Probably more than he knows. Valve was his only parent."

Gauge let Lexia's words linger between them, allowing her to vent that which plagued her thoughts.

"Valve once offered me twice as much for Tempest silk if I swore to stay away from his son."

It wasn't a surprise, but Gauge couldn't stop himself from saying, "That's despicable," and he actually spat on Valve's grave. "His death wasn't slow enough."

Lexia turned and finally looked at Gauge. Their eyes met through his lenses, and a bitter smirk spread on her black-painted lips. She said, "Thanks to Snow's Finest he died painfully, at least."

Yes.

The unrefined copper had done the trick.

"What did you say?" Lexia's eyes widened.

Had Gauge said that aloud? He shook his head and peered back up at the memorial, keeping his expression as clean as a slate. "It's nothing for you to concern yourself with, Ms. Tempest. I was just remarking on a settled score." He changed the subject to something lighter and more distracting. "You look beautiful, tonight."

Taken aback, Lexia seemed to forget Gauge's slip of the tongue. Instead, she said, "You are quite the troublemaker."

"A kindred spirit, then?" he asked, quirking a brow at her.

Lexia's laughter could end wars. How freely she gave the bright sound was another testament to the privilege of her upbringing. One she must never know the truth of if Gauge were to keep hearing that laugh. She looked away, but muttered, "Perhaps…"

Into the companionable silence which followed, Gauge said, "I meant the open invitation. You are always welcome at the Cathedral." He glanced over her.

Lexia looked over at him. Gauge wanted her to see the promise he offered—everything—but the lenses obstructed it—

Fuck it.

Gauge took his glasses off and let her see the sincerity in his eyes despite the painful glow emanating from the Flicker wicks backlighting Valve's memorial.

Desire.

Pleasure.

A night to remember, if not more…

Lexia's eyes filled with curiosity of the sensual variety. She didn't know what she'd yet to experience, but she wanted to.

Gauge wanted to make things clear between them. He said, "Let's broker an understanding. Axis is the man you go to when you want to make love. I'm the man you go to when you want to break the headboard. Be sure which one you want first before you come to me. Is that clear enough for you, Lexia? Tell me you understand."

Lexia understood.

Perhaps more than Gauge knew, and he was right about what he'd said earlier at the wake. The Count had no sense of appropriate timing.

Before Lexia could tease him about it, the Tempests' car pulled up to the curb. Rhyme glared at her from the driver's side with disapproval in the hard lines of his rugged face.

Busted.

Again.

"Break the headboard…"

In all this time with Axis, Lexia couldn't think of one instance of their lovemaking which she could describe in such a way. That was to say, Axis was thorough and stretched the definition of endurance. He would draw swell after swell from Lexia and never disappoint.

But she would be a liar if Lexia said Axis had met her every need.

This butterfly wanted to be pinned. To hurt and scream. Not in ecstasy, either.

And the starved look in Gauge's naked eyes said he could deliver.

Lexia was torn. However… "I understand you perfectly, Count Snow. Enjoy your evening in this lovely weather." She glanced over at the shadows, unsure of how she knew but she did… "Good night to you as well, Jan."

The shadow said, "Good night, Ms. Tempest."

Gauge only stared with those penetrating eyes as Lexia climbed into the backseat. Rhyme shot Gauge a nasty look before taking the wheel once again. The Count ignored him, watching Lexia drive away.

It wasn't a long drive home, but it gave her enough time to think about…everything. About Gauge's enticing offer. About her relationship with Axis. And about the truth of Valve's death.

Snow's Finest.

"The unrefined copper had done the trick."

"It's nothing for you to concern yourself with, Ms. Tempest."

But wasn't it?

How could Lexia not wonder about the cigars? To wonder about how frequently she'd seen Gauge dispense them to Valve despite their obvious adverse effects on the old bastard's health. And what kind of poison was copper to the inhaler's lungs?

A painful death, indeed.

But did Lexia disagree with the murder? Cold-blooded homicide—not an execution nor a duel—was against Winter's laws. Punishment would see Gauge in his own copper monument.

Was Axis right about the Count? Did he hold too much power in Winter?

Lexia wouldn't tell her fiance. Although Axis had entertained challenging Valve to a duel many times, he would never choose to kill his father in such a dishonorable manner as poison. No matter how much she thought the rotten Factory Master deserved it.

No.

Lexia would keep Gauge's secret, and one day, she planned to confirm her theory alone with the Count.

Soon.

Once at the manor, it was past curfew and Axis was hopefully asleep, so Lexia went to her favorite room in the house. Her father's study. It was all encased in rosewood, with a quaint fireplace and lots of cushy places to curl up and read one of the many books on the walls.

In this instance, Lexia sought a locked drawer in the desk. She felt around for the telltale splinter beneath the desktop and pressed the spring-loaded mechanism which released the lock. Inside the drawer, she followed the encoded indexing system to find Gauge's file.

Dr. Tempest wasn't privy to Lexia's knowledge of this sacred dossier, but she'd learned the secret within a year or two of living in the Manor. There was a trick to prying beneath her father's nose.

Lexia grabbed the file and the nearest book large enough to disguise it. Then she pushed the drawer closed and cozied up in an armchair, reading all the material Leon's spies had collected on Gauge Snow.

The father who was disgraced by several indiscretions, mostly involving his students but one which included a theory about a planet similar to their own. This one, according to Prof. Snow's research, was further behind in technology than Winter before the electromagnetic pulse reduced their vast and advanced civilization to their current steam-engineered community of only three cities. Prof. Snow was laughed out of seminars and conferences.

Next on the docket was Gauge's health.

Lexia didn't feel right reading that, so she skipped over to the part about the Founding of Winter. It mostly described arguments between Gauge and Valve from their first meeting on. Master Flicker wanted more land allocated to the Flicker name under the dome than Tempest, but Gauge assured him they could design the factories to take up minimal space whereas crops needed plenty of room to grow for material and food.

Wise decision.

Master Flicker also accused Gauge of…shaming his father to death?

Lexia blinked at the page.

It was a point of contention for some time until the Count threatened Valve with exile if he didn't stop mentioning it at every turn. Not surprisingly, Master Flicker had heeded Gauge's warning.

But according to Leon's notes, Prof. Snow died of mysterious circumstances which went unsolved because of the impropriety of the Snow name. The very same reason no one would listen to Gauge's warning regarding the EMP.

Wait…

Why was there a page on Lexia's mother—

"Lexia, dear, isn't it time for bed?"

She jumped so high in the chair she almost dropped the book concealing the file. Lexia said, "I-I'm sorry, father. Old habits, and all that."

Leon gave her a sympathetic smile. "I know it's hard watching Axis grieve, but look at it this way. If you two can survive losing a parent each, you can survive anything."

Given her conversation earlier with Gauge, Lexia almost winced at his words. She believed they were one hundred percent gospel, but was every person truly meant to have only one other? Why not two?

Lexia said, "Thank you. It's the very thing I needed to hear."

Dr. Tempest lingered in the doorway, saying, "We'll all need to be awake bright and early tomorrow morning. Apparently Snow has some surprise planned to 'lift Winter's spirits.' Whatever that could mean."

Lexia could think of a few ways Gauge could lift her spirits—

"Let me clean up in here, and then I'll head upstairs. Good night, father."

"Good night, dear."

Once Lexia heard Leon take the first steps to the second story landing, she rushed to the desk and returned the file as neatly as possible. One day, she would discover why Lya was mentioned in the Count's dossier, but disappointing her father twice in one night while he housed her grieving fiance seemed ungrateful.

Even to Lexia.

ELEVEN

Frozen Reprieve

EVERY DAY GOT A LITTLE EASIER, AND TODAY, AXIS WAS LOOKING FORWARD TO SETTING HIS GRIEF ASIDE AND ENJOYING HIS TIME WITH LEXIA AND DR. TEMPEST.

Even with Gauge.

In fact, Axis' curiosity about today's event was partially responsible for his resurrection. What could Gauge possibly have planned to 'lift Winter's spirits?' The only hint he'd given in his official announcement was, "Dress warm."

So Axis suited up in brown wool pants and a cream sweater he'd hope to keep Lexia from stealing a while longer. He accessorized with brown leather straps along his biceps, across his shoulders, and on his free wrist. Lexia's timepiece completed the ensemble.

When Axis opened the door to find his boots polished yet again, he was reminded of the conversation he kept postponing. Now that Gauge had approved of their engagement, the household talks could begin. Axis hoped Lexia would be understanding, and they would find some compromise in their shared lifestyle.

Bolt opened the door beside Axis' room and gave a half bow, saying, "Good morning, Prince Flicker. How are we anticipating the day?"

"Cautiously optimistic."

This brightened Bolt's demeanor, as Axis was sure everyone had been quite worried about him. He tried not to let the responsibility of others' happiness worm its way into his brain.

Instead, Axis slipped on his boots and said, "Let's see what the Tempests have prepared for breakfast, shall we?"

Bolt followed Axis down the stairs and into the breakfast nook of the dining room. There, Leon's servants filled his bowl of yogurt with fruit and granola and his glass with fresh squeezed juice.

The doctor said, "Good morning, son. Bolt, how did you find your room?"

Bolt shifted bashfully, a little uncomfortable with the special treatment. He said, "It was most grand, sir. Thank you for your generosity."

Leon gestured at a chair. "You're a guest in my house. Please make yourself at home."

Axis couldn't fathom how Leon could treat the Prince's valet so familiarly while still employing servants as paid slaves. It baffled him. Before one could prepare Axis a bowl of yogurt, he stopped them gently and tended to his own breakfast.

Leon smiled at the interaction as if he considered Axis a precocious child after all these years.

As Axis sat for breakfast, he considered the doctor's clothes. Brown wool pants and a cream sweater. All of Axis' life, Leon had served as more of a father than Valve ever could claim, and it lent itself to quiet moments such as this.

The sound of footsteps rushing down the stairs brought all three men's eyes to the entryway. Lexia appeared in it a moment later, dressed in a thick blouse the color of Gauge's eyes. The cobalt blue complimented her freckles and contrasted against the black leather under-bust corset and thick black leggings. Axis' timepiece swallowed her forearm in burgundy, while blue-dipped thigh-high boots covered her long legs. Her steam cannons jutted out from her hip holster, always preoccupied with the romantic notion of dueling without ever understanding the need for one.

Anticipation brightened Lexia's voice. "Good morning!" Her brilliant smile was infectious, reminding Axis of her mother. Winter's Diamond Heiress.

Leon looked similarly taken. "Good morning, my dear. New boots?"

A slight yellow blush kissed Lexia's cheeks. "Yes, father."

"Hmm."

Was Dr. Tempest concerned about something? Was Axis out of the loop? Well, after the last few days of fainting and spiraling, he supposed he would be.

Setting those thoughts aside for now, Axis said, "You look beautiful."

Several emotions flashed through Lexia's black eyes too quickly for Axis to discern them all, but they finally settled on warmth. She said, "Thank you, Prince."

Bolt snickered into his juice. Leon rolled his eyes and shook his head. Simultaneously, the older men said, "Love…" in a most condescending way.

Lexia vibrated with contagious energy all throughout breakfast. Honestly, Axis couldn't wait to see this surprise. So by the time they piled into their cars, he also hummed all the way to Snow Plaza.

A crowd had gathered at the topiary gardens, forming the Plaza's center. Bolt pulled up to the curb behind Rhyme in the Tempests' car. They all joined on the cobbles and parted through the throng to its beating heart where it smelled of frost and evergreens.

There, Gauge stood on a makeshift stage near a frozen lake in all his magnificent glory. He'd tossed back a black cloak with a fur-lined hood to reveal a black three-piece with gold brocade on the waistcoat. He'd twisted his braids into an intricate bun ornate with gold beads and ribbons, leaving his face bare to the cold. Gold-lensed glasses and gold gloves complimented his deep skin tone to perfection.

But it was Gauge's smile which commanded Axis' attention. In some ways, it was the same as Lexia's, alive and full of promises which they intended to keep. And that included promises made in the bedroom.

Wait…

What?

Why was Axis thinking that way about Gauge—

"Ladies, Gentlemen, and those who identify otherwise, thank you for joining us. Mourning came to Winter, and we paid our respects." Gauge's head tilted slightly toward Axis before saying, "But today, I want to introduce you to the dawn of that dark night. Last Founding Season, the late Master Flicker and I developed something extraordinary. And while we all recover from the shock, I think Valve would want us to embrace the good with the bad. So, I present you with a new sport designed entirely by Master Flicker. Ice skating."

Someone hopped onto the frozen lake and, to Axis' surprise, glided across it in an elegant arc. They spun on top of what looked like blades under the shoes. With a grand spiraling twirl, they completed the demonstration in the lake's frozen center.

The crowd gaped and clapped, oohed and awed to Gauge's delight. He beamed as he announced the rest. "In secret, Valve had manufactured enough so that everyone could have a free pair."

Axis didn't believe that for a second, and he wondered at Gauge's magnanimity for giving Valve all the credit.

Attendants descended upon the crowd en mass, passing out boxes. One handed a box to Axis, Bolt, Lexia, and Dr. Tempest, and when they opened them, they found a pair of bladed black shoes inside.

Gauge encouraged two more people onto the ice—They were Mrs. Tenz and her son. The youth's foot immediately slipped up into the air, with him landing promptly on his behind. Mrs. Tenz balanced clumsily beside him, while Gauge tied his skates on.

Others joined promptly across the many frozen lakes in the Plaza's gardens.

Dr. Tempest muttered, "I'll be too busy tending broken bones to enjoy this."

Bolt laughed, saying, "Sir, I think you can squeeze in some enjoyment."

Lexia leaned in and whispered so only Axis could hear, "The first one onto the ice gets to be on top tonight."

Well…

That was a win-win.

Gauge glided onto the ice like a man who'd had some practice to show off his skill while everyone else floundered. But of course. Little did the Count know, the Prince would conquer this sport like he'd done all the others. If only to show off for the Heiress' sake.

Certainly not for the Count.

Certainly not.

Gauge's chest swelled with pride as cries of delight and joyous laughter formed a chorus all around him. Winter could move on from grieving. Axis could move on from grieving, if he let himself enjoy this enough. And Gauge was sure Lexia would see to that.

He circled over to Mrs. Tenz and her son, who held onto each other for support. They beamed with rosy cheeks as he added a twirl for some flare to his approach. Gauge said, "How is my new forewoman faring?"

Mrs. Tenz's laughter came freer with Valve dead. "Wonderfully, Count Snow. Except—"

The younger Tenz "whooped" as he fell sprawling out on the ice again.

Even though the cold would eventually get to Gauge's bones, he spared the muscle to help the young man up, saying, "It took me quite a while, I must admit."

The teenager, blushing and flustered, ducked his eyes. He promised, "I'll get the knack for it."

Mrs. Tenz beamed beside them. "Prince Axis is joining the fun."

Oh, Gauge didn't want to miss this.

The crème de la crème, the pinnacle of athletic prowess under the capital's dome, stilt-walked his way to the ice and approached it with determination in his soft green eyes.

Gauge admired Axis so much. How did it feel to have such confidence in one's own body?

Lexia was more tentative, following Axis as he led her by the hand onto the ice. From here, Gauge could hear the Prince say, "It's a matter of balance. There, you've got the right idea."

Many people stopped and watched Winter's royal couple attempt the sport. The romantic moment would inspire songs at the very least, if not a new entry in their current newspaper serial.

Gauge craved the attention, and after so much restraint over the last few days, couldn't resist tormenting dear Axis. Not to mention, Lexia deserved a compliment for such a beautiful ensemble. They'd worn each other's signatures completely by coincidence, or perhaps they were on each other's minds.

Either way...

"Mrs. Tenz. Young Mr. Tenz. Would you care to join me across the lake?" Gauge held out his arm for his forewoman.

When her son gripped her shoulders to prevent the splits, Mrs. Tenz assured, "You go on. We'll learn the form first. Tell our Prince I said 'hello.'"

Gauge gave her a nod before gliding, oh so perfectly, across the ice toward the adorable pair. One he'd wanted to be in the middle of for as long as he could remember.

Axis and Lexia...

"Hello, Ms. Tempest. Prince Axis."

The latter was helping the former catch her balance. Lexia's black gaze sparkled as she tried to glimpse Gauge's eyes through the golden lenses. She said, "Count Snow, what a wonderful surprise!"

Axis said, almost begrudgingly, "Yes. Although, you'll understand if I have my doubts about the origins."

Gauge tipped his head at the Prince. "You'd be right, but good taste and all that," he said while executing a perfect spin.

Lexia gazed at Gauge in admiration and wonder, asking, "How long did it take you to find your balance?" She seemed to struggle with hers despite her fit and lithe physique.

Should Gauge be honest, or should he torment Axis with a lie? Torment was always so delicious. Gauge said, "Well, I took to it quite naturally, you know? I'd say I was skating figure eights by the end of the first day." Or more like the first month.

Axis let out an incredulous laugh, but said nothing to the contrary. He let it exude from his doubting expression.

Despite the fun in teasing Axis, the Prince stood with his sturdy legs and a straight back in a balanced stance while supporting Lexia, who was also coming into it.

What Gauge wouldn't give...

"Prince Axis, I challenge you to a race."

Another incredulous laugh escaped Axis, while Lexia grinned at the Count.

Axis said, "You can't expect me to race on my first day against someone who's had at least a few months' practice."

Lexia, standing on her own now, gripped Axis by the bicep. "Oh, please, Axis! I'm sure you can win. You're already moving about with ease."

It was true. Axis glided about with Lexia in a tight circle, grating on Gauge's envy. The man was simply magnificent.

After a thoughtful silence, Axis asked, "What're the stakes?"

"The same as our fencing match. A dinner with Ms. Tempest, and I'll keep my good faith measure of extending the invitation to you."

Lexia bounced with excitement.

Gauge had Axis now. How could anyone resist her?

The Prince kissed the Heiress' cheek and faced the Count. "You're on."

Dr. Tempest waved from the lake's shore where he tended injuries to avoid the fun of falling on his ass in his middle age.

Coward.

Bolt, Jan, and Rhyme lingered close by in their boots, prepared to slip and slide across the lake to protect their charges at a moment's notice.

Gauge pointed to the other side of the lake. "That's our mark."

Axis lined up with him. "Ms. Tempest, would you be so kind?"

Lexia made for quite the prize as she glided before and between the two men. She raised an arm with entirely too much enjoyment and lowered it to flag the signal.

Gauge took off with far more practice than Axis on the ice, gaining the lead. The Prince, determined and true, faltered only on launch before gliding his way quickly to catch up. If not for the growing ache in Gauge's bones, he could crouch and push more speed from his quads. But his knees didn't want to give even an inch.

Meanwhile, Axis breached Gauge's field of vision beyond the shields of his glasses.

No.

Way.

The opposite shore was only a few meters away.

With everything in Gauge, he pressed down and forced his knees to let him have this one race. Just this one. A dinner with Lexia and Axis. Please—

Lexia let out a cry of delight as Gauge slid into the embankment, soggy from so much snow.

Axis halted with entirely too much grace and stood over his opponent. Gauge tried to hold in a groan of agony, but it escaped, interrupting the silence. After which, the Prince held out his hand to the Count.

When Gauge accepted the offer, Axis easily pulled the Count onto his skates, saying, "Well done."

Acceptance.

It was all Gauge could ever ask for.

Lexia punched the air as Axis helped Gauge to his feet. The movement disrupted her balance, and the frozen lake traded places with the sky before her ass planted hard on the ice.

Male laughter erupted in a chorus from the opposite shore, and it was enough to make Lexia smile. She'd let her boys laugh at her.

For now.

It took more effort than Lexia wanted to admit getting back onto her feet. Practice. She needed practice to soar like Axis and Gauge. They glided toward her, muttering boyish banter to one another with stupid grins on their faces. It was wonderful to see Axis so happy, but even more so to see it in Gauge's presence.

This could work.

Lexia teased, "Are you boys done making fun of me?"

Gauge pressed a faint hand to his chest, saying, "Why, Ms. Tempest. Would I ever do such a thing?"

Axis winked at Lexia. "Never."

With all three of them together like this, Lexia had a difficult time keeping her mind off the way Gauge peered at Axis face with a warm smile. Or the way Axis returned it with more color in his cheeks. With sudden fantasies abound, lust made her blush, and Lexia knew she wouldn't sleep tonight.

She asked them both, "Will you teach me your technique?"

Axis and Gauge shared a look before both gentlemen took Lexia by her gloved hands and guided her across the ice. Axis gently instructed, "It's mostly in the legs."

Gauge added, "Try to keep your balance—There you go."

After a few good minutes of Lexia getting the knack, she feigned deficiency if only to stay between them longer. The three smiled at one another in the frozen vista with their close friends watching from shore. She glimpsed Bolt, Jan, Rhyme, and Dr. Tempest watching. Two of the four beamed, one glared through narrowed eyes, and the last...

Why was there so much trepidation on her father's face? It reminded Lexia of Lya's page in Gauge's dossier hidden in Leon's desk—

A gunshot sounded in the air, and Lexia's pulse quickened. "A duel."

Gauge breathed, "On the ice. Look!" He nodded toward a pair of skaters across the lake. People cleared the surrounding ice.

Axis muttered, "They're using swords," with perhaps too much excitement.

Lexia gasped as the duelists withdrew their rapiers and held them up to their faces. How could anyone learn to ice skate well enough in a day to perform in a life-or-death situation? She certainly wouldn't take that chance.

The crowd waited with bated breath as the fighters faced off with one another. Lexia touched a steam cannon on her hip, grateful for always coming prepared—

The first clang of metal against metal resonated through the wintry paradise. They met in a blade lock, seething at one another between the 'X' of their swords. Lexia could feel the tension in Axis as the two fighters demonstrated their strength. Gauge watched the whole fair with an affinity for the spectacle.

But Lexia wondered at the consequence. What could motivate a man to choose death if his opponent proved more skilled?

Speaking of...

One of the duelists pushed his opponent away with such force, it sent the skaters gliding backwards. Quick to regain the upper hand, the stronger man rushed in with a flurry of offensive attacks, barely parried by his weaker opponent. Unless the weaker one proved more agile, his fate was surely sealed.

Each clash awkwardly sent them back with opposing force. Accounting for that, the strong one kept coming back at a curve to take his weaker opponent by the side.

During one of these flourished maneuvers, the weaker opponent withdrew a small dagger and held it out. The stronger man wasn't skilled enough at ice skating to stop his velocity or correct his trajectory. He glided right onto the blade into his stomach.

Gauge winced, and Axis shook his head, muttering, "He's done for."

Lexia...

Well...

She glided toward the two men as the weaker one positioned his rapier for a final thrust. Lexia could hear Gauge and Axis soar after her, so she forced everything into her legs to move faster.

Please make it in time.

Please make it in time—

Lexia barreled into both duelists sending them all careening onto the ice. The stronger one painted the frozen lake in a crimson streak.

"Ms. Tempest!" the weaker one called in total confusion.

But Lexia was already checking the fallen adversary, asking, "Can you hear me? Are you with me?"

He groaned without a coherent response other than blinking in her face. This close, Lexia recognized the citrus farmer. He was the foreman who petitioned the union before the start of the Founding Season. His name was Kol, and he had three children.

"Please don't die."

"Lexia…"

Axis' concern left a waver in his voice from behind her. Gauge crouched and put his golden lenses level to her eyes. There was a wince in the motion, but he quirked a brow over the copper frames, asking a silent question.

What in the world was Lexia doing?

Funnily enough, Lexia didn't really have an answer to that question herself.

Except…

"No more."

Gauge looked taken aback, and Axis sounded more confused now than concerned. "What was that?"

Lexia said, "Get my father, and Count Snow, I hope you don't mind, but I'm about to change Winter's law on dueling."

"You're what?"

Lexia ignored the incredulity and the slight hint of fascination in Gauge's voice as she stood and addressed the crowd. She said, "No more! You can still duel in Winter, but only until one fighter draws first blood. There will be no more duels to the death."

Axis, halfway to Lexia's father, did a double-take and gaped at his fiance.

The winner of the duel went to his knees and peered up at Lexia, saying, "But this man slept with my wife."

The gathering crowd whispered and muttered.

"He has every right."

"Cuckolding a man is quite the offense."

"But is it worth the other man's life?"

Lexia shook her head. "No. Not every slight should result in a funeral. Think of the children left behind. I won't let this go on any longer."

People had more to say.

"What does Count Snow think?"

"Yes, Ms. Tempest. With all due respect, you can't change Winter's laws."

"What else do you think you can change?"

Lexia winced at the last. Surely more people supported the idea—

"I lost my husband to a duel." Mrs. Tenz glided up with her son beside her. She pulled him snug against her side as she said, "After the fifth Founding Day, I was made a widow over a misunderstanding and left to raise our son on my own. It's been hard work to garner benefits for his future without the help of another. I agree with Ms. Tempest."

More shouted in tandem.

"My daughter was shot over time off benefits."

"Every year without my son gets harder."

Lexia said, "Count Snow meant today's event to move on from mourning, not give it more cause. I petition to end duels to the death."

"As do I," Leon said on the approach as he walked across the ice to the bleeding man.

Next, Axis shouted, "I as well. What say you, Count Snow?"

Gauge stood and looked out at the crowd. Behind his glasses, his expression was unreadable. But the approving lilt at the corners of his full and soft mouth encouraged Lexia. He said, "Ms. Tempest is wise beyond years, far earning her title as Heiress to Winter's Diamond. Yes, let it be that from this day forward, duels end at first blood. Any duels which end in death will require investigation and possibly rehabilitation per Prince Axis' new reformation plans. This is a moment of maturation for Winter. We will learn from our past to make for a better future."

Bolt shouted, "Here, here!" And the crowd joined in jubilation.

Lexia caught Rhyme's eye across the ice. Even as a renowned duelist, he slow-clapped with an impressed grin. Jan beamed and nodded for Lexia. Everyone beamed at her, for that matter. But she wanted to do one thing more than anything.

Lexia skated over and embraced Mrs. Tenz.

For a better future.

"So, now that you've transformed my dueling laws, Ms. Tempest, would you and Prince Axis care to join me for dinner tonight?"

Axis blinked, baffled. Gauge moved on so fast from things. Lexia was right up to speed, also baffling her fiance.

She said, "We would love to."

Dr. Tempest interrupted, "Unfortunately, tonight is too sudden, Count Snow. Dinner is already in motion at the Manor, and we wouldn't want to waste food."

What was the expression on Leon's face? Axis had seen nothing like it. Was Lexia's father…afraid? Afraid of what—

"Quite right, Leon. So perhaps you can transport this feast to the Cathedral. I'll be expecting the food and my guests promptly at seven." Gauge's shaded stare settled on Leon and added gravity to his words.

Almost like a warning.

One Lexia had noticed, judging by her fervent glance in Axis' direction.

The Prince wasn't sure what was taking place, but it felt momentous. As if Gauge had poised Leon's answer on some brink.

Dr. Tempest gave in. "Very well." And he didn't look happy about it. There was a frown on his face Axis had only seen on rare occasions, mostly when Valve openly berated Axis at the conference table. Or anytime someone mentioned Lya's death.

Not the tributes or the memorials. No, Leon beamed at those. But if anyone asked the good doctor about the illness which had taken Mrs. Tempest from Winter, he shut down.

Like he was doing right now.

Lexia threw her arms around her father's neck and squeezed, melting the expression away. "Thank you."

Axis felt a pang in his chest. Twofold, even. Valve had been a bastard, devoid of any emotion other than the sinful variety, deriving pleasure from Axis' pain. There were no hugs in his household. The second pang came from his father's insistence that Axis himself would not make for a good father.

Would Axis hug freely? Or would he snap at his child for all the same excuses Valve found to beat his son—

Gauge likewise looked away from the paternal embrace in front of them. By chance, he met Axis' eyes through those golden lenses. For a moment, an understanding passed between them.

Apparently hugs were infrequent in household Snow, but the two men could be happy for Lexia.

Before father and daughter parted, Lexia whispered something to Leon which Axis couldn't hear. The man recoiled and searched her eyes. Louder, Lexia said, "If I am to inherit Tempest crops, I need to stand among giants on my own."

A flicker of pride flashed in Dr. Tempest's gray eyes, and he kissed her forehead in response.

Gauge said, "So, I take it you won't be joining us, doctor."

"It seems I will not." Leon didn't sound entirely enthused. It dampened an otherwise perfect day. "Besides, I'll need to tend these injuries at the infirmary." There was an implied, 'thanks to you.'

Axis frowned. He'd never noticed so much tension between Gauge and Leon before today. But Axis supposed their equal contention with Valve had acted as a buffer.

Without the old Factory Master?

Glares and frowns all around.

Leon broke the tension with a tired sigh and helped the wounded duelist onto a stretcher. He said, "We'll get him all patched up. Kol will survive."

Lexia beamed.

Axis tucked her against his side and kissed her wavy hair. She'd been amazing today.

Commotion transpired in the corner of Axis' eye. It was a slight, a falter, a small thing—But suddenly Gauge was leaning against Jan. It was only noticeable because the butler stood on the ice in loafers a good six-inches shorter than his ward.

Gauge said, "If you'll excuse us, we'll prepare the Cathedral for your arrival. Is two hours enough time to transfer dinner from the Manor, Dr. Tempest?"

Leon humphed in the affirmative, keeping his focus on his patient. When they headed for the shore, the old doctor said, "Come along, you two lovebirds. You're still my responsibility for the next two hours."

After parting nods, they followed to shore, excited for where the evening would take them.

The kitchens smelled of rotisserie meat and honeyed carrots which Axis had insisted on cooking himself. He would not let servants wait on him hand and foot.

"Love, why are you pushing the cooks out of the kitchen?" Lexia asked it teasingly, but Axis feared the direction of the conversation.

He turned away from where she was leaning across the butcher block counters. Instead, he focused on cooking at the Flicker steel stove, saying, "I think since Gauge approved our engagement, we should talk about the lifestyle we want. Namely, self-serviced or waited on by servants."

Lexia's natural kindness warmed the sweetness of her voice. "If you're adamant about it, we won't have servants, but I want you to consider how many people will go without beneficial labor positions if we choose to go that route."

Axis turned and blinked at her. "What do you mean?"

Again, she sounded patient with him. "Well, if we don't have servants, that's at least fifteen people without jobs which give them benefits such as living in our home with all the luxuries that come with it. Tempest Manor employs over a hundred people if you include the gardens. They all live in nice cottages on our land, close to their employers, and accumulate plenty of time off and free admittance into father's university for them and their children. We survey them anonymously regarding their happiness here and what increases they'd like to see. They complain about father and I eating in the kitchens more than anything else, which is why I'm here now. Sami wanted to finish packing up for the Copper Cathedral before her date with Rhyme, but she can't do that if you're here in her way."

Axis had never thought cooking for himself would get in someone's way. He said, "Well, I'll be damned if I impede on Rhyme's date."

Lexia grinned. "We'll poll around and see if anyone wants to work in our future home wherever that should be. If it seems unfavorable to the people, then I can certainly take after you and learn to look after myself." She leaned across the counter poised for a kiss. Eyes closed and everything.

Axis leaned across the countertop, his mouth a breath away from hers. She smelled so fresh and bright, like days gone by. Days Winter would never see again.

"You know I'm right, boy. Lexia...She would make a wonderful wife and mother, but you..."

Cigar smoke.

A noxious cough.

Words from the grave.

A haunting of malignant ghosts speaking half-truths. But even if they were only half, they were still the truth nonetheless.

Axis kissed Lexia and stole her breath away. The thief that he was... Or worse.

Perhaps Axis knew Valve was right all along.

Gauge stepped out of the shower after treating his exhausted bones to a long soak in the tub. Revived, he dressed in a black silk button-down and black leather pants. Black lenses set in copper frames protected his sore eyes. He added one golden cuff to his bicep for Lexia, and one burgundy one to his wrist for Axis. Gauge meant to symbolize the beginning of their business partnership, but also, hopefully, the start of a friendship.

Skating on the ice with the two of them this afternoon had meant the world to Gauge. More than they could know, but he suspected they'd sensed it, too. Hence the dinner.

Leon had told the truth. Tempest Manor had prepared a feast for this evening, and Gauge was happy to steal it out from under the old man. Leon had sided with Valve over Tija and had encouraged Axis and Lexia's relationship in a gambit to diminish Gauge's influence in the triumvirate.

So, now let the good doctor spend the night toiling over the secrets Gauge might feel compelled to spill to the young Ms. Tempest. Lexia deserved to know the truth, after all. But as much as Gauge enjoyed taunting Leon, he would never endanger the balance of power by exposing the man's most guarded truth.

Winter's Diamond…

"Little Snow, you've done well for yourself. Founding Winter, establishing a society, and supporting it with everything I know that ails you."

"Don't worry, Mrs. Tempest. No one can hurt me now."

"No one, indeed."

Lya had possessed a way with words. So acute and succinct. And she was right. Gauge was untouchable in all the best and the worst ways.

It made him think of Tija and how Gauge had wished she'd seen him win the race today. There was plenty of gossip about the whole affair to make it to sector ten. Some even contemplated the nature of the relationship between the Heiress, the Prince, and the Count. Some of their theories bordered on scandalous, yet amused Gauge all the same.

If the mighty triumvirate graduated into a power throuple—Well, that would suit Gauge just fine.

With that amusing thought, Gauge tucked his hands into his pockets and smirked the entire way downstairs to the foyer. The butler waited at the bottom, smiling.

Gauge teased, "Why Jan, if I didn't know any better, I'd say you were in high spirits. I wonder if it has to do with a certain young lady in our presence tonight."

Jan didn't hide his growing fondness for Lexia. He said, "I've prepared everything to the last detail, sir, including a dinner plate already served and set aside for your testing."

"Splendid. I don't want anyone to notice the particulars." Gauge would test it out of sight before sitting down to eat in front of his guests. He couldn't keep the excitement from his voice when he asked, "Are they on their way?"

The old spy gave a deep nod with a sparkle in his warm brown eyes. He said, "They're walking here *without* their chaperons."

How controversial.

"Send them to the conservatory when they arrive, would you? I feel a melody coming on."

"Very good, sir."

Gauge went to the piano in the glass atrium and settled his gloved fingers on the keys. He considered, if only for a moment, taking off a glove and feeling the gloss of the keys beneath. Instead, he gave himself over to a minuet. A bright tune filled with promise, like the evening ahead of him.

It wasn't until Gauge's second coda that he'd sensed his guests in the room with him. Jan knew better than to interrupt his music with announcements. It was a small gasp of delight which had alerted Gauge to their presence.

He stopped on a chord and looked over at Lexia and Axis. They wore the same clothes as earlier in the day, but Axis added a burgundy tie and brown waistcoat for good measure. Nothing on Lexia needed changing. Her hands were together and pressed against her lips to stifle the obvious joy glittering in her eyes. And Axis...

What could Gauge say?

The Prince always looked impressed when the Count danced with the ivories. Only this time he didn't hide it. Axis said, "Well done, Count Snow."

"Yes! Can you pass along the music?" Lexia beamed. "My students would love it."

Ah. So the rumors of the Heiress' virtues were all true. First and only to Axis and a saint for teaching children to play instruments. How infatuating.

Gauge said, "Of course. Anything for you, Ms. Tempest."

Prior to the last few days, that one-liner would've sent Axis' magnificent jaw to clench. But here they were…smiling at each other from across the room.

Power throuple, eh?

Jan interrupted the moment. "Dinner is ready, sir."

"Thank you, Jan." Gauge lowered the fallboard over the keys and stood with a flourishing gesture. "Shall we?" He held out the crook of an elbow to Ms. Tempest. And for good measure, the other one to Axis.

Why not?

Wonderfully, perfectly, they both accepted, and the power throuple glided across the foyer and into the dining room. Once inside the long room, Lexia pointed at the stained glass centered in the bowed window with a cry. "It's a butterfly!"

Gauge grinned at her even while he kept the painful memory the window represented to himself. There was no need to spoil the evening. Instead, he said, "You two sit down. I have one last item to attend to."

Axis pulled out Lexia's chair for her as Gauge rounded the corner to where Jan held his covered tray. While he quickly tested it with his tubes and vials, he listened to the couple admiring his home.

"It's all going well, isn't it, Jan?"

"So it is, sir."

Gauge smiled and said, "Try to contain your excitement, old friend. I don't see them moving in anytime soon."

"One can always hope."

The old spy's candidness almost made Gauge bark out a laugh. He clapped Jan on the shoulder before returning to the dining room. Understanding his ward perfectly, the butler followed with no opportunity for him to switch the trays. Other servants proceeded to lay out the feast for Lexia and Axis.

While they watched their food arrive and politely set about eating, Gauge wondered what it must be like to taste without the metallic tang of a test kit in their food and drinks. For them to feel the details engraved into the copperware sans overstimulation.

"Gauge?"

Gauge blinked and met Axis' soft green eyes. "Hm? Forgive me. I must've drifted off."

Lexia's voice held a hint of—mischief? naughtiness?—as she asked, "Are we not stimulating enough for you?"

Oh, the fire this girl was playing with…

Gauge said, "You're both plenty stimulating for me." He shot her a wink. "Now, tell me what I've missed."

Axis sounded as if he wanted to roll his eyes. "It's about Ms. Cloud. I wish to revoke her exile and have her return to my factories, if you deem it so." The last came out as a bit of a challenge, but in the best way.

Stimulating, indeed.

"Well, *Master* Flicker, your wish is mine to fulfill." When Axis' clenched his jaw in that famous expression, Gauge leaned toward him across the table. Akin to his name, something flickered in Axis' eyes.

Curiosity.

Gauge stared a long while before asking, "Are there any other wishes you would make of me tonight?"

Lexia choked into her drink, disrupting the moment in the cutest possible way. She smiled bashfully. "Don't mind me. Please. Do go on."

Both men laughed at the hope on her face until Axis said, "As it were, I do have something in mind."

Lexia and Gauge peered over at him, both holding their breath.

Axis' smirk said he knew exactly what was on their minds and took great pleasure in disappointing them. "Sector twelve. Let's discuss some of Lexia's ideas on the location of the factories and the farms."

Lexia eagerly told Gauge about her recommended updates to sector twelve's designs, and he readily agreed.

"Of course, we should move the farms to the northern, eastern, and western points. We'll isolate the mines and the factories to the south. I'll have to reroute some transportation, obviously, but it will keep the pollution off the crops. Why hadn't I thought of that, Jan?"

Without hesitation, Jan said, "Because Ms. Tempest is brilliant."

While Gauge and Axis beamed at her, Lexia hopped from the table and hugged the old butler, completely unaware of what kind of man she held in her arms. He blushed and deigned to squeeze back, because who could ever resist her?

Gauge peered over his glasses at the people in the room. He held up his pre-tested drink. "To Ms. Tempest for bringing us together tonight."

"Here, here," Axis said as he held up his glass.

Lexia blushed as she sat back at her place and held up her drink. "To a new beginning."

Gauge and Axis echoed her, "To a new beginning."

They ate, they talked, and they made plans for more. It was a wonderful evening, but by the time Gauge let them out the copper Wall of Pain, his body ached for rest. Axis freely shook Gauge's gloved hand, and Lexia winked at him on the way out the door. So much promise awaited them, and he couldn't remember the last time he'd smiled so much. Jan had even said so as he brought Gauge a cane to make it up all those stairs.

He'd barely stripped out of his clothes before a knock sounded at the door. "Come in, Jan."

The butler entered, saying, "Sir, a message for you. It's from Ms. Cloud."

Tija.

Jan dismissed himself as Gauge read it.

Dearest Count,

Please be careful with that heart of yours.

Always yours truly,

Tija Cloud.

So, Tija had heard the gossip already, and she knew Gauge well enough to warn him off. It's too bad he didn't know the meaning of the word 'careful.'

 TWELVE

Turbulent Mercury

Impossibly soft hands held Lexia down while rougher ones covered her mouth from screaming in ecstasy—

Lexia opened her eyes and blinked at her bedroom ceiling. What in the world was happening to her? Had she lost all sense and reason?

"Axis is the man you go to when you want to make love. I'm the man you go to when you want to break the headboard."

But what if Lexia could have both?

All the gossip about the triumvirate must've gotten to her head. If Lexia wasn't dreaming about Axis and Gauge, she was dreaming memories of forgotten arguments between her parents. Awful ones.

Father had once told Lexia the old electronic technology couldn't save Lya from the end. That the electromagnetic pulse didn't cause her disease. But Lexia had so many questions still left unanswered, including but not limited to questions about the disease and why her parents had never discussed it with Lexia.

Afflicted with insomnia, she walked over to her desk and sat down at her sketches.

The wedding dress.

Lexia and the seamstresses would work all day today on fabric for the gown, holsters for her cannons, and materials for the wings.

Lexia was glad Axis would reconsider the self-sufficient lifestyle. It was a privilege to live with servants, but it was a symbiotic relationship. Servants who worked in a triumvirate household were also privileged to do so, and without those opportunities, Lexia would lose contact with certain labor divisions in Winter.

With a sigh, Lexia rested an elbow on the table and plunged her hand into her wavy hair. She set about coloring. This should distract her from Gauge's touch, Axis' thoroughness, her father's suspicious behavior, and the file on Lya in the Count's dossier.

Shade here. Gold there. A sweetheart neckline on a corset-tied bodice with a full skirt.

Slits? Or no slits? With them, Lexia could still fight should a duel arise, but with the stakes lowered by her own decree, she felt less threatened by the notion.

Mother would have an opinion. She would make suggestions, attend the fittings, and tell Lexia how much the gown became her. Maybe Lya would do Lexia's hair for the ceremony. Most of it left down and wavy aside from two fluffy braids pulled back from her face.

"Mommy, why do you like to braid my hair so much?"

"Because it's home, Lexia. You are my home."

A tear fell on the sketches, and Lexia set them aside for their protection. What passed for sunlight in Winter breached through the windows, and she gathered a robe around her before walking outside on the balcony. Right now, she wanted nothing more than to sneak into Axis' bed and hold him close. To listen to him breathe in his sleep against her—

Did Gauge sleep alone—

Lexia scrunched her hands in her hair and squeezed her eyes shut. All these intrusive, conflicting thoughts bouncing about her mind was giving Lexia a headache.

Caffeine.

She left the chill dawn air to dress for a cup of morning tea. Leggings and another of Axis' stolen sweaters was enough for today…No, wait. She belted the sweater in black leather and a chunky buckle.

There.

Lexia opened the door onto the fifth floor landing and peered down at Axis' door on the second floor. Rhyme slept in a chair outside of it to guard the pre-marital laws. They need not worry. She wouldn't disrupt Gauge's engagement requirements further.

The kitchen staff busied themselves with breakfast as Lexia tried not to disrupt their workflow. She took her tea to the music room and curled up on the window seat, staring out at the gardens dressed in white. The frost-kissed window felt cold to the touch, and Lexia hugged her teacup closer. The aroma of bergamot and lemon had revived her.

Caffeine made everything better.

Axis would wake soon. Her fiance was an early riser. He'd start with push-ups, then sit-ups, and if he were at his apartments, he'd use a bar he'd installed for pull-ups. She'd never seen his routine in person, but he'd tried to encourage her to do the same.

As if.

Aside from this bout of insomnia, Lexia enjoyed her lazy sleep-in mornings. But maybe, when they lived together, he could convert her.

Speaking of conversion…

Was it Lexia's imagination or was Gauge the cure to Axis' public phobia?

By Axis' own admission, he couldn't propose to Lexia until he saw her dancing with Gauge. Ever since then, Axis hadn't minded getting closer and closer to her in public. There's also the ice skating. Despite all the gossip caused by the trio's fun, Axis had held Lexia through the entire lesson.

What she wouldn't give to bottle this magic for Axis' sake. It could only mean more exposure to the Count would improve the Prince's phobia. And how could Lexia not benefit from that?

Still…

Lexia needed to find the connection between her mother and Gauge before she could fully trust the Count. Did they share a secret?

Lexia glimpsed the trademark blue freckles in the window's frosty reflection and wondered at it. Unable to bear it any longer, she quit the music room to pilfer her father's study. She would sort this out—

Locked.

Lexia frowned and tried the door handle again. No, it was definitely locked. She knocked on the door. It was too well-made to hear anything beyond, but eventually Dr. Tempest answered it.

He said, "Good morning, my dear," and kissed her forehead. "You're up early." Tears glistened in his eyes. The last time he'd looked this way was when he broke the news of Lya's death.

"So are you." Lexia could barely conceal the concern in her voice as she asked, "Is something wrong?"

Leon moved out of the door in such a way to close it immediately behind him. "No, darling. Let's see what the cooks are preparing for breakfast. I smell cinnamon, and we both know how much I love that."

Lexia frowned at him but took the arm he offered. What else could she do?

Axis came down the stairs right on time and smiled. "Good morning."

Leon almost cut him off to say, "Axis, if you don't mind, there's a matter I wish to discuss with you after breakfast." There was a touch of urgency to his voice.

Axis peered between Lexia and Leon. "Of course. Is there anything wrong?"

But Dr. Tempest gave the same answer as he'd given Lexia. "Not at all. Just some matters to go over for your father's affairs."

Oh.

Perhaps that's why Leon looked so distressed. On Axis' behalf.

Her fiancé's face fell at the unfortunate reminder, but he soldiered on. "After breakfast then."

Lexia wouldn't have Axis' good mood ruined. She took his arm and kissed his cheek. "C'mon, gentlemen. We have a vast world ahead of us, and we shouldn't face it on an empty stomach."

Leon and Axis both smiled down at Lexia, completely oblivious to her growing list of concerns.

Something was bothering Lexia and Leon, and Axis didn't believe it was all to do with his father's affairs. A tension strained between the Tempests at breakfast, and Axis recognized it as Lexia's trademark. She had questions that needed answering, and the person she needed the answers from—Leon, in this case—wasn't providing them to her. She'd been the same way about Lya's death for months after.

Axis hoped they resolved it soon, and perhaps he could help during his post-breakfast one-on-one with Leon.

Bolt arrived toward the end of the meal, saying, "My apologies to all. I'm not quite the early riser as our Prince, here."

"Have a seat and eat your fill." Leon gestured at Axis. "Your ward and I have some business to attend to, and then he's all yours for the day."

Lexia stared without a word at her uneaten cinnamon roll and fresh juice, dejected.

Yes, Axis would help. There was no way he would let Lexia plan her dress today with a frown on her face. Not if he could help it.

Axis stood, asking, "Ms. Tempest, will you join me on the veranda for a moment?"

She blinked in surprise at his request but politely excused herself from the table. Leon and Bolt watched the couple walk out onto the terrace with warm smiles on their faces. Another lovebirds moment. Little did they know...

"What is it you want me to get out of your father? Because I will do anything to ease your troubles."

A little smile lilted the corners of Lexia's lips. "Is the friction that obvious?"

Axis winced and said, "Painfully so."

Lexia sighed and leaned on the cleared balustrade, peering out over the snowy landscape. She said, "I think father is hiding something about mother from me."

This again.

Axis placed his hands on her shoulders and kissed her freckled temple, promising, "I'll do what I can."

"Thank you." Lexia turned in his arms and squeezed him.

Axis muttered, "I knew you'd get that sweater somehow. I picked it out with you in mind."

Leon's study was a warm familiar place, but likewise a place of punishment. Whenever the kids had pulled a prank too astronomical to ignore, the adults would place them in this wooden room filled with leather tomes until they grew bored and fell asleep.

Punishments in Tempest Manor were welcomed compared to the ones in the Flicker household. At least here, the only smell Axis had to stomach was musty books rather than burnt flesh and cigar smoke.

The good doctor stood at his desk chair and gestured for Axis to take a seat across from him. When Axis did, Leon sat and said, "I know this is a difficult time for you, but there are some things I think we should discuss. For instance, how will Ms. Cloud play into unionizing the factories?"

Work.

How many days had Axis gone without thinking of work? The Tempests had been very generous providing him a space to heal, but Leon was right. It was time to jump back into things. Valve's disruptive legacy wouldn't resolve itself.

Axis laced his fingers together over the desktop and leaned forward to say, "I discovered Ms. Cloud was a double agent in our operation. She part-timed for Snow. Admittedly, this should upset me, but she'd acted so well as a liaison between us that her absence hasn't gone unnoticed. I would like to reinstate her officially in that capacity. As all three of our industries transition into this union model, I think she'd make for the perfect advocate between leadership and labor."

Leon hiked up a pants leg to lay one ankle out over his knee as he pondered. After a moment, he said, "So she will work with Phoro on the Flicker wick's line and Mrs. Tenz's jurisdiction in the mines. I suppose I could employ her over the orchard union with Kol where Lexia had recently agreed to let them unionize. It should mesh out seamlessly."

There was something wrong with Dr. Tempest. Axis wasn't certain of it when they first walked in the room, but the man's eyes kept sliding away for brief periods toward...

Axis turned and looked over his shoulder. It was a covered portrait, and he knew who was behind it. Axis asked, "Sir, if you don't mind me prying, what has you in such a state?"

The smile Leon gave Axis was not happy. There was so much sadness and even…fear…in his eyes. He said, "Truth be told, I am perturbed by the progression of your relationship with Gauge Snow."

That took Axis aback, and he frowned at his mentor. Truly, a man Axis considered a father figure. "Please confide in me what troubles you so. Does it have anything to do with what's bothering Lexia?"

"My daughter is so intelligent and capable, but she doesn't always think of the consequences ahead of her actions. Consider Winter's dueling law, for example. It needs refinement, of course, but to revise it completely in one beautiful act is reckless. Yes, that's how I'd describe Lexia. Especially of late."

Axis wouldn't go as far as calling Lexia reckless, but here lately she seemed more…alive than usual. He said, "I think it's only in Lexia's nature as she gets a feel for stepping into your shoes. She'll make mistakes, but I know she'll also work to rectify them."

Leon stared at the covered portrait and let out a heavy sigh. "She is so much like her mother."

It had been said, but something about the way Leon sighed with it and the shadow over his gray eyes raised the hair on Axis' arms. "Is there something wrong with Lexia?"

The doctor met the Prince's eyes and asked, "Son, what do you know of Lya's death?"

Again, Axis recoiled, straightening in his chair. "Nothing, sir. I was shocked to hear the news. She never seemed ill, but I know there are plenty of ailments which strike the healthy to the quick. I always figured it was like that."

"Axis, what I am about to tell you can never leave this room. Do you understand? Lexia can never know the truth."

"Axis, you never have to go home again. Not if you don't want to. You can stay here with us, and I'll protect you."

"Thank you, Mrs. Tempest, but I'm old enough to stand up to him now."

"I'll be here for you if you need me."

After the shock wore off, Axis swallowed and nodded his head.

Dearest Count,

I am not saddened by the news of Master Flicker's passing, only mournful of what I understand it has done to the People's Prince. I hope he recovers soon.

Of course, I will return to the capital and resume my role as soon as I conclude my business here in sector ten.

We should meet to celebrate. I long to hear of your adventures from your lips... among other things.

Yours forever and always,

Tija Cloud.

Gauge couldn't help but smile at the blue missive. Tija was a spectacular friend, and he looked forward to having her close again.

That being said, Gauge was distracted with news from Tempest Manor today. Word was the doctor looked troubled this morning, and

Ms. Tempest seemed equally preoccupied despite a day of happy plans ahead of her. Someone with her sense of fashion would surely enjoy designing a wedding dress. So why all the long faces?

Gauge straightened in the tufted leather chair and stared across the vault at the slots labeled, 'Tempest.' Would Leon do it? Would he finally confess his sins and negate all the material Gauge held over him? Perhaps it was time to free the truth.

What would Lexia think?

Of Gauge?

Of Leon?

Gauge relaxed back into the chair and took another sip of his crystal tumbler. He feared the truth from Dr. Tempest's mouth, because any narrative he'd weave would paint him as some victim and Gauge as a villain—As one does.

"Leon won't understand."

"Mrs. Tempest, I worry you're not thinking clearly."

"The next inferior man to say that to me will come to understand how hard a diamond can be."

So many secrets…

On the brink of Founding Day and the promise of a new city, would everything fall through Gauge's gloved fingers like sand?

Lexia's carefree smile.

Axis' understated strength.

Gauge brought his drink with him as he exited the vault—

"Sir." Jan waited down the spiral stairs in the library with a grave expression.

Gauge couldn't keep the concern from his voice as he asked, "What's wrong?"

The butler said, "Prince Axis is here, and he's upset. He demands to speak with you. Alone."

No.

Leon, you rat.

Gauge hurried down the stairs and into the conservatory where Axis stood with a hand on his hip, staring out the windows. Gauge asked, "How can I help you—"

"Don't. I don't want your games today." The ice in Axis' voice brought Gauge to a halt.

What could he say to absolve himself? To bring things back to yesterday?

When Axis turned and faced Gauge, the soft green of his eyes had hardened into shards of emeralds, dark with anger. He asked, "Is it true?"

Gauge had to ask, "How much has Leon told you? Has he told anyone else?" Namely, Lexia.

Axis took this as confirmation and clenched his jaw, looking away in disgust. "How fucking could you?"

This was cause to frown. What exactly had the doctor put in the Prince's head? Gauge took a step toward Axis, beseeching, "I'm not sure what Dr. Tempest said, but I've done nothing worth your personal ire—"

"Lexia."

Her name hung between them as Axis' rage began to make sense. The Prince accused, "You've lied to her face and still claimed to be her friend."

Gauge wanted to argue semantics. Since the night of the Founding Ball, he'd decided he would tell Lexia the truth should she ask him directly. But the situation had yet to arise. So, *technically*, Gauge had never lied to her face, but Axis was in no mood to split hairs. Clearly.

Salvage.

Gauge *needed* to salvage this. He wanted their friendship so badly. "Please, give me the benefit of the doubt. You don't understand my position in this conspiracy."

"But you admit to having one?" Axis asked.

Yes, clearly in no mood.

This was it.

Gauge had failed. Again. "There is nothing I can say. It's obvious you've made up your mind about me, and no matter—" Gauge's voice failed him momentarily, on the brink of tears. "No matter how many ways I try, you can only see me as a monster. That's fine, I suppose. But what about Lexia?" Could Gauge afford to lose her, too?

Axis clicked his tongue in disgust before letting his breath out in an aggravated sigh. He said, "I can't believe you. What do you think? That I would keep this secret from her a moment longer? Because that would only further prove your self-delusion. I only wanted confirmation from you before I brought her all the facts."

Oh, to be the bearer of that news.

"How will you break it to Lexia? You speak of delusions. Consider the life she's led, built entirely on secrets and lies. Do you think she'll thank you?" This was exactly why Gauge hadn't wanted to be the one.

A sliver of doubt thawed some of the frost in Axis' resolve. He said, "Lexia deserves to know the truth."

Gauge swallowed hard and dared to nod along. "You're absolutely right, but you know what they say about the truth. You tell her; you hurt her. I wish you luck in delivering the news, and I'll await your return."

Axis' eyes narrowed a touch as he asked, "Why?"

"Because once you break her heart, you'll need ideas on how to mend it. For that, I'll be waiting."

Lexia and her seamstresses pinned fabric to a dress form and compared the textures of certain materials. Some were matte and drank all the light. Others were glittery and refracting.

Which did Lexia prefer?

One woman said, "You would look beautiful in any of these, Ms. Tempest."

The other added, "It's really up to your preference. What sort of statement are you looking to make? Radiant like a diamond? Silky like a black pearl? Or perhaps the young mistress would like something with more danger to it?" She pointed to the darkest matte fabric.

It was too bad Lexia couldn't focus on much. Even though her father had said the discussion with Axis would wrap up some of Valve's affairs, Lexia didn't like the way Axis had stormed out of the Manor. He still hadn't come back, yet.

And Leon?

Well, he'd locked himself in his study again, and Lexia couldn't feel more worried.

Oh, no.

What if Axis had discovered Gauge's complicity in Valve's death?

No, surely Leon would've been more public about the announcement.

"Mistress, are you all right?"

Lexia sank in a chair, propped her chin in her hands, and sighed. "My heart's not really in it today, ladies. I'm sorry."

They glanced at one another before sitting down beside her. One smoothed a hand over Lexia's back, and it was such a maternal gesture that it almost brought tears to her eyes.

The seamstress said, "That's fine, Ms. Tempest. We have plenty of time to reschedule."

But the longer Lexia waited, the less time her people had to prepare, and that simply wasn't fair to them. She pointed at a fabric and said, "That's it. That's the one."

The ladies perked up and beamed. One said, "It's a fine choice, mistress."

The other one tugged for Lexia to stand. "Now, come on. Let's measure and drape. Are you still thinking slits in the skirt?"

Lexia nodded and let them pull her onto the fitting platform. "I don't want the gown to hinder any movement."

"We understand. And there's nothing wrong with a little...slink."

The women snickered at one another, eliciting a smile from Lexia.

One said, "It will complement the bodice; although, I fear your father won't approve of the design."

Right now, Lexia wasn't sure she cared, but dared not voice it. "I want this for Axis."

"Yes, mistress." That would be the last she heard about her father's opinion on the gown.

The other said, "As for the wings…"

The fitting carried on for hours until Lexia—exhausted from falsifying her enthusiasm—stumbled off the platform.

"Ms. Tempest! Are you all right?"

She waved them off gently. "Yes. Yes. I'm fine, ladies. Forgive me. I only ask for a minute alone."

This was not like Lexia, and the look the seamstresses exchanged reflected that. But Lexia simply could *not* carry on this way a minute longer, and she hated her mood had affected such a joyous occasion at all.

They left Lexia alone in the sewing room, drifting in her thoughts. She trailed her fingers along various fabrics, rugs, and beads—

"Ouch!"

Lexia brought her finger to her lips and sucked on it. An errant pin had left a small bead of blood on the tip. Yellow blood… same as her mother's. Blue freckles. And a scent like summer rain.

Winter's Diamond Heiress.

Lexia stared out the window while Lya brushed her daughter's hair. "Mother, why are we different from other people?"

"What do you mean, dear?" Lya asked in a way which sounded as if she already knew the answer, but she wanted Lexia to articulate it.

The curious child said, "Axis, Gauge, and father bleed red. So do the cooks when they make a mistake in the kitchen. And no one else I've met has blue freckles. They're always brown on others. So, why are we different?"

Lya stopped brushing and turned Lexia round to face her. "It's true. We are blessed with special features, but does it matter? The other people accept us and never question our differences. Plus, you know what I think?"

"What?"

Lya's smile broadened into a mischievous grin. "I think Gauge and Axis like your freckles."

"Mommy!"

Lexia blushed yellow now as she'd done then, but she understood the situation from an adult's perspective. One Lya had avoided. She and Lexia were accepted because of privilege. Pretty privilege and station. They were exotic gems in Winter's frozen wasteland, and no doubt Gauge encouraged Lexia's marriage to perpetuate her genetics. She couldn't remember ever being sick or breaking a bone. Not even a finger or a chipped tooth. Not so much as a cold.

Could that have something to do with the secret between Diamond and Snow?

Lexia peered in a mirror, her wedding gown half-formed around her. She slipped some of it off and pulled the rest over her head. Next, went the shift, all while staring into the mirror.

White hair.

Black eyes.

White skin.

Blue freckles.

Yellow blood.

Never sick.

No broken bones.

What could it all mean—

"Lexia, I have to speak with you—"

Axis stopped halfway through the door and stared at Lexia in her lingerie. Hand-sewn, it was blue lace.

Yes.

Snow blue.

Lexia crossed her arms over her breasts, feeling vulnerable and exposed—Caught in a moment of introspection and the deepest confusion.

Axis sensed her discomfort and asked, "Would you like me to wait outside?"

"No! No. Please, come in." She could use the presence of someone she trusted. "I don't think I should be alone right now."

Axis stepped into the room and closed the door behind him. He maintained a respectable distance, looking both concerned and upset.

Unable to stand it any longer, Lexia rushed across the room and threw her arms around his neck. Her words came out muffled against his shoulders. "Oh, Axis! I don't know what's wrong with me, but I'm scared."

Scared of the intrusive thoughts.

Scared they might hold some merit.

And scared everyone in Lexia's life knew why but her.

Axis' heart broke. He'd never heard Lexia admit to fearing anything. Not even a future without her mother. She took everything in stride and reined life around her whims. Fearless. Maybe even reckless. It's part of why he loved her.

Truly, Lexia trembled as Axis embraced her. He wanted to tell her it would be all right. That they could face anything together. But as the sentiments formed, the weighty truth banished them away.

It would not be all right, and this crisis Lexia would certainly face on her own.

"How will you break it to Lexia? You speak of delusions. Consider the life she's led, built entirely on secrets and lies. Do you think she'll thank you?"

Axis winced as the love of his life held onto him for a strength he couldn't give. She would need it, too, to cope with the reality from which he couldn't protect her. Except...

"You tell her; you hurt her."

Damn Gauge.

Damn Leon.

Axis would do this for Lexia. When he opened his mouth to tell her, it dried up, and his throat squeezed closed. He wet his lips, cleared his throat, and tried again. "Lexia?"

She inhaled and said, "Do you know you smell like polished leather and steel? Simply breathing you in brings me comfort."

There was the dry mouth and tight throat again. Axis clenched his jaw and gently took Lexia by the biceps. He parted them enough to meet her eyes. Tears glistened against the black irises, and as he watched, one brimmed her lashes.

Axis caught it before it spilled down her cheek. Almost as tall as he, Lexia had never looked so small. Not since her mother's funeral. He said, "I have to tell you something."

Lexia blinked up at him rapidly enough to lose a few more tears, and Axis wanted to kill Leon and Gauge. This wouldn't only test the couple's relationship. It would test Axis' resolve.

Tell Lexia the truth and shatter her existence.

Or carry on with the deception and keep her safe.

Axis brushed his fingertips along the blue freckles on her temples, and when Lexia leaned into his hand with her eyes closed, soaking in the comfort, Axis knew.

He couldn't do it.

An entire life poised on a delicate balance of deceit and privilege. The privilege of not knowing the truth, and the deceit of never having the chance to decide for herself if she wanted to know it.

And now Axis was another bearer of this unhappy burden.

"Lexia, I'm moving back to my apartments, and I think we should reconsider some aspects of our engagement."

When she opened her eyes, Axis could see her heart fracture within them.

Lexia stepped back and covered herself again, claiming a stray piece of fabric. She asked, "What do you mean? Why?" She sounded so fragile, on the verge of breaking.

Axis would break Lexia this way to keep from breaking her in a way which wouldn't mend. He swallowed hard to keep from choking on his next words, but eventually got them out. "I am unfit as your partner. More to the point, your father has enlightened me of some health matters which make me unfit as a father. And I would never ask you to accept a life without children—"

"We can adopt."

Axis blinked at Lexia.

She took a step toward him, hopeful as she repeated. "Orphans aren't common anymore, but there are still plenty of children in need of parents. We can adopt."

Could Axis love Lexia more? It only made this harder. He balled his hands into fists and said, "Forgive me if I find this difficult to move beyond. I ask for a few days to think on it."

Tears rolled down Lexia's cheek, and yet she broke into a warm smile. "Of course. Yes. Please give the idea some thought. I could go forever without children, but please don't ask me to go a lifetime without you."

The first of many tears fell on Axis' cheek, and he clenched his jaw to stifle a sob. Unable to say anything further, he gave a curt nod and left the only woman he'd ever loved raw and naked—in every sense of the word—alone in the room to cope on her own.

Rank bastard that he was.

Axis stomped up the stairs, stone faced, holding it all in until he reached his room on the second floor. There, he sat down on the bed, stiff as a board, and stared at the far wall.

One hot tear.

Then another.

Frustration and anguish forced their way through Axis' clenched teeth in an animal sound he would never admit to making. He picked up a pillow and screamed into it.

This was too much.

It was all too much—

A knock sounded.

Oh, what more could fate ask of Axis this day?

Bolt's voice came through the door. "Sir, I just heard the news."

How fast it traveled.

Axis' valet continued, "Will we be leaving then?"

Air.

Axis needed some space and air. Miserable, he opened the door and asked, "Bolt, would you mind doing me a favor?"

"Why, of course, Prince Flicker."

It took a hard swallow and licking his lips for Axis to ask, "Would you please pack my bags for me? I'll walk back to the apartments and meet you there."

Bolt's eyes widened. Never had Axis asked him to perform any task other than driving, and that's because Axis had yet to learn how. Bolt said, "Absolutely, sir."

"Thank you." Axis managed to get the words out before he shuffled down the stairs like a zombie and walked out of Tempest Manor. Perhaps for the last time.

Gauge and Leon would pay for this.

Thirteen

Diamond Secret

W INTER MOURNED. Not over Valve Flicker's passing, but over the potential dissolution of its royal couple. News of Lexia and Axis' quiet separation had traveled at lightning speed across the three existing sectors in only two days. People sang of the loss and wrote operas on the tragedy. Every individual citizen voiced an opinion, and none of them were hopeful.

Gauge hated this.

Never had he meant Lexia and Axis any harm. Obviously, the Prince didn't tell the Heiress the truth, so now the Count wondered why on Winter Axis would withhold himself from Lexia.

No.

Gauge knew why. The stupid boy scout couldn't lie to her face. Did that make him a better man than—

The Count didn't even finish the thought before realizing the answer.

But of course Axis was a better man than Gauge, who'd looked Lexia in the eyes—kissed her—and lied to her. By omission, but a lie nonetheless.

The train pulled into the mine.

Shirt.

Waistcoat.

Tie.

Slacks.

While Gauge fastened his cufflinks, a knock sounded from the door. He called, "Come in, Jan."

"Sir, Ms. Cloud has arrived."

Gauge had sent his personal railcars to fetch her this morning. While staring out the window, he said, "Very good. Please see her to my room."

"I'm already here, dear Count."

The sound of Tija's voice always made Gauge smile even amid all this stress. He turned to see Jan give a bow before leaving the pair alone. Tija looked gorgeous stripping out of her gloves and knee-length coat. It hid the short, tight dress beneath which accentuated her legs in those black tights.

"You look fantastic." Gauge never lied in his compliments.

Tija's smile was girlish with the hint of a blush. "Thank you. And thank you for the special escort. Tomorrow, I can take my things to my old apartments on my own—"

No waiting.

No games.

Gauge crossed the room in three strides, buried his hand in Tija's black hair, and kissed her like she could ease his troubles.

She always answered in kind, letting him inside. Before Tija could run her fingers through Gauge's braids, he gripped both her wrists and pinned them behind her back. She moaned for him, and he backed them against a wall.

When Gauge broke their kiss only to nip her neck, Tija gasped out, "I see the Prince and the Heiress haven't fully replaced me yet."

He found it in him to chuckle. Tija could always bring that out in Gauge. Breathing against the soft skin of her neck, he said, "I promised you there would always be a place for you in my bed, and I meant it."

Hours later, they laid in the ruin of Gauge's sheets on the floor *next* to his bed, propped up against it. Hair messy. Clothes gone. It felt good to seek comfort in Tija.

She held up his hand and peered at it as she laced her naked fingers with his gloved ones. Tija asked, "How much of the rumors are true?"

With a half-chuckle, Gauge scoffed, "'How much did you believe' I think is the better question." To soak in her warmth and genuineness, he tucked her closer to him.

Tija nudged Gauge playfully. "You know, I used some of it for masturbation material."

Gauge barked out a laugh and snorted. This made her burst out in bright laughter and snuggle him more. She kissed his chest before nudging him again. The spy wanted her intel.

It was easy to indulge Tija with such a brilliant smile. Gauge said, "We skated on the ice and had dinner together. We planned the new city and how to rectify complaints within our current industries. It wasn't better than sex with you, but it was certainly better than some others I've had."

Tija grinned at him and shook her head incredulously. "How steamy. But truly, it would do Winter wonders for the three of you to get along."

Ah.

The decline of Gauge's good spirits had finally arrived. It was time to talk business with his oldest partner. He sighed. "I want that more than you could know, but there's simply too much friction and static between us. Axis is so quick to judge—even himself."

Tija nodded along knowingly.

Gauge continued, "And Lexia…Anything I do with her *not* in Axis' presence begs for trouble."

"The best kind?" Tija asked, but as if she already knew the answer.

"The best kind."

She nodded sagely, having guessed correctly. Tija sat up and peered down at Gauge with a glimmer in her gorgeous blue eyes. An idea had struck her. "Obviously, there's only one cure for this."

Gauge waved his hand, at a loss. "Please enlighten me, because I don't see it."

"Air it all out in the open, then spend a few days with the three of you in bed together."

Again, Tija could make Gauge laugh like no other. It was downright wholesome, and Eternity did he need it. Incredulous, he asked, "All of it? Even the secrets I keep from you? And you would be fine with this?"

Tija's feminine laughter implied she knew Gauge better than he knew himself. "Yes. Everything. The gloves. The glasses. And the domes over Winter. Everything, love. It's the only way you'll ever truly find happiness. Trust someone completely."

Gauge stared into Tija's eyes and brushed a strand of her hair behind her ear. Something about the way she said it hurt. He asked, "You think I don't trust you?"

Tija captured his hand and leaned her face into it so that Gauge cupped her cheek. Her voice was soft, loving, and full of understanding. "You carry so much with you, Gauge. I'm not sorry you don't see it in me to shoulder some of the burden, but I think a girl like Lexia is exactly what you need. Someone fearless. Even a little reckless. She'll rattle your foundation, and I think you should let her."

Wow.

Tija smiled a little and kissed the tip of Gauge's nose before saying, "Besides. I'll be around to keep you grounded. You and Axis both. Ooo…Yeah. I like the sound of that—"

Gauge smacked her with a fallen pillow.

Even as snow fell onto Lexia's hair, she refused to let up. Her flat boots pounded the cleared cobbles as she pushed with her quads to gain more speed. Tied back from her face, the weight of her ponytail swayed with her rhythm. The pace punished her calves but cleared her mind.

Tempest Boulevard.

Snow Plaza.

Flicker Avenue.

Again and again, Lexia ran the triangle in the capital's center seeking solace in the physical activity. It proved far better medicine than crying in her bed. Here, the puffs of frosty air from her breath hid the tears.

However.

There were cons to this trek.

Triangulated as it was, it placed Lexia in the heart of her own conspiracy. Father knew something she didn't. Gauge knew something she didn't. But now, Lexia could only guess Axis was in on the secret, and that's why he'd yet to answer her missives.

All forty-six of them within the last seventy-two hours.

Silence.

It broke Lexia's heart.

Run.

Breathe.

Don't think.

Don't let the weight of the lies crush Lexia's mind as well.

Perhaps, it might prove easier if Rhyme would quit following her in the car. Hovering in her peripheral vision, he was a constant reminder of Lexia's current state.

Never mind.

Lexia passed Axis' apartments and tried not to glance up at his window in an obvious way or risk another sonnet. The warm glow from his Flicker wick lamps illuminated them through the gauzy curtains, and it took everything in her not to leave the cold and seek shelter in his arms.

This wasn't the time for Lexia's impulsiveness—

Oh, who was she fooling?!

She took the stairs of his stoop two steps at a time and knocked—no, banged desperately—on the door. The sound of the car pulling up to the curb set her heart beating faster than the run.

Please, don't interrupt, Rhyme.

An eternity passed while Lexia awaited an answer—

The door opened...

To reveal Bolt.

Lexia couldn't find it in her to smile at the valet, but she tried to let her regard for him show in her eyes until...

Bolt's crestfallen expression matched the solemnity in which he shook his head before he closed the door in her face.

Glass.

Lexia's heart was made of glass and now it was in pieces, cutting her with every squeeze of blood.

"Heiress?"

It hurt to swallow Lexia's disappointment and force some composure before she turned and faced Rhyme. He stood on the cobbled sidewalk holding an umbrella out for her to take.

"Are you ready to come home?"

Home.

No, Tempest Manor wasn't home to Lexia right now. Rather it was a house of cards waiting to fall apart. If not Axis, where could she seek refuge?

A chime played through the triangle as it had done every hour prompting Lexia to face its origin. The Copper Cathedral's clock tower called as if in answer to her question.

"I meant the open invitation. You are always welcome at the Cathedral."

If Lexia asked directly, would Gauge answer her honestly? He seemed so...

Misunderstood.

But... What if Lexia didn't like his answers? Where would she run to then?

A chill passed over her which had nothing to do with the snow. Lexia said, "Rhyme, please take me back to the Manor." She couldn't bring herself to call it 'home.'

True, even as they pulled through the front gates, Lexia felt like an intruder on someone else's life. Especially as the servants stopped mid-task and watched her take the stairs up to her suites. Five floors of gawking left her tense between the shoulder blades.

A hot shower.

That would do the trick.

The Snow copper pipes hissed as the Flicker wick pilot light heated the water into steam where Lexia lathered Tempest botanicals in her hair and along her skin. A heady haze thickened the air in the en suite, dizzying her.

Or maybe Lexia was simply nauseous.

At times like these, she would usually seek bittersweet comfort in thoughts of her mother. How would Lya soothe her daughter in this situation?

Brush Lexia's hair. Sing to her. Warm her with hugs.

But not today.

Today, Winter's Diamond provided no solace. Thoughts of her were only another source of anguish and confusion.

There was only one remedy for it.

Six chimes of the Copper Cathedral's tower later, Lexia went out onto the balcony. Although she hadn't seen her father in days, she assumed Leon still took tea in his suites and had gone to bed two hours ago. It would leave the study vulnerable.

In black leather pants and a black blouse with puffed sleeves, Lexia climbed over the balustrade and sidled along the roofline to the first gable. This was tricky since the study was on the opposite side of the house from her room on the first floor, but Lexia had snuck out hundreds of times. It only took confidence, patience, and a shit ton of physical prowess.

All of it, in fact.

Lexia bunched her biceps to climb onto the gable's pinnacle and ran along the apex to the other end of the house. All the while, wooden shingles covered in ice threatened to claim her life. It was a relief when she climbed down onto the wraparound porch on the fourth floor. After that, it took a mere handful of acrobat stunts to climb down onto the first floor's veranda.

Lexia landed right at the study's window. She snitched a small knife out of her ankle-high boot and shimmed it under the window until...

Yes!

It gave. Lexia lifted the window up, climbed inside, and shut it quietly behind her. Still. She went still, listening for any sound aside from the rapid beat of her heart and the rush of her exerted breath.

When nothing came, Lexia went to the desk and triggered the mechanism—

No.

A knock came from the window. Stilted, Lexia turned and faced… Rhyme. He knocked again before pointing behind her where the door opened.

"Father…" Lexia breathed.

Leon's disappointment was in his frown as he closed the door behind him. "Lexia, please step away from my desk."

Close.

Lexia was so close to answers. Her voice came out as a strangled croak as she asked, "Why?"

Her father shook his head, took off glasses, and cleaned them on his pajamas. He peered through them before settling them on his face again.

This was all too surreal for Lexia. Frustrated, she reached for the drawer again.

"Don't. Please."

"Why not, father? What are you keeping from me, and how on Winter can you justify it now?" A sob broke from her on the last.

Leon didn't placate Lexia or reach out to her. He kept his distance, but he looked desperate to get her away from the drawer of secrets. He said, "There are some truths too painful to know. I ask that you heed what I say and forget this unpleasantness."

Exasperated, Lexia threw her hands up in the air. "This 'unpleasantness' is costing me my relationship with Axis—One you orchestrated, mind you, but one I cherish. And the only bastion of safety I can seek is behind a monument of death. At least Gauge keeping secrets seems normal compared to this absurdity. My own *father*!"

Wounded, Leon winced. He took a step toward the fireplace, produced a file folder, and activated the Flicker wick. Flames consumed the logs in place within a heartbeat.

No.

Lexia rushed across the room, but too late.

Leon tossed the file into the fire, and it proved equally efficient with the paper as it had with the wood.

Lexia watched the flames burn away the name 'Snow' on the tab. The light from the fire bounced across the room, final in its devastation. Due for some tears, Lexia asked, "Why...?"

"If you are to hear the truth, it won't be from me."

Unable to say another word, Lexia glared up at her father.

Leon's eyes widened with shock and sadness as he breathed, "Your eyes. You look just like your mother the last time I saw her..."

That was it.

Lexia ran out of the study, through the kitchen door, and climbed the wrought-iron fence.

Escape.

Flee.

To somewhere.

To nowhere.

To anywhere but here.

Axis couldn't face Lexia. He couldn't face any of this. It was all so fresh.

Losing his father.

The shocking truth and the disillusion which followed.

And now his severance from the only person Axis had ever wanted with all his being.

Every wound felt raw and cankered with pain and lies. To top it all off? All of Winter's souls knew, watched, and consumed the infection hollowing out Axis' heart.

He tried to bury himself in work, writing up counterstrike offers based on Phoro's suggestions. But it all felt so...

Empty.

A knock sounded on the door to Axis' inner apartment. He said, "Come in, Bolt." There would be no other visitors for the unforeseeable future.

"Sir..."

The sorrow in the word brought Axis around from his desk. Bolt stood there in the door, dejected and a little heartbroken. He echoed his employer's mood.

Axis asked, "Was it..." He swallowed, unable to say her name.

Bolt could only nod solemnly.

Axis' hands fell from the desk, his arms too heavy to hold them up any longer. Dozens of missives and now an in-person attempt at communication. But Axis could not—*would not*—be the one to shatter Lexia's world.

Fucking Leon.

"There's more…"

Axis met Bolt's eyes once more, and they looked graver than before as he held out a red envelope.

No.

More bad news?

Axis crossed the room in two strides to take it and opened it with shaky hands.

My dearest love,

Forgive my lack of decorum, but I've found little use of it lately. Everything feels wrong, Axis. Please, tell me what is right?

You won't return my messages? Fine.

I'll get to the truth on my own.

Tonight.

But I swear to you, my love, nothing will devastate me so much to wish us apart. Find it in your heart to see that.

Love always and forever,

Your butterfly.

Tonight.

Coward that Axis was, he hoped Lexia did in fact get to the bottom of it on her own, hash it out with Leon, and come through the other side.

Eventually.

But until then, the distance was necessary for Axis to cope.

Nothing would devastate *her* enough, perhaps, but it had been enough for him.

At least for now.

So fresh.

So raw.

It was all too much, and Axis needed the space. He needed not to look in Lexia's eyes and see a woman searching for truth where he could only offer her more lies.

Silence was better.

Wasn't it?

"Mrs. Tempest—"

"Don't call me by that name again, Little Snow."

"Well, if you'd reconsider your endearment for me, I'll do the same. As you can see, Lya, I am no longer little."

"You'll always be small to me, child."

Gauge woke with a start powerful enough to stir Tija in his arms. In a voice thick with sleep, she asked "What is it?"

Something...

Had Gauge heard something?

When no other sound came and he resigned it to his imagination, Gauge said, "Nothing, go back to sleep." He kissed her hair and nestled her back against him—

A knock resounded.

They peered at each other before Gauge called, "Jan?" What could disturb them at this late hour?

The butler walked in looking…nervous.

Gauge bolted upright. "What is it?"

"Ms. Tempest is in the foyer without her chaperons asking for… sanctuary."

Lexia must not know the truth or she wouldn't seek it from Gauge. Every instinct told him to tread carefully. He didn't want her to run away, but he also didn't want to tell her.

And Tija…

"Don't worry about me, dear Count." She kissed his cheek and whispered, "Remember what I said."

How could Gauge forget?

"But I think a girl like Lexia is exactly what you need. Someone fearless. Even a little reckless. She'll rattle your foundation, and I think you should let her."

Without another word, Tija stood naked to the room and collected the traces of her clothes thrown here and there.

Jan dismissed himself for her sake.

A little nervous, Gauge dressed, donned a fresh pair of gloves, and tried to make himself presentable.

Lexia…

Sought sanctuary.

With Gauge.

Once again in her stylish coat and boots, Tija took Gauge by the gloved hand with a reassuring squeeze. "Be gentle with Lexia. She's wounded and alone."

"Right."

While still holding his hand, Tija made to leave, but Gauge pulled her back into his arms for a parting hug. He said, "Thank you."

Understanding wasn't easy to come by, and Tija could claim to have seen more pieces of the puzzle that was the Copper Count than any soul on Winter. She didn't run in fear or scold him. Gauge needed her, but right now...

"Don't keep Lexia waiting."

"Yes, ma'am."

They walked out onto the stairs together, and there was no hiding the reason why they were together at two in the morning. Before reaching the bottom, Gauge called below, "Ms. Tempest, how may I help you—"

Oh...

Poor Lexia.

She looked up from where she was curled up on a sofa, hugging her knees to her chest. Even though Lexia was almost as tall as Gauge, she looked small. Tears reddened her eyes, but not so much as the anger seething deep in the black.

Tija left Gauge staring on the stairs and went to the door where Jan waited. She said, "Until next time, Count Snow. And Ms. Tempest?" Lexia's eyes flicked over to Tija, who said, "Please consider me a friend anytime you like. I've returned to the capital, and I'm never too busy to lend an ear."

Lexia only nodded, and Tija left. The younger woman buried her face in her knees again as if this world were too bright for her.

Gauge could understand that. "Jan, lower the lights. Please." Even through his amber lenses, the dim was more preferable to his corneas, anyway.

In the privacy of the dark, Gauge walked down the last few steps slowly, keeping his eyes on the distraught girl in his foyer. He feared any quicker, and she might burst into a fresh bout of tears.

When Lexia didn't bolt like a skittish kitten, Gauge sat down beside her and reached out. She didn't flinch, so he smoothed a gloved hand down her back.

Lexia said, "Mmm…Ahh…Hmm. Mmm."

Gauge wanted to laugh at the muffled communication, but tried to keep it out of his voice as he said, "Ms. Tempest, you'll need to come out of your shelter for me to understand you."

Lexia lifted her head from her knees, blew the bangs out of her face in a habitual gesture which Gauge loved, and met his eyes. "I didn't know where else to go. Axis…He won't…" She choked on a sob.

"Sh…Don't upset yourself further. You owe me no explanation why you're here. You're welcome to stay as long as you like." Gauge glanced up at his butler. "Will you please prepare a room for our guest?"

"Of course, sir. Ms. Tempest, should you need anything, please ask."

Astonishingly, she held out her arms to the old spy, so much like a child seeking a parent. Jan, choked by the gesture but unable to resist, hugged Lexia where she sat on the sofa. Over her shoulder, he shot Gauge a warning glance.

Vulnerable.

Lexia needed protection, and they would give it expecting no form of reciprocity.

Yes.

Gauge understood. He nodded, and the pair parted. Lexia managed probably her first smile in days, though weak, at the butler. "Thank you."

"Yes, miss. Excuse me—"

"Please put her in the room across from mine," Gauge instructed.

There were only two rooms on the top floor, both identical in their magnificence, but the one had remained unused for a decade. Jan's eyes widened a touch, but he nodded and went about his duties.

Lexia stayed curled in a ball, but relaxed by centimeters the longer she sat there. She said, "Thank you, Count Snow."

"Come now. There are no chaperons to impress. You can call me, 'Gauge.'" He tried to say it cheerfully to bolster her out of this slump, but perhaps there was too much unsaid between them.

Still, Lexia whispered, "Gauge," like she was trying the feel of his name on her lips.

Unfortunately, it reminded him of the last time she'd said his name. The kiss.

Lexia's eyes slowly rose to meet Gauge's, and they stared at one another as if they were recalling it at the same time. Yet while the Count was quite the rogue, he wouldn't kiss one woman with the taste of another on his lips.

Gauge said, "Let's get you to bed—To sleep. I'll show you to your room. Did you bring any bags?"

Lexia shook her head as she unfurled her long legs in those attractive leather pants she so much enjoyed. Gauge held out his hand, and her smaller one curled slender fingers around his glove.

They stood together. She peered up at him, so open and raw. He stared down at her, eager to make her forget. After a few heartbeats passed between them, Gauge led her up the stairs.

Oh, what scandal awaited them in the morning.

The Heiress, distraught by her separation from the Prince, sought sanctuary in the Copper Cathedral, a slave to the Count's every whim.

While Gauge enjoyed spectacle, this coming onslaught was enough to make him roll his eyes.

Nothing would happen between them tonight.

Even so, a little voice whispered in Gauge's head, 'But what about tomorrow?'

Lexia followed Gauge upstairs in silence. Scooped out as she was, she couldn't form words for conversation. Besides, anything she would say would come out as questions about the lies among the men in her life. And maybe, for now, Lexia simply needed to rest.

The Copper Cathedral's stairs climbed forever to the very top, and Lexia noticed Gauge's slight gait without his cane. All the while, the dusty shaft of a gilded elevator followed their climb as a decorative hint of the Count's waning health. She wouldn't pry.

Not yet.

"Here we are." Gauge gestured toward a door Jan was holding open for her.

There was only one other door on the floor, and it was across the staircase. Only a few steps away. Gauge's room.

Lexia mumbled, "Thank you," before stepping inside. It surprised her to see the Count didn't follow. "Uhm..."

She could see Gauge swallow before he said, "Yes?" What was he suppressing? Impulse? Desire—

No.

Lexia shouldn't think those thoughts. Not with her life in so much turmoil. And what about Gauge's part in this conspiracy?

She shook her head and went inside.

All alone—

"Lexia..."

Gauge's voice came softly from behind her in the doorway. She peered over her shoulder at him, and he swallowed again. He said, "Take this time to consider things and clear your mind. We can always revisit..." He gestured between them. "This tomorrow."

"I'm the man you go to when you want to break the headboard. Be sure which one you want first before you come to me. Is that clear enough for you, Lexia? Tell me you understand."

"I understand."

Gauge shut Lexia in the room without offering himself across the hall. It was probably best this way. She turned and finally took in her surroundings.

Beautiful.

They'd decorated the room in black, grays, and white, which suited Lexia just fine. A plush black rug gave a softness to the pale gray parquet floors. The white walls brightened the space, and this high up it felt airy. Easier for Lexia to breathe. She touched a massive post on the enormous bed and traced the detail carved into the black wood. With white sheets, it beckoned like a seductive cloud.

The room smelled a little stuffy, and despite the blizzard outside, she opened the stained-glass balcony door...

To a breathtaking view.

Few buildings climbed as high as the Copper Cathedral's tower. From up here, the apartments, houses, factories, and lawns twinkled below, Flicker wicks and fireplaces hard at work to keep out the cold and the dark. The copper-capped of the Cathedral's eaves and gables glinted, reflecting the light.

It enchanted Lexia.

She left the balcony door open and snuggled into an armchair to gaze out over Winter's capital city. A freshly washed throw blanket kept her warm as she lost herself in the sights.

Father was the enemy.

Axis was compromised.

And Gauge—Well...

He and Lexia shared a secret, didn't they? She could easily be executed as an accomplice to Valve's murder after learning the truth and not bringing it to light.

Was Lexia any better than Axis? Or Gauge, for that matter?

Perhaps whatever inside her—the impulsivity, the sympathy for the devil, that blackness which lived in her eyes—sought Gauge for companionship.

Yellow blood.

Blue freckles.

Never sick and no broken bones.

Inheritor to Winter's Diamond and all her secrets.

On a powerful gust of wind, frost blew into the room. As the snow claimed her, Lexia snuggled into the chair and finally fell asleep with unshed tears in her eyes.

Tomorrow waited.

FOURTEEN

Open Invitation

THE MORNING GREETED AXIS WITH A PERVADING LOSS OF SENSATION THROUGHOUT HIS ENTIRE BODY. Numb, he hadn't slept all night. Instead, he'd worked himself into a strange coma of city planning and unionizing the future. All the while ignoring the stack of papers dedicated to wedding preparations.

Lexia entered his thoughts. Often.

Axis couldn't help but drift to the vision of her in a wedding gown. Black and gold of course. Her white hair in loose waves. A radiant smile on her face.

But then, Axis would remember the last time he'd seen her. The state he'd left her in, standing in that room. Naked but for lingerie the color of Snow's eyes. So alone with tears streaming down her face. And that hopeful smile which would haunt Axis forever.

"Please give the idea some thought. I could go forever without children, but please don't ask me to go a lifetime without you."

Axis could grind his teeth over Gauge and Leon all day long, but he couldn't escape the truth. Axis was as much a bastard for keeping this secret as either of those fools.

This thought followed him through his morning routine: workout, coffee, mail—

A message from Leon.

Son,

I know you're upset with me, but I want us to put our differences aside. We share a common threat to my daughter, and I fear we may already be too late. Lexia confronted me last night, and when I proved too cowardly to confess my sins, she ran.

Axis—Lexia fled to the Cathedral.

Avoid the papers. Don't believe the headlines.

I know without a doubt she loves only you, but a scandal on this scale cannot be contained or regarded kindly. Please respond to this missive with ideas on how to return Lexia home where she belongs.

In your debt,

Dr. Tempest.

Lexia… Ran to Gauge…

Axis didn't bother putting on a shirt to run outside in the cold and grab the morning paper. He stared at it in his hand and gasped, "No."

Distressed Heiress seeks refuge in Copper Cathedral: Winter's Diamond, Multi-Faceted.

"Why, Prince Axis…"

Blinking in shock, he barely registered the woman's voice, yet recognized it immediately.

Tija stood on the cobbled sidewalk outside Axis' door and gestured to his apartments. She asked, "Would you kindly invite me inside?"

Bolt appeared in the doorway, wiping sleep from his eyes, asking, "What's wrong, sir?"

Everything.

A few minutes later, the three—Axis, Bolt, and Tija—sat in Axis' living room sipping coffee in uncomfortable silence. Everyone knew why. Absolutely everyone.

All of Winter knew of Axis and Lexia's troubles, and now they believed her unfaithful with Gauge in this hour of weakness.

Tija's arrival was both welcome and a harbinger of bad news, no doubt. After setting down her cup of coffee, she went first. "Prince Axis, I felt the need to come here today outside of my liaison duties to discuss matters of which you are now aware."

So much official speech to simplify the situation.

Tija cleared her throat to say the rest. "But I'm afraid I find it difficult to converse with you while you are…" She gestured at him.

What?

Bolt clicked his tongue and repeated the gesture at Axis.

Oh, right.

He'd forgotten to put on a shirt.

Fuck.

The scars.

Tija's eyes didn't rove over him, in fact she averted them as best she could. Her pink blush was nothing as beautiful as the yellow color which often kissed Lexia's cheek, but it was endearing nonetheless. Axis left to find his robe and belted it for good measure.

As he reentered the room, he said, "My apologies, Ms. Cloud."

She muttered something under her breath like, 'No apology needed,' before she straightened and said, "I'll be frank. Last night during my visit with our Count Snow—"

Axis clenched his jaw at 'our.'

"—Lexia arrived quite distressed. I was very concerned for the state she was in."

Damn it.

How could Leon let it go this far? How could Axis?!

Tija went on. "I'm close friends with several people who staff the Cathedral, and I can say she only stayed the night in a guest room. There was nothing inappropriate about her visit aside from the lack of a chaperon, much to her reputation's detriment. Do you understand me?"

Axis blinked a few times as he absorbed this information. He peered up at Bolt, who offered a reassuring smile. This was good news. Though truly, Axis hardly doubted Lexia would act so...

Recklessly.

He swallowed loud enough for the two in the room to hear, and the sound made Tija say, "I think you understand the gravity of the situation. No, nothing has happened, but there's every chance something might. I only come here as a friend to say I saw the state of her. She's vulnerable and rash. I fear her infamous impulsivity for your sake, not hers. I believe whatever is happening between the three of you, Lexia will make a decision on it today which will impact your relationship forever. But I also believe she's well within her rights to make it."

That cleared the fog for Axis. "What do you think I can do?"

A knock sounded at the door, and Bolt said, "Excuse me," before leaving to answer, much to Axis' relief. He couldn't face anyone today of all days.

Tija watched him leave, waiting until she and Axis were alone before saying, "I'll tell you the same thing I told Gauge. Air it all out in the open and throw yourselves at each other."

Axis recoiled like she'd slapped him, and he suffered the worst kind of emotional whiplash. He spat out his coffee in the middle of it and choked out, "I beg your pardon?!"

"Sir!" Bolt burst into the room. "Sir, outside…"

Axis set aside his coffee and went to the window. "No…"

Dozens of people waited outside with tiny notebooks in their hands, vying for an audience with the Prince. They spotted him at the window and started their barrage of calls through it.

"Sir, can we speak with you?"

"Prince Axis, tell us your thoughts on Ms. Tempest's betrayal?"

"Is the wedding off? Or postponed until you can include Count Snow?"

Everyone had an opinion, and everyone came to share it with Axis.

This was his worst nightmare.

____

Gauge finished the metallic-tasting breakfast with his tongue coated in the blue testing powder. He peered out the nearest window, overlooking the mines, and considered the state of things.

What the hell was happening?

Lexia Tempest was in his home unchaperoned, and Gauge could only think of how Axis was handling it all.

As of one hour ago, Lexia had left her room and wandered down to the kitchens—much to the cooks' distress—and took breakfast there. A cup of tea and a muffin. This was all according to Jan's account, as Gauge had asked the old spy to report her every move.

The butler last stated Lexia went out into the courtyard in one of Jan's coats to see how the plants faired in their dormancy. That should occupy her for an hour at least while Gauge considered what exactly to do with her.

By all advice and his own desires, the answer was obvious.

Yet…

Gauge couldn't bring himself to leave his room. There was too much in the middle, clouding the space between them with a fog of confusion and doubt. Did he really want to press matters with Lexia when the waters were so murky?

Thinking of water reminded Gauge that Jan had mentioned Lexia's hair was wet this morning. Presumably from showering. Here…In the Cathedral. And for the first time since his years as a starved teenager,

Gauge imagined a woman under the hot spray. Lexia's long white hair soaked down her back. The sounds she'd make as her tense shoulders relaxed in private relief and the water traveled where it pleased—

Damn him.

Gauge burst from his bistro set, grabbed a cane, and left the security of his room in search of rattled foundations. Before he took the stairs, he heard…

A melody.

A bright, cheerful tune coming from Gauge's piano. There was a falsity to the song. One of those ironically optimistic ones where the lyrics described something disastrous. Tragedy beneath the facade.

Lexia…

Gauge took the stairs as fast as his bones would let him. Jan waited down in the foyer, staring off at the conservatory. There was a worried crease to his frown, and Gauge knew his butler was quite taken.

Who wouldn't be?

The old spy glanced up as Gauge finished the last of the stairs. Jan nodded in a way which said so much.

Gauge peered over at the conservatory, at a loss for words. This was it, and well…

Gauge gave the faintest of nods, and Jan went to work sealing off the Cathedral from prying eyes. Rumors were impossible to staunch completely, but at least no one needed to know the details of this encounter. Jan would dismiss the servants for the day and make himself scarce.

Gauge swallowed and forced himself to step into the glass room.

Lexia was wearing nothing but a silk robe—A detail Jan had omitted. Perhaps intentionally. She'd left her hair down, and the dried waves framed her fresh face in an unmade way which left her more exposed than the robe. From here, Gauge could see both her wrists were free. No timepiece. No restraints.

Uninhibited and unhindered, Lexia continued to play while gently swaying to the music. Even with her eyes closed, she heard his approach, and said, "I was wondering when you would stop hiding from me."

No one.

Not a single soul on Winter.

Talked to the Count this way.

Lexia opened her eyes and pegged Gauge with a challenge in her stare. Almost a defiance. This was her wrath.

And Gauge deserved it. "Lexia—"

"Don't tell me." She closed her eyes again and squeezed out a tear. "I... I... Whatever this secret is, I don't think I'm ready to know it. Whatever could drive Axis from me and force my father to lie to my face must be awful. And if it has anything to do with my mother—I don't think I could bear it. Not yet."

Lexia continued to play for a while as a quiet stretched between them. In a silent invitation, she scooted over on the bench. Gauge set his cane aside and sat down beside her. This was truly inappropriate. She wasn't dressed enough for any proximity, let alone one so close, but . . .

Gauge caught the rhythm of Lexia's melody and played along on the lower notes while she took the higher octaves. It suited them. Heavy and dark; bright and light. But if they couldn't have honesty between them in words, then Gauge would bring it to them in song.

He slowed the tempo down and prolonged the notes.

Lexia's playing became more erratic. Her fingers fluttered across the higher keys like a butterfly trapped in a net. It took on a dark tone as she escaped through the notes in ways she couldn't from reality.

Gauge was Lexia's escape, and he anchored her with the gravity of it all. Passionately and more fierce, she expressed her uncertainty and anguish.

Gauge wanted to feel it. He paused only long enough to bite his gloves off and splayed his fingers across the glossy keys. Immediately, the vibrations stimulated the nerves in his hands to an almost painful sensation. The only similar sensation he could liken it to was walking after depriving the feet of circulation for too long. Needles tingled along his fingertips, but it felt real.

It felt alive.

Lexia's fingers moved more elegantly on the ivories, but she couldn't match Gauge's ferocity. It was a complement to one another, and it let their music soar.

They'd both exerted themselves to breathing heavily by the time they slowed down. One slow key. And another. Until they stopped.

Lexia panted as she lowered her hands from the keys, and Gauge quietly closed the fallboard. She watched his hands as he did it, a paler gray than his kohl complexion. Then her eyes shot up and met his. They stared at one another, barely able to catch their breath.

They met each other in the middle, claiming one another in a kiss. Fierce, as always, Lexia gripped Gauge by his shirt and pulled him tight against her. He gripped a fistful of her hair in kind, so silky and soft against his sensitive fingers.

Lexia parted her lips and moaned as Gauge took the invitation.

He couldn't withstand the angle any longer and broke their kiss to lift Lexia by the waist and sit her down on the fallboard before him. She gave a cute 'yip' in the process and peered down at Gauge with expectant heat in her stunning black eyes.

Thirsty, he drank in the sight of her in that robe and let out a curse before tearing off his glasses. Daylight pierced through Gauge's corneas, but he ignored it for the clearer view of Lexia Tempest. She held her breath as she met his eyes, unfiltered.

Poised on the brink once again, they stared at one another in breathy silence.

Gauge watched Lexia for any signs of distress or regret as he reached up and untied the belt to her robe. When she didn't stop him, he pulled it open and…

Lexia was completely bare underneath, and every perfect centimeter was on display atop Gauge's piano. A yellow blush kissed her cheeks, and he reached up to cup her face. She leaned into his hand with something in her eyes.

It was warm and unbridled.

But it couldn't be…

No one could give their heart so freely in such a short amount of time. Especially under these circumstances. It would be…

Reckless.

Lexia reached out and ran her fingers through Gauge's braids. He turned his face in her hand and kissed her palm. Then he kissed her knee. Up her firm thighs. In between.

Both Lexia's hands formed fists in Gauge's hair as her head went back on a loud gasp when he reached his destination. Passionate in every way, it didn't take long to bring her close to the edge.

Gauge stopped and nipped her thigh.

Lexia cried out his name in the sexiest sigh he'd ever heard.

They played this game again and again until Gauge was satisfied Lexia wouldn't run away. Until reality set in that yes, this was in fact happening. Here, in his conservatory, Gauge Snow would fuck Lexia Tempest until she went out of her mind with ecstasy.

Or until Gauge's legs gave out.

Whichever happened first.

Letting Gauge Snow pleasure Lexia was exhilarating, wrong, and oh, so good. Wave after wave crashed into her, washing away the sediment of her anxieties. He knew it, too.

Lexia could tell by the way Gauge peered up at her every so often, checking to see if she was enjoying herself or if she was on the verge of saying 'stop.'

No.

Lexia didn't understand the word 'stop.' Call it impulsiveness or recklessness, but once she gave herself up to something, there was no backing down.

So, yes.

Lexia would fuck Gauge in his conservatory, library, bedroom, bathtub—everywhere in this Cathedral—until she lost her mind in ecstasy. That had been her plan since she'd chosen to wear a robe this morning rather than repeat yesterday's ensemble.

Forget the lies.

Forget the truth.

Get lost in this fantasy come true, and don't look back.

Gauge stood, making their height even for when he kissed Lexia with the taste of her on his lips. It made her purr against him. This close, he smelled like the frost from last night. His hands were unnaturally soft where they cupped her face. So different from Axis' more calloused skin from regular sword play and the occasional day of manual labor. The softness felt silken, but the roughness had its advantages, too.

Lexia reached for the buttons on Gauge's shirt, and he broke their kiss to stop her—Oh, no. Please, not now—

The buttons from Gauge's shirt flew everywhere as he ripped it open to Lexia's touch. A giggle bubbled from her for the first time in days, and she smiled into their next kiss. Her hands traveled up his bare chest to his shoulders, where Lexia held on as Gauge guided her legs around him and lifted her off the piano.

With little effort, he spun them around the conservatory, dizzying Lexia. It wasn't until her back hit the glass that she realized Gauge had pinned her wrists to it.

People could see in from the street to glimpse the Heiress struggle a bit against the Count. Just a wiggle.

Gauge grinned and held Lexia firmly before kissing the delicate skin of her neck—

He bit down, and she arched her neck with a gasp.

This was it.

This was something Lexia had wanted from Axis for so long, and Gauge gave it to her without her having to ask. If Axis were here, would he see and understand? Would he join them—

"Lexia."

She had to admit, "Gauge, you feel too good to be wrong."

He kissed her shoulder, saying, "But even now I'm keeping secrets from you."

Gauge was giving Lexia a choice. Accept the lie and join him in bed. Or fight everyone tooth and nail for the truth at the expense of her happiness. At the expense of what was happening right now.

He squeezed her wrists and ground his hips against hers, and Lexia's eyes rolled in the back of her head as she moaned, "I don't care. Just don't take your hands off me."

Gauge growled and twirled them once again before setting Lexia down on the conference table. Far gentler than she wanted, he cupped her throat and pushed her until she laid down across it. She kept her eyes on his as she pressed her neck tighter in his grip.

"Everything about you is flawless," Gauge said before squeezing her throat.

Lexia tightened her legs around him while simultaneously arching her back to give him better access.

Please.

Please.

Make her forget.

Desperation left Gauge's piercing blue eyes wild. He said, "Tell me to stop."

Lexia let him see the resolve in her eyes as she shook her head.

"Then we're both damned." He let the words out through clenched teeth as he kicked out of his pants.

Gauge took what Lexia gave and buried them together in an ecstatic grave filled with lies, betrayal, and foundation-rattling sex.

Tija asked, "But Axis, where are we going?"

"To the Cathedral."

She said, "Surely, you must know if anyone sees us together it will only make the story more sensational," and she was right.

Axis froze. His throat tightened until he couldn't breathe, and his palms began to sweat.

A panic attack.

Breathe in.

Breathe out.

Few people had seen Axis this way—Dr. Tempest, Lya, and Lexia. Each of them had told him the same: take deep breaths and try to distract. It proved rather difficult with people shouting their very public and exaggerated opinions on the matter—

"Get away. Shoo! You should all be ashamed of yourselves!"

Tija?

The sound of a steam cannon went off right outside the door, and Axis burst into the hallway. He stared at the spectacle.

Bolt's cannon was steaming from a fresh firing, and Tija glared at the fleeing intruders. She humphed. "Serves them right."

Bolt beamed at her.

What the hell was happening around this place?

Although, Axis had to admit, the gunshot and the dismissal of the paparazzi had distracted him from the panic attack.

Bolt stepped off the curb and opened the backseat door to the car, saying, "Ms. Cloud."

"Why, thank you, Bolt." She slid inside and called, "Are you coming Prince Axis?"

Axis slipped into his coat and climbed inside. They rode to Snow Plaza in silence. All the while, Axis thought of what to say to Lexia. How to reach her.

As they arrived, Tija took Axis' hand before he could climb out. She said, "Be gentle with Lexia, and please don't fault our Count for the natural progression of things."

It sent Axis to frowning as they exited the car together. He'd considered a detour to Tempest Manor to pick up Leon, but not only was he still angry with Lexia's father, Axis imagined Lexia was, too. And rightly so.

Nothing could return to the way it was after this.

The trio climbed the stairs to the Wall of Pain with Axis exercising all his restraint not to run up and bang on the despicable copper monument, demanding to see Lexia. It was his fault, wasn't it? He'd turned her away from his apartments and left her with nowhere else to go.

Tija knocked. That was best. Axis clenched his jaw and ground his teeth the longer it took for someone to answer. By the time Jan cracked the door a notch, the Prince's molars had turned to dust.

"Hello, Ms. Cloud, did we forget some of your luggage?"

Tija smiled at the butler, saying, "No, Jan. Prince Axis and I are here to see Ms. Tempest."

"Now," Bolt added, straight out of Axis' mind.

The older man peered between the three of them, but there was something about the way he did it. Assessing a threat? Eventually, he said, "I'm afraid Ms. Tempest is indisposed, and the Count isn't taking visitors today."

Indisposed.

Tija glanced at Axis. Perhaps she heard his teeth grinding, or maybe she sensed the pending eruption. Because Axis couldn't contain it anymore.

"Lexia! Lexia! Forgive me!"

Bolt grabbed Axis by one arm, and Tija grabbed him by the other. They had to drag Axis away from the copper monument. He still shouted, "Lexia! Please! I need to see you!"

Jan closed the door in their faces as Axis' friends pulled him onto the street. His heart pounded, and tears burned his eyes.

"Lexia! Lexia…Oh, no. Lexia…"

A crowd formed, but Axis could barely take notice. His voice cracked as he continued screaming her name—

"Axis." Tija whispered against his ear. "While you railed against the unfairness of it all, Jan slipped this in my hand."

It was a copper envelope, but sealed with a gilded butterfly. Without consideration for their audience, Axis opened it immediately.

My love,

I have failed in my mission to obtain the truth and find myself adrift with no anchor. It's the morning after my arrival at the Copper Cathedral, and you are in my thoughts. My dreams.

No power on this planet could take me from you but yourself. I won't force our engagement if you truly feel we are no longer a match, but not a day will go by that I won't miss your smile and your laughter.

Please don't deny me your friendship.

Until you decide you can stand my presence again, please find it in your heart to forgive me for the mistakes I will make in the meantime.

I seek refuge from the storm, and I've found it in Snow.

Still, forever yours,

Lexia Tempest.

No.

Lexia…

Dizzy, Axis stumbled against the balustrade. The crowd gasped and cried. The crush of their presence overwhelmed him, and no matter how Tija and Bolt tried, it proved impossible to keep the people away.

Someone shouted, "Is it over?"

Another cried, "Has the Heiress left you for the Count?"

Everyone knew.

Axis had fucked up.

Too much.

It was all too much.

The cobbled street traded places with the sky, and darkness carried the Prince away.

Gauge and Lexia didn't stop.

Not even to eat.

Not even as his bones and overly sensitized fingertips begged him to do so.

They made their way through several rooms in the Copper Cathedral before finding their way to the bed in Lexia's room. There, they carried on with the balcony door open for all of Winter to hear their cries of mutual ecstasy. It was as if they kept on with each other to put off what would follow.

The self-questioning and doubt.

Maybe even regret.

No, those things were for later. Long after they awakened from passing out.

Lexia was silk beneath Gauge, soft and supple. She was also generous, insisting on returning the pleasure from earlier with an hour focused purely on him. It was a rest to recuperate from all this physical expenditure.

Gauge knew Lexia was accustomed to a certain level of exceptional performance from Axis. There would be little in the way of measuring up to the most athletically capable man in Winter. But Gauge found ways to please Lexia in which he could tell she'd been neglected.

The butterfly enjoyed being pinned.

Bitten.

Choked.

Every time Gauge pulled Lexia's hair, she arched her neck and released the most satisfying sigh. When he crushed her hips with his hands at a punishing pace, orgasm racked her body until her spine bowed. And once, he held his hand over her mouth, stifling her moans, until she gripped him to release.

They didn't break the headboard, sturdy as it was, but they certainly gave it a ride it would never forget. Lexia had scored the deep-colored wood with her nails and left scratches in the grain.

Gauge wanted to frame it. A literal notch in his headboard.

Bedpost.

Conference table.

Eternity, Lexia would be the end of him. His bones hurt from the wild ride, but there was no stopping it. Over and over again, he buried himself in the scent of summer rain, and over and over again, Lexia came for him.

Before too long, Gauge would need a shot of adrenaline just to keep up.

But finally, after countless rounds together, Lexia's eyes could barely stay open as she gazed up from beneath Gauge. She swallowed hard, glowing from the exertion and release. She breathed, "I'm afraid to sleep. I'm afraid of tomorrow."

Gauge kissed her briefly and said, "Don't be. I'll be here when you wake."

The last thing Lexia said before falling asleep in his arms was, "That's what I'm afraid of." Then her eyes closed, and her breathing came evenly.

Ah.

The pre-marital laws.

Lexia had stayed true to them and never spent the night with Axis. If she awakened to Gauge in the morning, it meant her betrayal was complete.

How to remedy this?

Gauge knew the best way he could come up with. Gently, he laid Lexia on the bed, went to his room to find a shirt, and dressed her in it. It was far too cold to leave her in the nude, and this way she could derive some comfort from his scent without breaking any vows to Axis.

After covering Lexia in the blankets, Gauge peered over at the open balcony door. Outside, Winter slept, but tomorrow it would awaken with fresh appetites. Hungry for news of the Heiress and the Count.

Poor Prince.

Gauge showered and dressed in pajama bottoms and a robe before Jan knocked on the door. Gauge said, "Come in."

"Sir, I brought your dinner."

It prompted Gauge to glance at the clock. One in the morning. He and Lexia had started this affair sometime after breakfast.

Wow.

His stomach growled. As he tested his food, he said, "The servants can return tomorrow. I know there's no stopping the rumors, but I want them to steer clear of Lexia—Ms. Tempest."

The butler gave a half bow. "Of course, sir. And what about our other guests?"

The mercenaries.

Before Gauge could stop himself, he laughed. He'd completely forgotten they existed, but then he remembered Axis' request for mercy and frowned. He said, "Leave them for now. Feed them once a day, and see they have water—Jan. I mean it."

There was a hint of disappointment in the old spy's voice. "Very well." After a pause, he asked, "Is Ms. Tempest to become a permanent resident of the Copper Cathedral?"

Uncertain.

Everything was so uncertain.

Gauge liked the idea of walking into a room in his home and smelling traces of a relieving shower on a hot summer's day. To see their complexions contrasting together in the throes of passion. And to see her smile across every meal.

But something told Gauge that was further out of reach than he realized. And perhaps their total abandon today had only made it worse.

"Why are you coming to me for help, Lya?"

"Because you're the only one with enough power to free me now."

"You talk as if you hate your husband—your family."

"I only hate that which keeps me here."

Gauge sighed. "I don't know, Jan. I just don't know."

Too much weighed in the balance, and Lexia might forgive herself in the moment, but regret awaited her in the morning.

Or maybe not.

Who was to say with a wild sprite such as her? Perhaps there was a chance this could all still come together. But Gauge knew one thing.

That all depended on Lexia Tempest.

EPILOGUE

*"*Mommy, are we good people?"

"Yes, dear, why do you ask?"

"Well, sometimes I get confused. I know Axis is good people, but his father is not. I don't always understand. What makes people good?"

"My sweet girl, what makes us good are our actions. You're right about Valve and Axis. But not everyone will be so black and white your entire life. Like Gauge..." Lya retrieved something from a drawer and handed it to Lexia.

It was the pinboard of butterflies, and Lexia felt her heart break all over again. "Mommy? I don't understand."

Lya smoothed a hand down Lexia's hair, saying, "Sh. Look closer."

Monarchs and Zebras.

Peacocks and Admirals.

There were at least two dozen unique varieties in a rainbow of colors, and they were labeled with care.

Lexia peered up at her mother and asked, "Gauge wasn't trying to be mean?"

"No, baby. He meant it to be sweet, but Little Snow has his own way. One day, you might come to understand. You can't be good without a little gray."

Lexia opened her eyes and blinked at the guest room's vaulted ceiling from where she lay in the enormous cloud of a bed. The gentle sound of Winter waking came to her from the open balcony door.

Gauge had understood Lexia and left her alone in the bed. After everything they'd done together, feeling this way couldn't be wrong, but it didn't feel right.

It felt gray.

Lexia understood and didn't understand all at once. Perhaps that's what growing up was all about. She hoped Jan had delivered her letter, and that Axis was all right. The truth waited across the hall from Lexia, and when she was ready, she would seek it in Gauge. Then together they could revive Axis from his mourning and self-doubt.

Winter would have its story.

The Prince, the Heiress, and the Count weren't finished just yet.

Author's Note

I hope the ending didn't kill your desire to finish the story. Please continue reading *Polar Axis* to reach the conclusion of Winter's Verse.

Please visit my website at https://nicolehayeswriter.com/. There you can purchase autographed copies and special edition packages. You can also sign up for my newsletter, if you're interested.

If this is your first introduction to my writing, please consider checking out my 13-book Sci-Fi epic, *The Vast Collective Series*. You can find the entire series on Amazon by scanning the QR code below.